Carnival Macabre

An Anthology of Gothic Horror

Edited by

Cassandra L. Thompson
Damon Barret Roe

CARNIVAL MACABRE

An Anthology of Gothic Horror

EDITED BY
CASSANDRA L. THOMPSON
DAMON BARRET ROE

QUILL & CROW PUBLISHING HOUSE

CARNIVAL MACABRE: AN ANTHOLOGY OF GOTHIC HORROR
EDITED BY CASSANDRA L. THOMPSON, DAMON BARRET ROE
PUBLISHED BY QUILL & CROW PUBLISHING HOUSE

While some of the stories included in this anthology are based on historical fact, the stories in this novel are works of fiction. All incidents, dialogue, and characters, except for some well-known historical and public figures, are either products of the author's imagination or used in a fictitious manner. Any resemblance to actual persons, living or dead, or actual events is purely coincidental.

Content Disclaimer: Please be advised that the stories included in this anthology fall under the genres of horror and Gothic fiction. As such, there are elements and themes that may be triggering. You will find an index of triggers at the end of the book should you wish to apply your own personal discretion. We have done our best to identify potential triggers, but we apologize deeply if we missed something. We understand the importance of communicating transparently with our readers and establishing our community as a safe space.

Cover Design & Interior by Marie Casey
Printed in the United States of America

ISBN: 979-8-9851285-8-1
ISBN (ebook): 979-8-9851285-7-4
Publisher's Website: www.quillandcrowpublishinghouse.com

TABLE OF CONTENTS

FOREWORD
Brad Acevedo

"A clown is funny in the circus ring. But what would be the normal reaction to opening a door at midnight, and finding the same clown standing there in the moonlight?"

Intriguing words uttered by the enigmatic Lon Chaney, The Man of 1000 Faces. But let's explore that for a moment. Why does coulrophobia, the intense fear of these grinning grease-painted jesters, run rampant in our society? Why do we cast a gaze of mistrust toward the clattering amusement behemoths of metal rivets and garish neon lights that seem to appear overnight?

After all, a carnival is meant to amuse, to elicit smiles and laughter. Might there just be something wicked lurking beneath the candy-colored veneer? Rusted metal, grease-laden miasma, and sideshows seem designed to inflict the suspicion that all just might not be as we think.

I currently work with the marketing team at Quill & Crow Publishing House. Perhaps you've seen me on social media, touting our gloriously Gothic tomes, likely smeared in greasepaint and stage blood. As an individual who is awkward in a social context, I often find comfort behind the mask and paint. To transform, to disturb, to amuse. To put on a show.

For me personally, it started with deception. Close up sleight-of-hand magic to be precise, practiced by my own father right before he would don a costume and perform for children at schools in state-mandated drug education programs.

Before their downfall, we would frequent the Ringling Bros & Barnum and Bailey Circus when they came to California, marveling at the wonders of trapeze artists and motorcycle stunts, the comedic capering of their famous clowns and yes, the questionable utilization of exotic animals.

Beyond this would be the sideshows booths of the state fair which we would visit every summer, far removed from the salt-pierced skies of the boardwalks and trolley parks of amusement heydays, now dropped unceremoniously between funnel cake stands and quarter-powered foot massage machines. It's only five dollars to witness the spider woman! Pay no heed to the human-head-sized hole carved in plywood above a puppet arachnid thorax. Seeds of distrust imbued at a young age, yet fascination instilled all the same.

Now I find myself personally ensconced between two known circus towns in Florida where one might find the bearded lady at the local Showman's pub or a decommissioned amusement ride on a suburban lawn. So, it would seem, for me at least, the Greatest Show is never far from where I dwell. It's an intangible appeal, and I find unmitigated comfort within the sideshow tent or the warped wood of the leisure park boardwalk.

The Show exists in many forms, even now as curious bygone relics that still manage to scrape by. Street buskers performing on piers and parks for tips, or daredevils inflicting pain upon themselves for our benefit to be gawked at with equal measures of repulsion and reverence.

Rigged games of chance for which you have no chance.

And of course, ever traipsing on the fringe of frivolity, the most popular trope of the dark carnival. Clowns fascinate me as a societal study of what we make of glimpses that exist beyond what we see. They're garish, unsettling, and they dwell within the dales of the immortal uncanny valley. Human but then, not quite. Something else beyond the veil of what should be familiar.

And therein lies the cotton candy heart of our Carnival Macabre. To take what is an instrument of cheer and amusement, and contort and corrupt it into something that should be wholesome but just…isn't. To make you scream, but not with glee. To "Step Right Up," and never return.

Memories of youth tarnished with the corrosion of something truly wicked, indeed. Or perhaps, this is all in our heads. Clowns are just here to make us laugh. Those rides that appear overnight in your local abandoned parking lot are unequivocally safe. That man inviting you into a dark tent wants to show you something amazing and wonderful. Something you'll never, ever forget.

So hurry, hurry, hurry! Don't be shy. See what wondrous marvels await within our joyous playland. So much fun to be had and sights to be seen.

Join the show.

And never mind that the word Carnival is derived from a Latin etymology that roughly translates to "Goodbye to Meat."

There's nothing macabre about that whatsoever.

It's all in good fun.

Now then…

Tickets, please.

CHAPTER ONE

THE BONE KING

Craig E. Sawyer

Moses Dunning unfurled his bedroll onto the floor of the freezing boxcar. The wind outside was howling like a cornered wild animal, each chill draft whistling through rusted sheet metal like the bite of jagged teeth. Two sets of curious eyes followed the broad-shouldered teen's every movement. He wondered if he had made a mistake by accepting the train-hoppers' offer to share their car for the night, but the snowstorm limited his choices of where he could lay his head.

"What made you decide to hit the rails?" the taller of the two young drifters asked. Moses noticed that his hands were fidgeting. He had a spiky, bleached blonde mullet, nearly white in the shadowed car. The other had red hair, freckles, and a sullen silence about him. Moses thought the pair might be planning to rob him, or worse. He hadn't had much luck with white people—especially ones with mullets—since he hopped his first train a few months ago.

Moses shrugged, turning his back toward the worst of the biting wind that rattled past the door. His worn Patagonia jacket was still serviceable for most weather, but the storm's chill had quickly seeped through every hole and crease in the fabric. "I'm just a-roamin'. I got tired of working dead-end jobs that had me killin' myself for little pay." Moses's voice was deep and calm, with a drawl dipped in molasses. In his short time on the rails, he'd learned it was better to be vague, unassuming. Besides, the story was always the same.

Gas prices had risen exponentially. Rent and groceries too. Whether it was the draw of adventure, ditching low-paying jobs, or to escape a bad home-life, there was a new breed of nomadic roustabouts riding the rails, looking for that next experience that playing video games and making TikTok videos just couldn't provide.

Moses had learned a lot in the last few months. Usually, it was less 'grand adventure' and more gritty, sad, survival.

"You got that look," the freckled boy said.

"What look?"

"Like you're hiding something."

"Naw, just looking for a place to stay warm." Moses adjusted his newsboy cap, hoping that would be the last of it. Better he not confirm their suspicions. He had gotten into a bit of trouble in a town a few miles back when he'd jumped off a freight in search of a decent meal. He ran into a few local teens, who started calling him names, and soon had him backed into an alleyway. One of them had a knife. Moses had been forced to fight his way out. He'd disarmed and stabbed his attacker pretty deep—hightailing it to the train yard to take the next train out before he was caught.

The red-headed boy chuckled. "You seen a skinny kid 'round here, goes by Carl?"

"Naw, no one but you two."

"That's a nice soldier's bindle you got there. I used to have one just like it. I sold it to a kid a while back in Virginia," the blonde teen said. Blondie picked up a banjo, idly plucking the strings, fingers passing over the black skull-shaped sticker affixed to the white wood. The look in his eyes didn't appear easy-go-lucky. He was all business, and he rubbed Moses the wrong way; if there was going to be trouble, it was going to be with him.

"Yeah, I got it from my daddy. He fought in the Middle East," Moses said with a fair amount of pride. "He died last year, and I didn't have no good reason to stay in my hometown."

"How about a girl with a nose ring, named Ziggy?" the freckled one asked.

"I told you, I haven't run into anyone since I got here, just you two." It felt like an interrogation, but it was still better than being out in the elements. Moses would keep his mouth shut and take it, at least until they got to another town. By what he could tell, they were in the middle of bum-fuck-nowhere.

"My name is Gutter, and this freckle-faced fuck is Jimmy. We've been train-hopping together for over two years now. I wouldn't wish a night out in this storm on my worst enemy, so you're welcome to ride along with us to California," Blondie said. Despite his welcoming offer, Gutter's smile was like a hungry dog, and his gaze kept shifting toward Jimmy.

"Mighty cool of you. My name is Moses," he said neutrally. "So, why is this train stopped in the middle of nowhere?"

"They're probably here 'cause of the carnival," Jimmy said. "My guess is they're loading it, 'cause of the storm n' all."

"What carnival?"

"Didn't you see the lights from the Ferris wheel, just east of the tracks?"

Moses shook his head. "Naw, I didn't see any lights."

"You must be blinder than a bat, cause they're *bright*," Gutter said, humming a few bars as he tuned the banjo's strings. "You got something wrong with your eyes?"

"They must be taking it down," Moses said. He didn't take the bait as he braced his back against the opposite wall of the train car.

"Maybe that's it."

"Where's this train headed to?"

"Not absolutely sure, but definitely west. Our plans are to get to Sacramento Valley, California. A man can get three months of work in the orchards, picking avocados during the harvesting season. We want to get off the trains for a while. I don't like it that Harlow caught the Westbound, but you're welcome to ride the whole way with us."

"Why didn't you go with him?" Moses asked.

Gutter broke into a belly-laugh, and shook his shaggy head.

"What's so damn funny?" Moses grumbled, wishing there was a way to end this conversation and close his eyes for a minute.

"Catching the Westbound means he's dead, dumbass."

"Better watch who you callin' names," Moses warned, keeping his eyes on Gutter as he plopped down on a bedroll. Just because he had to keep his head down didn't mean he had to be a doormat. "Jesus, how did he die?" he asked, curious despite himself.

"Two days ago, the train we'd been on came to a sudden stop, not far from here. I think there was a dead deer laying on the tracks. We'd spotted the lights from the carnival's Ferris wheel on the ride in. Thought we might be able to find some work there. Harlow hurt his ankle when he hit the ground, so he decided to sit it out while we walked over to the lights. We hadn't walked that far when we heard him scream. We found him lying face down a few feet from the tracks. His head and body had been smashed in like a ripe melon. We'd have got back on the train, but it had already moved on. We spotted this one and been hiding out here ever since."

"What did you do with the body?" Moses asked.

"We drug him over and buried him in the middle of a grove of pines."

"You just buried him? What about his family?"

"Hell, we don't know his family. And the cops would accuse us. Besides, Harlow was his roustabout name. None of us use our real names. How would you have done it differently, boy?"

Before he could think better of it, Moses got to his feet, strode over to Gutter, rage clear in his face. "I ain't your boy!"

"The B-Bone King got 'im," Jimmy said, his eyes filled with fear.

Gutter whirled around, casting his anger toward his friend. "Shut up with that bullshit! There ain't no such thing."

"What happened to Carl and Ziggy, then?"

"You missing more people?" Moses asked.

"They've only been gone an hour. They went out to find some dry wood for a fire."

"What the hell is a Bone King?"

Gutter sighed. "An old roustabout told us a ghost story," he said, setting his banjo down. "He said that there was something that lurks at crossroads—near train tracks—waiting for train-hoppers or teen travelers. You can tell he's around by a loud whistle he gives off. The story goes that he was a carnival freak accused of killing a teenage girl. It was back in the late 40s or some shit."

Moses sat back on his bedroll, and found himself tuning out the rattling, chilly dullness of the train car to listen to and imagine the story Gutter was telling. Anything to pass the time, distract them from the bubbling tension.

It had been a beautiful spring day outside the town of Fairhope, Arkansas, a town set a little way south of the train tracks. The sky was a clear, vibrant blue, and a lush field of dandelions surrounded the Madame

Sinti Traveling Carnival. The carnival was owned by its namesake, a strong-willed woman of Romani heritage who had immigrated to the United States after the war. Most of the Romani people were persecuted by the Nazis during the late 1930s; nearly half a million died in concentration camps. America was a new start, but the general attitude toward those called 'gypsies' was not the best, worse still for a single woman who owned her own business.

Her adopted son had an ailment that made his bones brittle, but he wore a protective suit made from animal bone. The boy grew up in the carnival, and would often perform as an illusionist—the Bone King. His best trick was that he seemed able to change his features to look like someone else. Carnival tales and playbill legends said that Madame Sinti found him as a child wandering in the woods after a bright light fell from the heavens. She always said that God had sent him to her.

The carnival normally didn't journey so far south, but due to some sick animals and bad weather, they had to stop in the small, sleepy town of Fairhope, Arkansas, just south of the tracks. They didn't pay any mind to the signs posted outside of town, not when they had so little choice in the matter; *"Don't let the sun go down on you here if you're a Gypsy or Grifter!"*

To the locals, no doubt the traveling show represented both of those things, but many of the town's inhabitants would come out to see what all the hoopla was about anyway. That's all Madame Sinti needed to capture their attention and earn a few coins, just like every other town she'd passed through.

Sixteen-year-old June Morris was one of those curious villagers. She was so over the moon at seeing an ad for the traveling carnival that she ripped it down and stuck it in her pocket. June was a fresh and bright-eyed sixteen-year-old with long, straight, blonde hair, the very definition of a rebellious preacher's daughter. She was careful to keep the carnival's playbill from the gaze of her bad-tempered father, who most certainly would not have let her go. Against her father's wishes, she snuck off to the carnival with her boyfriend that very afternoon. Many of the townsfolk had taken the train from Fairhope to the carnival grounds. The roads that led to the carnival were rough, barely more than worn trails, and most people didn't own a car.

Her boyfriend, Rant Dowd, was no prize. He was notorious for his thievery and lying, and thus the perfect boyfriend for a defiant teen. He was drunk before the train even pulled into the dirt field near the brightly colored tents.

The young couple bickered the entire afternoon. Rant caught June smiling at the odd-looking illusionist with a black top hat who had pulled a bouquet of flowers from his sleeve. June gave the magician an impromptu peck on the cheek, barely visible through his skull-like mask.

Rant pushed his paramour off the carousel in a fit of drunken, jealous rage, unconcerned by how June's head hit its metal edge on the way down.

The Bone King tried to stop her bleeding, but it was too late—she died in his arms, a bouquet of flowers spilled across her blood-stained face and neck. It didn't take a genius to figure out who they blamed for her death.

The locals tied the struggling illusionist to the railroad tracks. Madame Sinti tried to stop them, but the mob wanted someone to pay for June Morris's murder. They didn't care if their victim was innocent, as long as they looked the part of an outsider.

Fearful of the consequences, Rant pressed his advantage. "This goddamned freak tried to get fresh with my girlfriend," he bellowed drunkenly, waving his arms. "He pushed her off the carousel to her death!"

Someone out of the mob handed Rant a hammer from a high striker strongman game, pushing him toward the helpless boy. Rant approached the carnival illusionist with wild eyes. Heedless of his pleas and cries for mercy, he brought the mallet down on both of the magician's knees. Over and over, Rant swung the hammer, smashing all the bones in the teen's limbs. Other teens—other *men*—took up the grisly hammer when Rant dropped it in exhaustion.

After the poor boy's bones were little more than powder, the father of the dead girl led the crowd in a ferocious spell of hate and mob justice, like he had done many times at the Fairhope church on Sundays. "Damn his soul to the pits of Hell!" He spat his hate and grief to the blood-thirsty crowd, stirring the teenagers to a murderous rage.

Seizing her chance, Madame Sinti snatched the hammer, held it high above her head, and let out a deep, primal scream. "I place a curse upon you all! The spirit of the Bone King has always dwelt within the Earth, and he will rise again against the murderous! The sinful! The debauchers! Pray for their lost souls all you want, but in the end, if they have killed in sin or lust, the King will turn their bones to dust." Madame Sinti pulled what remained of her son off the tracks, and took his limp body back to the carnival grounds.

She buried him with top hat and hammer, then took a knife and cut her palm. The blood dripped onto the dirt, onto the shattered bone brace that had once sheltered her son's body, just as the dirt would shelter him in death. She whistled three times, calling on every dark and vengeful energy she knew, chanting softly as she took the lanterns down, removed the safety glass, and set the canvas tent alight. Hate and grief made her indifferent to the screams, to the souls caught in burning tents as she set each one to oil and torch.

The flames licked and whistled as the carnival burned to ash. The smoke could be seen all the way into town and, ever since, the legend of the Bone King was told to any teen traveling through those parts.

In the boxcar, everyone was quiet.

Moses wasn't sure what to think about the story.

"Look, the new kid is scared," Gutter jeered.

Moses rolled his eyes. "You really believe that story?"

Jimmy took over, eager to add his two cents. "The old man s-said if you whistle three times and say his name, he'll come up from Hell for revenge. And he said the Bone King can play tricks on a person's mind, too."

"He won't whistle, he's too chicken-shit," Gutter said. He went back to strumming the banjo.

Moses gave a defiant smile. "I'm not scared." He whistled three times, making sure the trio of notes was louder than the wind that still blew through the car.

"Don't say it," Jimmy said.

The kid was wringing his hands. It was too hard to resist fucking with him, just a little bit. Maybe then they'd shut up and leave him be.

"Bone King!" Moses yelled.

"Dammit! Why did you do that?"

"Would you shut the fuck up, dumbass? The only trick on your mind was the story," he groused, winking at Jimmy as if he'd missed some kind of signal.

Ah, fuck, Moses thought, slowly moving his hand into his pocket, around the handle of his knife.

"Any requests?" Gutter asked, as Jimmy leaned back and picked up something from behind an old stack of boxes.

He wasn't very careful about going unnoticed—with all the cocky confidence of a white teenage boy. There was a pit growing in Moses's stomach, but he tried the best he could to stay calm. "Yeah, you know *Lies* by the Black Keys?"

"Naw, I don't know that one."

Moses readied himself for the attack, but before Jimmy raised whatever weapon he'd been hiding, there was a sharp, loud whistle outside the sliding metal doors.

All three of them jumped in surprise. Gutter raised a finger to his lips, motioning for silence. Moses stood up, pulling the small knife from his pocket.

"I thought you said you didn't have anything?" Jimmy hissed as he pulled out the wooden club he'd been hiding.

"Y'all didn't tell me about your weapons! You were planning on robbing me, weren't you?"

"Maybe you were planning on robbing us!" Gutter brandished a pair of tarnished knuckles between them, his intent clear.

"Both of you, shut up! Listen." Jimmy moved up to flank the cracked roll door.

Moses shook his head and exhaled a nervous breath. Gutter glanced over at him and nodded, both moving to the door.

It squealed loudly as they slid it open. The blast of air that hit Moses's face was so cold, it took his breath away. A flurry of snow blew in, followed by a scrawny, hooded figure.

Gutter and Jimmy jumped on the stranger, beating him about the head and shoulders for a few long seconds. "Stop hitting me," a high-pitched male voice yelled. "It's me, Carl!"

The two punched and hit him in the head a few more times before they stopped. "Why didn't you say that before you threw open the door?"

Moses was glad he hadn't started stabbing the kid. "Damn, you know this guy?"

A scarecrow-thin boy, about sixteen, stood shaking like a leaf in the wind. His nose had already started to swell, and a small stream of blood ran down his lips and chin. "I think you broke my fucking nose, you assholes!"

Maybe it was the train yard, but the frail-looking boy smelled funny to Moses, like sulfur or something. There were red stains on his boots. "I'm Moses."

Jimmy poked his head out and looked down the tracks in both directions before sliding the door closed again. "You see any train workers out there, Carl?"

"No! I didn't see nothing. It's colder than a witch's tit out there." The boy stomped his boots, knocking the snow from them, and rubbed his own shoulders furiously. "Oh, shit...I dropped the wood by the tracks."

"So, where's Ziggy?" Gutter asked.

Carl's eyes were wide, like a frightened rabbit.

"I asked you a question!" the blond teen snapped.

"She started going on and on about lights she was seeing. I told her that there were no lights over the hill, but she wouldn't listen. It's like she was obsessed. She started running up the hill. I chased after her, but when I reached the top and looked over, she was gone, and there were no lights anywhere, but there was this loud whistle."

"You foolin' with us, again?" Gutter shook his fist. "What really happened?"

"Wait...you heard a whistle?" Jimmy's eyes were wide as dinner plates.

Carl cleared his throat and nodded. "I can't explain it. It was just a crazy loud whistle."

Gutter leapt across the narrow car, grabbed Carl by his snow-slicked jacket, and pinned him against the door. "You did something to her!" he roared in the kid's face.

"Nothing! I didn't do anything to her! I think whoever killed Harlow might have done something to her," Carl pleaded helplessly, panicked spit flying from his mouth, mixed with blood from his nose.

"Let him be!" Jimmy yelled.

"Okay...okay!" Carl cried out. "I'll take you to the last place I saw her! Jesus!"

Gutter released him and turned to the others. "You! New guy! Time to earn your keep."

Moses wasn't in any hurry to help them. They had been about to mug him, for Chrissake, but he had little chance three against one, knife or no knife. He nodded. Besides, if there was a girl in danger, he should help anyway.

Gutter threw open the boxcar door, but stopped Carl as he walked past. "You sure you're telling me everything? I'm gonna find out if you're not."

"What are you getting at?"

"You have a thing for Ziggy."

"We all had a thing for Ziggy."

Gutter pushed past him. "It's funny you used the word *had*."

The snow had stopped, but it left a glowing blanket of white over the rural landscape. It didn't take long for the boys to make their way down the tracks, wound like a snake around a row of tall pines. The area that Carl had mentioned sat less than two hundred feet away, through a dense grove of cedars, and beyond that was the steep hill Carl had mentioned. Long icicles hung from the eaves of the train, but there was no sign of workers, or any life, for that matter. A chill ran down Moses's spine, something that went far beyond the cold.

Behind the trees, on the other side of the hill, a series of ghostly lights rotated, swirling and bouncing off the sheet of white and the night sky. It was hypnotic and beautiful.

Gutter pointed. "That's it...the carnival?"

"Man, how did I not see that before?" Moses spoke in a dazed voice. "It's amazing."

The cold night had sharper teeth than before, nipping through their inadequate jackets, as the three made their way past the side of the train and through the trees. Moses pulled his hood up, trying to warm his numb cheeks and keep his nose from icing over.

He had always hated the cold, but *this* terrain had a dream-like quality to it. A quarter moon shone down on the blanket of pale, cool earth, reflecting enough light to reveal their way. Moses kept his hand in his pocket, fingers curled around his knife. After all, this could be an elaborate trick to get him in the woods and kill him.

Snow crunched loudly under boots, and Moses felt moisture invading his socks. His feet were wet, making him tremble and his teeth chatter.

Gutter was leading the group. He abruptly stopped and bent down to inspect a patch of snow.

"What is it?" Jimmy asked.

"Tracks, I think they belong to Ziggy. They look about the right size for a girl," Gutter said, eyes following the marks. "Look there!" he yelled, pointing toward a dark, red hump in the snow. It was about twenty-five feet away, near a circle of trees. The bright lights of the carnival lay beyond the hill. "It's her red jacket!"

Snow was falling again. Moses could see his own warm breath, and he wondered what he had gotten himself into.

"Wait, is that...Ziggy?" Gutter pointed to the top of the hill. A pretty girl was looking down at them and waving, her face in shadow. She yelled and motioned for them to join her, the bright glow of the carnival silhouetting her.

"It's her!" Carl took off in a dead sprint toward her. "I told you I didn't do anything to her! What are you waiting for?"

"Wait!" Gutter said, but it was too late; Carl was already trudging up the snow-covered hill at a steady pace. "I should go after him," Gutter said. "You and Jimmy stay here."

"Wait! I can go with you!" Moses said. He didn't want them to get out of his sight.

"No, I'll be right back!" Gutter snapped, waving them back.

Jimmy looked sheepishly over at Moses. "This is getting weirder and weirder."

"Why isn't she wearing her jacket?"

"What did you say?" Jimmy asked between chattering teeth.

"It's freezing out here. Why would she not have her jacket on? She was on that hill dressed like it was a summer day," Moses said, pointing at the hump of a jacket buried in the snow. Something was terribly wrong. He moved towards it.

"What are you doing?"

Moses paused as he bent over the red hump in the snow. "What did you say about the Bone King? He could play tricks?"

Jimmy nodded. "Wait...you don't think?"

Moses touched the jacket with the tip of his knife.

Nothing happened.

Jimmy sighed with relief.

"I'm tripping," Moses said, and let out a relieved snicker.

A sharp loud whistle broke the silence, echoing through the trees, three high-pitched tones of alarm, of warning. Jimmy was pushed to one knee by the sound.

It felt like an icepick being plunged into Moses's eardrums.

"Jesus!" he yelled as he covered his ears. Moses moved closer to the lump of snow, took his fingers from his ears and pulled the jacket's hood back.

Underneath was the broken corpse of a young girl. She had a nose piercing and green eyes. Patches of stringy hair fluttered out from the sides of the fur-lined hood. Her face had been smashed in, her mouth left agape; caught in a scream of terror.

"Oh, Jesus, Z-Ziggy?" an equally pained Jimmy blurted.

"We've got to find the others! Let's go!" Moses urged, helping Jimmy to his feet.

They took off, running up the hill to where the lights beckoned.

They reached the top and looked down into the small valley. Less than fifty yards away was a fully functioning carnival. Pulsating lights and calliope music filled the air. Moses could smell popcorn, and the sweet sugary scent of cotton candy.

Entranced, the boys walked into the beckoning illusion. They stared in awe, transfixed by paintings of exotic animals, freaks and feats of magic, games of chance and skill, the smash and slam of nearby bumper cars. A row of tents at the back featured gaily-ribboned banners above stages. Rushing wind hit their faces from the tilt-a-whirl as its buckets spun and twirled.

"It's beautiful! How is this possible?" Moses whispered in confusion.

It didn't make sense, but Jimmy was soaking it all in, like a child dazzled by the colors in a kaleidoscope. He jumped up on an empty stage and looked inside one of the many tents. "Where are the people?"

Moses stopped at a cotton candy machine, tore off a piece, and stared at it. "This is fresh, like it was just made."

"Gutter! Carl?" Jimmy called out over the music. "Oh, my God... look," Jimmy said, his voice sounding child-like. "That is so cool!"

Straight ahead, through the ghostly lights, was an antique carousel. It was filled with horses and mermaids, spinning fast. Riding on several of them were Ziggy, Gutter, Harlow, and Carl. They looked like they were having the time of their lives.

"Come on, man! It's so much fun!" Gutter called out as he blurred past on a brightly painted unicorn.

Jimmy grabbed the fluffy piece of cotton candy from Moses's hand and took a bite, rubbing the remaining sugar on his sleeve. "You guys had me so worried! And here you are having fun without me!" He started walking toward the merry-go-round.

Moses snatched at his shoulder. "Don't go near it," he said, trying to keep the younger boy back. There was something evil about all of it, he just wasn't sure what.

"Why not?"

"It's not right. They're not right," he said in panicked exasperation. Something dark and shadowed stood in the middle of the spinning horses, like a spider in its web. "Do you see him?"

"See who?" Jimmy asked, distracted by the glimmering, spinning machine.

Moses raised his hand and pointed.

The happy faces of the riders turned to pure hate. With each pass, their faces and bodies became bloodier and more inhuman-looking. The horses and mermaids melted along with the flesh of their riders, until they were only bones. The merry-go-round spun faster and faster, blue flames gathering around the spinning base, whistling louder and louder as it picked up speed. A tall, shadowy figure stood untouched at the center of the flames, surrounded by burning bodies. He wore a top hat and carried a large hammer dripping with blood.

Whistling.

"We need to get back to the train, now!" Moses screamed, turning away from the horror. "Don't look at it!"

Jimmy kept walking toward the carousel, as if hypnotized.

"To hell with you," Moses said. He took off in a flat sprint toward the tracks. As he ran through the carnival grounds, the bright lights and music started to fade. His feet felt frozen and stiff, but he pushed through the pain, using it to ground him in reality and ignore the faltering illusions around him. The gleaming Ferris wheel was replaced by a rusted one. The cotton candy smell was overpowered by the stench of burning meat. Moses passed a water-damaged and bullet-riddled sign that read: *Madame Sinti Traveling Carnival.*

The whistling was slowly fading. Moses got closer and closer to the snake-like train. An out of breath Jimmy ran up beside him. Moses had gotten through to him after all. "Are there any others?" Moses asked, out of breath.

"No, they're all gone. It's just us. I saw the train engineer climbing aboard. I think the train is about to leave."

"Good, let's get the hell out of here."

Moses climbed into an empty box-car, and helped Jimmy inside. The boy pulled the door closed behind them, shutting out the wind and light.

"Wait, it's dark as hell in here. Do you have a flashlight, or a lighter?"

Jimmy was silent.

"Jimmy?"

Loud whistling and the crunch of bone filled the boxcar. Panicked, he fumbled in the darkness for the latch and handle. He finally found it and threw the door open.

The light from the moon was enough to see a man with a top hat standing beside him—the same figure from the carousel. His bones cracked terribly with every step, and those in his face protruded through sallow skin. His body was protected with a suit of animal bones. In his hands was a large hammer.

Moses turned to jump off the train, but tripped and landed badly, and a shock of pain in his knee brought him down. He glanced back at the Bone King, as he lumbered toward him.

"You are the one who called me!" The Bone King said, his eyes filled with hate. *"All who hear the whistle must die."*

Moses felt the words more than he heard them. "You don't have to do this," he cried, raising his hands. "I didn't mean to call you!"

"It was you who summoned me," the Bone King replied calmly. His yellow knuckles tightened on the hammer's grip as he grew closer.

"I didn't do nothing to you, man!" Moses heard a whistle in the distance, but not from the Bone King. It was a train whistle, one coming down a nearby track.

Moses turned to look out the open door. The train's smokestack was getting closer, winding through the hills as the rising sun peeked over the snowy and desolate landscape, which seemed like a million miles away from the dark interior of the box car. Moses planned to pull the door shut as he jumped out, but he realized it was jammed. He took out his pocket knife and worked on the door's mechanism, trying to get it unstuck.

The Bone King was almost upon him, only inches away from bringing his weapon down.

"Come on, dammit!" Moses swore, putting all his effort into it.

The door creaked as its rusted gears rumbled to life. Moses scooted underneath it, just as it slammed shut.

He fell hard to the ground, but the adrenaline pumping through his veins helped him to work through the pain. He was surprised to see the outside of the train had changed. It appeared old and abandoned now, like it had been that way for decades. Gnarled tree limbs were growing through its corroded holes and out of its smokestack.

The Bone King could play tricks on a person. He had been playing with their minds ever since they got here. This was all one big trap.

The painted letters on the side of the train car swam into sudden focus. *The Bone King is whistling for you!*

Moses bolted through the field, running as fast as he could manage toward the billowing smoke of the whining train.

Miraculously, he reached the moving locomotive, tried to hoist himself up and place a foot on the railing, like he'd done a hundred times before. But after a fifty-yard dash through the cold on a bum knee, it was an impossible task. Moses missed the step and tumbled into the tall, icy grass lining the tracks, his knife flying free of his grip in the fall. He lay there a moment, trying to catch his breath, but someone—or something—was stalking through the weeds toward him. The whistling was deafening this time, drowning out the droning rattle of the train. Moses searched frantically in the thick pampas for his knife, fingers closing only on damp, crinkling grass.

The shrill whistling stopped. Moses tried to control his panicked breathing—the silence was deafening, as still and cold as the snow beneath him.

He raised his head to peek over the swaying vegetation as the Bone King's hammer came swinging down.

CHAPTER TWO

RACLURE'S CURIOSITY

Amy Westphal

Soon, the night would lose grasp of the darkness, allowing the pale pink of morning to varnish the sky. In this fleeting Time Between, Coventry Lane appeared like any other street in the good portion of the city—dark, cold, and extravagant. Manicured shrubbery and homes wrought with ornate columns and delicate buttresses loomed ominously above the two cloaked figures scampering below their many-roomed interiors.

The small boy knew better than to stray towards street lamps and candle-lit windows, but he could not prevent his imagination from envisioning the honey-glow of the hearths held within. Undoubtedly warm and toasty, inside a home he would never have.

A girl with no such illusions remained watchful, for the scent in the air was not of a crackling wood stove but of wet ash hovering low in the atmosphere, revealing that not all was right on the lovely street in its early hours, where moonlight waned against the impending sunrise.

"I think we've found it, Vi. It reeks of ash, and wet towels and rotting food."

Vi knew the harrowing scent. It haunted her olfactory memories like a forlorn ghost. "It's the smell of decay, Tommy, even the frost can't hide it. We've indeed found the right street."

The siblings continued down the quiet lane, mindful of their thin shoes on the slick black pavement.

"I see it, Tommy. The end there, see how it leans in the direction of the wind? It may not last the night. We should hurry."

"Oh, I don't like this."

"I'm sorry, but if we come back to the Curiosity empty-handed, Raclure will punish us more surely than this old house ever could."

"That's not funny, Vi."

"It's not meant to be." Vi nudged her brother towards the wreckage, a once-grand home of two stories burnt to one skeletal half.

They felt the warmth emanating from the detritus. Spires of smoke slunk and curled from the collapsed veranda. Vi ungloved her hand for a finer touch. "It's quite warm, Tommy, but just. We shouldn't be in danger of burning."

"Just regular danger then?"

"We'll be quick. You know what to look for."

"I know, I know, jewels, art, and anything unnatural."

"Anything that can tell a story, yes, but nothing too obvious. And I know you know this, but it helps us keep focus on what's possible. People come to the Curiosity to revel, and to see the unbelievable; artifacts from far-off lands, gold from Egypt, relics from Rome. A simple ornamental box could be the snuff box of King Henry the VIII."

"But really, it's their own frilly novelties re-sold to them. People are silly."

"They don't even realize; they see something familiar made extraordinary. A bronze finial becomes a Tibetan ritual weapon when you add glass beads."

"I suppose when you want for nothing…" He squinted into the dark.

Vi let out a long puff of steam, the windchill stinging as she inhaled again. "Let's make it a good one, alright? A warm meal will lift your spirits."

Tommy nodded.

The shriveled door hung from charred hinges and swung open with a snap, sending flakes of crusted red paint into the air. Inside, the wind hissed through shattered windows.

"Light your lantern now, Tommy."

Vi lit her own and inspected the entryway. Although warped and blackened from damp soot and ash, its walls stood fairly intact. They had scavenged much worse.

Vi could feel the heat cooling by the moment and wondered if the coroner would make it before the home's inevitable collapse. "Strike while it's hot, Tommy. It won't be warm much longer. Stay focused," she whispered, entombing the terrible images deep in her mind.

They walked in tandem down the hall, the weak floorboards crackling underfoot, the smell of Bakelite and smoke burning their lungs. They kept their keen, practiced eyes moving, taking in the blistered olive wallpaper and tarnished bronze sconces. Muddy soot swirled in erratic patterns across the warped floor.

The siblings broke stride when they entered the living room. Tommy took a fancy to a charred cigar table while Vi carried on, testing the floorboards and skimming the ceiling as she counted viable rooms. The dining room was nothing but rubble. The scorched remains of a four-poster bed sat in place of the dining table while the moon gaped at the shimmering wreckage. Vi did not wish to gaze upon the waning spotlight, the thick plumes emanating from the pyre, or the piles of burnt sheets, so she passed to the next room.

The parlor appeared promising. The floor above had caved in and its contents slid out into the garden, leaving a slanted ceiling.

Through the rotting forest of blackened and crispy brocade upholstery and decimated wood furnishings was an unblemished portrait of a young girl, hanging inside a fine gilded frame. Vi's eyes lingered on the portrait for longer than prudent; the way it survived vexed her logic.

She shook her head, turning away to search the rest of the room, lamenting all the indiscernible charcoal armatures laid to waste.

Only an ugly set of tarnished silver candlesticks were salvageable from the mess. Vi tucked them into the pockets sewn inside her black cloak, then moved along.

The last assessable room was the kitchen, but kitchens seldom held anything of practical, transportable value. The fine china, and silver—if any—would more likely reside in the dining room, often under lock and key. But Vi and Tommy had no interest in obvious riches. They were instructed to make note of these but never take, for that was a dangerous game played by thieves. Vi and Tommy searched for a story, for subtlety, in exchange for room and board; a goldmine that good flatware could never buy. Vi did a quick survey of the kitchen's explosion of brick and tile, then an even quicker one of the dining room, before heading back to her brother.

She walked softly, her lantern painting strange pictures on the bubbled toile. She glanced at the fractured ceiling, and through the blackened and sagging support beams, to find the sky had turned gray. It was time to go.

Tommy was still in the living room, on his knees, covered in soot.

"Well now, little sir."

"Look, Vi." Tommy held his lantern over the bulging parquet floor, revealing several sets of cufflinks with real ivory and colorful jewels.

"Tommy, you're wonderful! Raclure will be so pleased. I found a dreadful set of candlesticks, but also a gorgeous portrait of a young girl."

Tommy shoved the cufflinks into a cut seam inside his own cloak before following Vi to the parlor.

Vi dusted the floor with her feet as she walked, mindful of the steps they left behind and the weak floorboards. "The wall is burnt, but the portrait is perfect, totally unblemished."

"Where is it?"

"Right there, above the curio. Do mind the shattered glass, it's quite a mess."

"I only see a mirror."

Vi looked up from the floor and held up her lantern.

The portrait was gone.

"Well, that's odd, I was quite sure..."

"Another room, perhaps?"

"Only the living room, dining room, kitchen, and stairs are accessible, and hardly so, the rest is collapsed. Even I don't trust those stairs."

The siblings took another lap around the ground floor but kept returning to the mirror. Same lovely gilded frame, but no lovely face within.

"Are you sure you saw what you saw?"

"I was certain," she mused. "Such a sad, pretty, young girl. She was in profile, like this." Vi tilted her head gently to show Tommy. "She looked as if she was pining for something, how could I forget?"

"Maybe it was your own reflection?"

"I'm far too old, and I've never been pretty a day in my life."

"You are to me. Like mum."

Vi gave Tommy a scant smile. "Perhaps I'm seeing things. It's freezing and so noxious in here, my head is spinning. The mirror will be just as good, better if it's haunted." Vi held her lantern above her head and gave him a ghoulish grin with all her teeth showing.

Tommy shuddered appropriately. "Oh, a haunted mirror, Vi! That will be quite the attraction indeed. Very smart. Raclure will eat it up! Let's grab it and go before any early risers see us over their morning tea."

Vi unhooked the mirror, still warm on her ungloved hand. "You know, brother, you're so covered in soot, I don't think you'll be visible anyway."

The boy giggled in his mittens and sighed. "I sure miss Malcolm, Vi."

She froze. Laughter always brought memories of Malcolm. "I do too," she replied with a sharp intake of frosty breath.

She tucked the mirror under her woolen sweater before adjusting her cloak. Then, with their treasures secure, the Lords of the Time Between made their way away from Coventry Lane. The sun ached to rise, and they could not be seen in such a fine neighborhood.

They dashed past quiet lane after lofty avenue, until the distance between buildings shrunk to a sliver. In the heart of the city at dawn, they skirted the sturdy beggars and yellow glow of street lamps deftly without so much as a jingle in their hidden pockets. For nothing could wake a man down on his luck like clinking metal.

They arrived at the Curiosity as the sun bloomed over the horizon, both starved and chilled to the bone, but unscathed by vagrants or the law.

It was a good haul, enough for a hot meal and a hot bath, Vi wagered, but not without the approval of their warden, Cornelius M. Raclure. A jovial, engaging man to his many patrons, but a vulture of a father figure once the door of his beloved museum locked shut.

Vi unsheathed her key to unlock the door, but Tommy pulled her away.

"Vi, look! Raclure used our papier-mâché cat skulls for the window this week."

"Shrunken heads, you mean?"

"Shrunken heads…yes…from Peru."

"Yes, Peru. Very good, brother." She smiled before leaving him to marvel in the cold. Raclure would be in the office, waiting for the siblings to arrive and present their findings. Vi hung her cloak and mittens on the hat rack, releasing a tumble of damp curls as she did so.

"Well, if it isn't the Lords of the Time Between."

"Malcolm?" The name unraveled from Vi's lips like an escaped sigh. "You're here." She brushed and dusted herself in harried fashion.

Malcolm grinned. "Yes, spring holiday."

"How…how is it?" Vi blustered, collecting her composure before it spilled on the floor with ungainly affect. "University, I mean." She kept her hands tight to her treasure like a talisman.

"It's really good, Vi. I've brought home last term's books. For you." Malcolm felt the same pull, but stood still, a fumble of hand-wringing.

"Thank you." She exhaled, keenly aware of the door to her left. The door that stood between them, the one that divided them.

"Well, actually, there's one for Tommy, about pirates."

"He'll love it, of course." She smiled, digging her heels into the floor. "You know, Tommy just remarked how much he missed you. When you were with us. I can't believe it's been what…three years?"

"Yes. Three. And almost two since I left…I miss it too, always."

They exhaled at the same time. "Although," he continued, "the last time was one too many, I think."

"That atrocious tear-down, yes. Your foot went right through the floorboards into the cellar and you twisted your ankle. You looked ridiculous." Vi chuckled and the mirror thumped against her chest. She held it tighter, her body longing to fall into the comfort and ease of a different time.

"Neither of you could lift me. I think I'd grown half a foot that year. So, you fashioned me a crutch from a rake and a flour sack. You were always so brilliant, Vi." Malcolm's handsome face flushed, but he did not look away. "Who'd have thought I'd turn out so clunky and gangly? I was such a runt."

"No, you've become a fine man, Malcolm." Her eyes held firmly on his.

"And you, Vi." He took a single step forward, the desire to drop all pretense aching in his fingers. "You've become a fine lady, though as petite and light of foot as ever, I see."

Vi held her ground. "I'm grown, yes, but I will never be a lady."

"You are to me."

Vi licked her suddenly-parched lips, her eyes burning. "Your father finally let you have a holiday at home, I see."

"Yes. Raclure seems to feel enough time has passed. We have made many good acquisitions, and many fortuitous connections—but it hasn't changed anything. No time or distance could." He took another step forward. "Someday, Vi."

"Yes?"

"Someday, soon, it will be you and I...and Tommy." He grinned, placing another foot forward, the distance of Raclure's door frame between them, the only distance that ever mattered.

Vi smiled, a single tear escaping from her stormy eyes.

Malcolm glanced at his father's office door. "We'll have a real carnival one day. With real treasures from real places where we've adventured. And rides. Like we've always dreamed."

"Rides?"

"That go round and round and..."

"And?"

The door creaked.

Vi jumped back.

Malcolm reached out and wiped the tear from her cheek. He stepped back, his hand pressed to his heart. "Find me in the Time Between," he whispered.

Vi pursed her lips in the delight of his touch, the soft scent of bay and lemon lingering. She turned around as she drew a long, ragged breath before retrieving her brother, who was not outside but peeking through the door with a smug grin on his sooty face.

She ushered him in as their warden emerged from his office. Raclure gave them a curt nod and gestured for them to enter. Vi cradled the mirror under her sweater, the warmth of it like a tender embrace as she and her brother walked single file to offer their tribute.

The old man returned to his desk and scratched a few more marks in his ledger with swift and decisive strokes. When he finally lifted his gaze to the siblings, his expression was unreadable, nothing more than brows and thin lips pressed into a straight line.

He huffed. "Virginia?"

Vi gulped in the heady aroma of dust and snuff, and curtsied. "This morning, I present to you, sir, these unassuming candlesticks of real silver. They are stout in shape and not of current fashion, but I imagine they were too valuable to be discarded, making their age and value quite intriguing under the tarnish."

35

Raclure nodded, the lines between his tidy silver brows vaguely etched; not terribly impressed, but not angry either. He scratched a few more marks into his books. Vi held her breath.

"Thomas?"

"Sir, I think you will quite enjoy these items today." Tommy stepped forward with optimistic confidence unusual for his station. "I present to you these three sets of cufflinks, found by a smoldering cigar stand."

Raclure inclined his head. "Go on."

"Well, sir, when we entered the location, I noticed a hat-stand and coat rack and thought, this is a man who hangs his own hat. He's a working man, but in a fine home. You see, sir, from the coat rack, there was a progression, the remains of a pair of leather shoes sat next to a fireside chair with the cigar table nearby."

"And what makes that cigar table stand out, Thomas?"

"Well, now. This man, who hangs his own hat, he is the picture of well-earned comforts, like yourself, sir. A man who would sit, roll up his sleeves, and smoke a fine cigar after a long day."

Raclure grinned, the type that made one's arm hair stand on end. His hands were absentmindedly rolling up the sleeves of his own impeccably starched shirt.

"And this man, sir, would have finery to take off, wouldn't he?"

The old man took a magnifying glass to the boy's findings. "Yes. Ivory. Real. Enamel and 18 karat gold. These are good. Very good, but not too good. Well done." Raclure sat back in his imposing chair, possibilities dancing in his dark eyes.

"We have another item, sir," Vi added, pleased that her brother had impressed him so.

"Go on," he mused, his gaze perusing the menagerie of artifacts on his overstuffed shelves.

"This." Vi untucked her thick woolen sweater and revealed her treasure.

"A mirror?"

"Yes. It was inside the parlor, in the most perfect condition. Look." She presented the frame with both hands. Raclure stood up and reached over his desk. His fingers brushed the still-warm metal and recoiled in anguish upon its touch. Vi felt the electricity.

"Static, fascinating," he whispered, rubbing his hand. He reached for it again and took the frame in his wizened fingers, scrutinizing each inch of its splendor. "I see. It is magnificent. And in fine condition for surviving a fire. Extraordinary, really. It should have shattered. I'm impressed today." His tone surprised even himself.

"Indeed, sir. The house was teetering as we left. I'm sure it will collapse soon with whatever strongbox it may contain. There's also a bed where the dining table should be, and all of it still smoldering where I'm sure the silverware would be."

Raclure squinted in acknowledgement of their reconnaissance, their truest purpose. Then he looked at the mirror again, his mind spinning new webs of deceit before their eyes, his interest ebbing in its purveyors.

Vi pressed harder against his rare mood. "I thought at first, sir, that the mirror was a portrait, so real it could have been a photograph. Just a lovely, melancholy girl."

The old man peeled his eyes away from the mirror. "But when you came closer, there wasn't a girl? Intriguing."

"Yes. Perhaps it was a trick of the light or my own reflection, but perhaps it's haunted. A spirit girl trapped in a mirror, only revealing herself to whom, I wonder?" Vi clenched her teeth against her desire to smile.

"Yes," he hissed. "She reveals herself, but to whom? Whom..." He skulked around the room between the siblings in a dance with the mirror. "She only reveals herself to the most depraved individuals." He lowered his voice to a whisper. "Yes. A curse on their name if they see her. People will yearn to look, but fear it even more, yes!"

Raclure cackled at his own reflection, his own brilliance. "They will remark on their virtue and tell their friends, whose indulgent hearts will want to measure their own!" He bellowed with self-satisfaction, perspiration beading at the temples of his severely parted hair.

The siblings clapped. "Brilliant, sir. Brilliant," they cried in unison, Vi's smirk disguised in admiration.

"Well, I'll say, I think that has earned you a spot of tea and breakfast. And most certainly a bath. Off you go."

"Yes, sir. Thank you, sir." The siblings bowed and left the sweltering office for the kitchen, glowing from the grace bestowed upon them by their fickle warden.

Matilda, the housekeeper, would be pleased. She enjoyed good days as much as they did.

"Tommy! Vi, you're here! That's good news."

"Raclure is pleased with us, and we're starved." Tommy salivated over Matilda's prep counter.

"I couldn't be happier, a good week for you is a good week for me."

"You're too kind, I couldn't bear another week of cold broth for Tommy."

"A nice break is long overdue. Every week is another burn-down, move, or probate, it seems. Can't anyone stay still?"

"Nothing is more certain to us in life than death, and days are busy when you thrive in the misfortune of others."

"Well, I like that." She huffed. "How droll, Vi. You're growing quite the edge around you."

Tommy frowned as he spooned mountains of porridge into two bowls. Dark circles rimmed his blue eyes.

Vi sighed. "I'm sorry. Every day, I go through the motions, but today…"

"What?"

"Do you ever miss it, Mati?"

"Miss what?"

"Being a Lord?"

"Me? Gracious, no. I was dreadful. I was a much more efficient pickpocket. Silly, clumsy girls always are." She winked.

"Well, luckily you're a marvelous cook."

"And gratefully so. It's been…five years now?"

Vi furrowed her brows, recalling her years under the twilight. "Yes. Five for you, and Auggie and Abel, of course. It's unbelievable, isn't it? Ten Lords in all—down to us two."

"Six years and counting, I remember it well."

"Me too, I'd have sold my soul to the Devil himself to get off the street. And, alas, wishes do come true." She beamed artificially.

"Careful, Vi, there's only six of us left, don't make it five."

She bristled. "I should've run."

"Run. What for? What's one man for another? Even the worst of them are frightfully predictable. We're safe where we have purpose."

"In the armor of roasted beef," Vi replied with a hollow laugh before scooping large spoonfuls of porridge and bacon into her mouth.

"Indeed." Matilda chuckled. "You don't forget what medium-rare looks like after a go in the heave."

"As if a normal corset isn't torture enough," she said, muffled through a large gulp.

"Indeed, indeed. I haven't seen the main attraction since."

Tommy's eyes rose briefly from his bowl as he continued to eat with vigor.

"There are good men, you know," Vi mused.

"There are, I suppose, but not for girls like us." Matilda's words cut sharper than the knife she wielded so deftly. "You'll be the last Lords, I believe," she continued, as if rehearsed. "The master has made great strides in polite society. He's expanded the Curiosity and earned himself quite a position. I can only hope that will bode well for us. We must remain useful, and loyal. Keep that in mind if I were you."

"I will."

"You can ask, you know." A sly smile stretched across Matilda's ruddy face.

Vi smirked. "Ask what?"

"You know very well that Malcolm's back, said he saw you this morning."

"He's taken breakfast already, then?" Vi frowned, unabashed by her disappointment.

"Yes. And he'll be working in the box office for the school holiday. The master is quite intent on Malcolm partnering with him after he graduates."

"Naturally."

"He, also, my little pixie, is as smitten with you today as the day he first laid eyes on you. And you he, but you must hide it. You know that, right, Vi?" To soften the blow, Matilda gave Vi a spoonful of the tart filling she was preparing for afternoon tea. "The master thinks Malcolm's outgrown you, and you must act as if you've outgrown him. Your future depends on it. I fear his wrath for you, I really do. He won't just take Malcolm on another tour for holiday, not anymore. Your skill and size won't save you, and you know what happens when you no longer have purpose. Please, Vi, for you and Tommy. For all of us."

"I understand." She always had.

Matilda took the spoon from Vi and sent the siblings upstairs to rest. Vi helped Tommy under his covers with his shoes still on, then collapsed on her own bed.

For being newly fed, she was empty.

"Why can't you and Malcolm just get married now?" Tommy asked while kicking his shoes to the floor with a thump. "I really want to go to Australia and see the bushmen."

"Tommy! We're far too young and it isn't so simple."

"He loves you. You love him. Why does anything else have to matter?"

"Raclure has worked many years making the Curiosity what it is today. He was the ward of his brother, you know, the kidsman? He was a pickpocket, just like we were."

"I thought he axed his brother?" Tommy whispered.

"Yes, and everyone who ever crossed him, brothers, wives, thieves and Lords." The words crept over Tommy's skin, sending shivers down his spine. He pulled his tatty covers close.

"But now, our silent servitude is more crucial than ever. He's accepted in good society and is an esteemed businessman. And Malcolm is his heir. I'm a woman with no dowry or worth. He can't marry me."

"I shall never understand the evil or the rich, Vi."

"I know it's hard."

"Do you think we're bad people?"

Vi considered her answer. "No." She let the word linger in the air, choosing her next with equal care. "We didn't choose this life, regardless of how adept we are. We did *not* choose it. And some day…"

"Soon?"

"Someday, things will change for us."

"You must listen to Matilda then, Vi."

"I know. I'll be careful."

Tommy nodded, his eyes swimming in the promise of something better before closing again. Only moments passed before his breaths evened and deepened. Vi sighed and curled up with her threadbare quilts, but her thin pillow was harder than usual. She moved it aside to reveal several textbooks.

Malcolm's books.

She picked one up and held it to her lips, his familiar scent faint on the leather cover as she inhaled it with honeyed gulps.

"You know, Vi," Tommy garbled from a half sleep, "you said you've never been a lady. That's not true. I remember."

"Remember what, Tommy?"

"Before."

"How? I don't remember at all."

"Before we left the village. I was wearing entirely too much clothing that all itched. I remember waiting a fortnight for a piece of cake and everyone was sad. And you, sister, were wearing a frilly dress."

"Aunt Elizabeth's funeral? It was only two hours for cake. A fortnight, gracious."

"Well, all the same, I was four. So, I don't believe you don't remember our life before."

"Fair enough, but all the same, when everyone thinks you burned down your house, brother, you stop being regarded as a lady, or even a human."

Tommy frowned. "Soon, Vi."

"Yes," she replied, desperate to mean it.

Vi closed her eyes with Malcolm's books tucked under her arm. Sleep found her swiftly, and so did her dreams.

She found herself in a white nightgown that did not belong to her. In it, she glided, weightless, down a dark and unfamiliar hallway. Down, down, until she stood before Raclure's office door.

She opened it without concern of invitation or intrusion. Inside, the mirror beckoned to her from her warden's desk, a plume of white smoke surrounding it. She gazed at her pale reflection in the smooth glass, her blue eyes tired and dark-circled, her hair unruly.

And then the image in the mirror changed, a whirling shift, like a window seat in a swift carriage ride. Now the mirror held a new corridor, verdant with warmth and possibility. Malcolm was waiting for her there, with outstretched arms, a Ferris wheel in the distance and popcorn fragrant in the air. She reached for him, but the image changed again.

This time, her finger slipped through the mirror, the sensation like testing the temperature of a warm glass of milk. She pulled back and, through the ripples, saw the girl again, terror vivid in her eyes. She banged her blackened hands against the glass, in the same nightgown as Vi, but filthy and spattered with congealed blood and soot. The girl silently begged for help through stilted coughs and heaves. Vi banged and clawed the mirror in return, until the girl pressed both hands to it and looked Vi straight in the eyes. Vi pressed back, the girl's agony her own. A girl as real as herself, trapped somewhere. Somewhere dark, rank with wood rot and ash. Vi screamed and pounded again, the glass hard as iron on her coiled fists.

Then the mirror changed once more, revealing what appeared like a blighted glen in winter, bloated with splintered wood, poisoned by black decay.

Vi bolted from her slumber tangled in blankets and feverish with sweat. Her hands ached. Unable to shake the dream or the scent of smoke and ash burrowed in her skin, she got up and prepared a bath. She scrubbed her skin raw, crying into the tepid water as she did so. Until it turned cold and her skin wrinkled. She then dressed and styled her hair with extra care before waking her brother to do the same, her mind still bound to the mirror.

She went downstairs to try and sneak a peek, preparing an excuse that could explain her presence in Raclure's office. She pressed her nose against the frosted glass window. She could see his form milling about, hands in his hair and pacing. He was speaking to someone, but she could not see anyone else in the gray glass. She pressed her ear to it. Was he talking to himself? Vi's heart thrummed hard in her chest and in her ears. He was angry, but why?

Afraid of catching him in a temper, Vi backed away and stood in the stairwell, her back pressed against the wall. Slight and thin, she would see him before he saw her.

So, she waited.

Five minutes.

Ten.

And then he emerged, his hair unruly and his shirt untucked, not yet in the finery he wore for his patrons; his crimson velvet suit and matching top hat. He wore no rouge, no powder, nor kohl to enliven in his aging face. No. He paced back and forth through the doorway, his hands raking his face before he stormed outside and took a sharp left into the cold afternoon.

Vi waited still, for the other person to come out of the room. Was it Auggie, the gentle and obedient young man with scars at his temples, who no longer spoke after losing his twin? Was it Malcolm? Surely not Matilda. Then who?

Vi grew anxious and went inside. But no one was there.

Nothing but the stale odor of perspiration and smoke. Vi looked around the office. The mirror was propped against books on his desk, the very same spot as her dream. She touched it with her fingertip, waiting for the reflection to liquefy, but the warm glass remained solid. She ran her fingers around the fine grooves of its decadent frame, recalling the fire from her own memory. The oily kerosine stain on her nightgown from over filling a lamp the week prior. The looks of anger and suspicion from the fire brigade as they pried Tommy from her arms before yanking her from the iron strongbox they used to hide from the flames engulfing their home.

It wasn't her fault.

No one believed her.

Vi wiped her eyes and, for a moment, saw the girl in herself. Her blue eyes brown, her expression the deepest sadness.

"I can't do this anymore. I'm certainly going mad."

Vi left the office and paced the entryway in dizzying circles. She wished she could go to Malcolm's bedroom, huddle on his bed, and look at maps of places they dreamed of exploring. But those days were gone.

All they had were the hours in the Time Between.

Vi glimpsed out the front door of the Curiosity's housing. Raclure had still not returned, so she went to the showroom across the way to peruse the treasures and recall the stories that evolved from them.

Blinding sunlight bleached the sidewalk as Vi walked from one door to the other. She smiled at the shrunken head display between the two entrances and wondered when the mirror would take stage.

"Thank goodness I found you here."

Vi turned around and smiled weakly. "You shouldn't be seen with me."

"I know. But Raclure hasn't returned from wherever he went this afternoon. Was he pleased this morning?"

Vi looked around to be certain. "This morning, yes. It went very well. He was practically giddy. We needed it."

A shadow of hatred grew over Malcolm's kind face. "How badly? Have you seen the main attraction recently?"

Vi sighed. "Let's not call it that, Malcolm. Not anymore. I can't bear it today. It's a torture chamber."

Malcolm took her callused hands in his and gently held them to his lips before checking her wrists; yellowed bruising and fine scabs afflicted her otherwise delicate skin. "The stretcher?"

"A few weeks ago."

"The others?" he asked through his teeth. The muscles in his jaw tensed and defined.

"Only me, as far as I know. Never Tommy. You know fear has always been enough for the children. And, as his acclaim grows, he relies on so few. I wouldn't recognize any of his thieves."

"He's grown leerier since I left, but today he's strange, since after breakfast, which is why I ask. He added another lock to the…chamber, and I caught him talking to himself at his desk. He's never been so disheveled."

"I saw the same through the office window. And Malcolm…I think it's the mirror. I thought I saw a girl in it when we found it and just dreamed of her too. A terrible nightmare. And with your father acting strange? Could it be cursed? We can't both be going mad?"

"I'm more inclined to believe it's simply stress. You carry such burdens, Vi. And Raclure? He should worry…"

"I just want to run, let's run together."

"What about Tommy and Auggie and Mati? We can't all run. You said it yourself, we don't know what kind of illicit network he has. No. We must wait and take what belongs to us. This is ours. We've built it and we *will* make it right, Vi."

"I want that to. But I'm scared. I'm afraid of what we've done."

"You're not a bad person, Vi. I know you. Now, the doors open in thirty minutes. We will play our parts. Then, after, we can figure this out—"

"—in the Time Between," they whispered to each other.

Before leaving, Malcolm pulled her into his arms and lifted her, catching her breath on his soft lips. And time waited for them, a love forged in moonlight, patient and true.

The oscillating whistle of an ancient and foreboding pipe organ set the tone for the Friday evening showcase. Five minutes remained before the doors would open to Raclure's Curiosity, a spectacle of oddities and treasures; coin-operated fortune tellers, exotic live mushrooms in terrariums, sacred skulls, tubes of ectoplasm, canopic jars, and more. Patrons clamored to explore the red velvet kingdom while their eccentric host riveted them with tales of his escapades across continents.

But with the Lords of the Time Between stationed at their posts, and guests waiting, Raclure was nowhere to be seen.

Malcolm left the box office and pulled Vi and Tommy from the gift shop. "Where's Raclure? He's never late."

"I don't know."

The trio retreated to the short hallway separating the showroom from the office, like a tunnel between two worlds.

Raclure was there, garbling to himself before the gilded mirror.

"Sir, it's time. May we assist you?" asked Tommy.

"The devil are you doing here?" the old man bellowed. "I am never late. Ridiculous, insolent." He turned around and Vi clasped both hands over her mouth.

Malcolm gaped in horror while cupping a hand over Tommy's mouth. "Father, your face."

"Are you daft? Have you been away too long? It's show time, boy. You have much to learn about showmanship," he sputtered, his eyes like oily black pits.

"But Father, your eyes, your rouge, it's smeared around your mouth and all over your teeth. And the white powder, it's so caked and heavy."

For a moment, Vi thought Raclure would strike his son, but instead, he turned to face the mirror again, seeing for the first time the clown before him.

The old man slumped back in his chair and removed a blue silk handkerchief from his breast pocket. All traces of anger dissolved into silent, petulant horror as he scrubbed his face. The trio stood silent as he removed the garish display.

In a voice reserved for his finest patrons, he said, "Thank you for your recommendations. Please, man your stations and I will greet our guests." He beckoned them.

Terror etched their faces as they stumbled back into the showroom.

"Grand, sir, grand," Malcolm replied. He lowered his voice, raking his face. "Vi, what do we do?"

"I-I don't know."

"I've never been more horrified by him," Tommy murmured.

"We have to do something, Malcolm."

"Alright, we'll think of something. Let's get through this evening. There are people everywhere. I'll host if I have to."

Vi nodded and dragged Tommy back to their post selling sundries and souvenirs. Malcolm strolled stiffly back to the box office.

Matilda and Auggie met Vi at the counter but before Matilda could say a word, Vi put a finger to her lips. "Everything is fine. I promise.

Back to your stations, okay?" Auggie nodded and lumbered back to his watch, but Matilda stalled, her eyes wide with concern. "It's alright, Mati, I promise. Go back to the coat room, please."

Matilda narrowed her eyes but nodded.

Tommy waited for Matilda to be out of sight before speaking, the poor boy pale with fear. "There's something wrong here, Vi. It's sour in the air. I can taste ash. What's happening? What's wrong with Raclure? What's wrong with you?"

She took him in her arms and kissed his head as their mother would so long ago. "Listen to me. We're together. We'll be okay. But I'm going to tell you truthfully, I think it's the mirror. We shouldn't have taken it. I think we did something very wrong—*I* did something very wrong..." Vi waited for her brother to laugh, but he didn't.

"We should take it back, Vi."

Vi nodded then held her brother's hand and waited, the pipe organ a shrieking banshee to their nerves.

And then they heard it. Raclure's booming voice followed by a sea of other voices. Jubilant chatter crashed into the showroom like a tidal wave. Vi let the sound wash over her. Calm her. Help her fall into her duty and survive the night.

Yet time seemed to move backwards as Vi and Tommy smiled and upsold their wares. Vi painstakingly wrapped parchment paper around fanciful replicas of featured exhibits while Tommy handed out packages of salted nuts and taffy.

Then, at the last excruciating stroke of ten, when Raclure ushered out his last guests and locked the door, Vi exhaled.

It was a very good night; guests spent a fortune in the shop. Vi hoped it was enough for their greedy warden. Enough for him to retire early with a celebratory brandy or three. Enough to leave them to their own nocturnal devices.

Vi left their bedroom at the blackest pitch. Every creak and crack of the floor lit up in her mind, a maze she knew like the back of her hand. Not a swish of cloth followed her movements as she slipped a piece of paper under Malcolm's door, alerting him it was time.

Vi hoped he remembered the steps.

Tommy joined behind Malcolm at the stairway as they marched in reticence towards the office. Vi went to the ground floor alone in reconnaissance before the others followed.

The small frosted window to the office was dark. A good sign. She put her hand in her trouser pocket to double-check for the key she should not have. Next, she tiptoed to the other door in the entryway. A door she would sooner forget.

The entrance to the main attraction had a shiny new lock. Three deadbolts in all.

And all unlatched.

Vi's spine stiffened and her breath caught in her throat. She stepped back towards the stairway, but a cold hand grabbed her by the throat and snatched her off the floor.

"*You*," he hissed.

Vi let out a muffled cry while dangling in the air, muzzled by her warden, Raclure.

He shoved the girl down the stairs while she thrashed and clawed in the dark. A burnt orange glow emanated from the dark cellar as Vi fought her way down the narrow and misshapen stairwell, the putrescence of formaldehyde and smoke gagging her.

In Raclure's most evil, secret space was a hellscape of insidious contraptions. Where a certain type of patron could explore their most delinquent machinations and revel in the most repugnant practices of the Middle Ages. Little did they know those contraptions from a seemingly crueler, more barbaric time were iron welded and forged by the madman among them; their jolly host in his blood-red suit and painted mask.

Blind to the truth that those who cross him never return.

Blind in the graveyard of his depravity.

The Knee Splitter, the Head Crusher, The Heave, The Stretcher, The Hat.

Raclure dragged Vi through the channels of his evil while rasping in tongues, "Your fault, you did this…" The showman buckled Vi into his iron chair and placed a Scold's bridle over her face before sweeping out of view, his curses and taunts echoing through the chamber. She searched through her iron mask for the object of his obscenities. "You don't know what I've sacrificed, what I've done," he cried before his voice faded under a fury of footsteps.

Vi strained against the straps and finally saw it.

The mirror, gleaming upon a pyre of tinder and sticks below Raclure's most prized mechanical feat. The one wielding the infinite, impossible power of electricity...

The Hat.

Simple. Innocuous. But inside the black felt, metal plates and copper wire wrapped and coiled around iron nails that secured at the temples of the wearer. Elegant, refined, brilliant.

A hat, a single switch.

A most docile creature created.

A human without words, without worry, without memory.

Vi often wondered what it would be like to forget...

She gazed at her warden's most cruel and beguiling punishment, and then the mirror, symbols emblazoned on it. "EM PLEH."

Help me...

A dark shroud befell the mirror's glass, then the blighted glen of her dreams, and then the girl, her fair skin paler than ever. The girl pressed her hand to the glass and nodded. Vi's eyes filled with tears.

"Stupid children. Ruinous idiocy."

"Father, please, you're not yourself. We never, ever spoke a word, any of us."

"Our loyalty is yours," Tommy cried, "please, sir!"

"No. No, everyone knows, I am ruined! The mirror told me everything, everything... I know it all and I will not be taken. I will burn it all and start anew. Alone."

Vi strained her neck to see the stairwell. The silhouettes of her brother and Malcolm marched into view with their hands above their heads, Raclure's with a pistol to his own son's back.

"Vi, no!" Malcolm cried before his father bashed his head with the blunt end of his weapon. Malcolm stumbled but remained upright as they were shoved forward at the mercy of a bullet.

Raclure pistol-whipped Malcolm again and the young man fell splayed on the foundation at Vi's feet. Raclure shoved Tommy into a gibbet cage above them, all while cursing them and the mirror. "It seems it was a mistake to bring my young Lords in proximity again. Foolish children. But, you, Virginia, *you* have damned us all. And you will watch it burn. All of this and everyone in it. You will burn for destroying my sacrifice. My dreams. The girl has shown me the way. She knows all and has shown all."

Vi looked for the girl. *No. Please.* The girl put a finger to her dry, cracked lips.

"Father, please," Malcolm sputtered in fading consciousness. "You're not well. A holiday, perhaps, you and I, Constantinople, India, anywhere. We'll find riches beyond imagination."

"No boy. I will—what?" Raclure spun around and grabbed the mirror. It sizzled red-hot in his grip. "No, no, it's not too late. I have done everything you said. Please. No!"

The Lords gagged in horror as Raclure fried his hands. Then, when he could bear no more, it released him. He then turned to his beloved Hat, picked it up, and shoved it on his own head.

He screamed in anguish as he twisted the nails into his temples. Bright blood oozed from the wounds.

The trio watched, too afraid to look away.

Raclure wept. A garbled plea dripped from lips as he rested a single, charred finger on the shiny switch.

Vi closed her eyes, waiting for the impossible.

The scent of metal and grass filled the chamber. Vi opened her eyes. Raclure was slumped on the floor with his head between his knees, the Hat on the floor beneath him. Above, Tommy had pin-picked the lock of the cage door and swung down. He helped Malcolm to his feet.

They worked together to release Vi from her bondage. With her hands free, she touched Malcolm's face gingerly before hugging them both. "We have to return the mirror. We must take her home."

Malcolm nodded, woozy and dazed.

"Tommy, I want you to get Auggie and Matilda to help you take Raclure to his bed. Tell them he's had an accident with the Hat but nothing else. Malcolm and I will return the mirror together."

"With the cufflinks and candlesticks too, Vi."

"Of course."

Tommy hugged his sister and raced upstairs. Vi picked up the mirror and, for the first time, it was cold.

No.

"We have to hurry."

They collected the other items from the drawer in Raclure's office then fled into the frigid night.

Vi kept a watchful eye on the mirror as they ran in the dazzling light of the full moon. Pale fingertips pressed against the dark cold glass. "Please hold on, we're coming."

The Lords streaked down Coventry Lane to the precarious house at the end, amazed it still stood.

"Wait!" she cried.

"What?" Malcolm slurred.

Vi crunched through the scorched lawn around the collapsed veranda, searching for what she knew she must find.

And there…

Between overgrown weeds and destroyed wood and debris, she saw it. Flakes of ash danced in the moonlight like snowfall. The blighted glen was not a glen at all, but the wreckage of a cellar door.

"Malcolm. Here." Vi dropped to her knees and ripped away the ruptured pieces of door to reveal the stairwell within.

Together they slipped down the staircase by dodging jutting wood, mangled wire, and broken steps.

"Hello?" Vi's voice echoed into the darkness. "Hello, are you here?"

"Vi?" Malcolm whispered, caressing her arm in lament.

"Wait." Vi took Malcolm's hand and put it on the mirror.

He shook his head, as though he didn't want to believe. But before pulling away, he felt it. *Thump, thump. Thump, thump.* Malcolm's mouth fell open, his eyes wide. He gently took the mirror and cradled it in his arms. "Find her, Vi."

Vi tucked into the ruins with delicate grace. Removing debris piece by piece until she could shimmy deeper into the cave of shrapnel. Nails and splinters tore her clothes and scraped her skin while she slithered, further and further until an alcove revealed itself, cloaked in darkness, freckled in moonlight. A small hand lay open-palmed in the glow.

Vi reached for her, the girl's downy hair a shroud upon her own face. A finger's breadth lay between them.

The girl's hand snapped around Vi's wrist and a wide bloodshot eye met hers. "Your turn."

Vi screamed.

A cacophony of shattered glass.

Malcolm's ears bled from the din. The mirror sibilated. "No!" he cried as the glass boiled and swirled a new image.

A portrait of his love, forever trapped in the Time Between.

CHAPTER THREE

HUMBUG

Brad Acevedo

CERRINA

Marvelous Wonders! Wondrous Marvels!
Sirenic birdsong of seldom spoken words!

Oh, it was music to my ears. Upon stepping off the trolley onto the warped wooden planks, one was privy to find their senses overwhelmed as they entered a world of clattering claptraps and salt-tinged miasma.

The sights! The smells! The aura of unmitigated wonder beneath a starry canvas of amber lights strung on slack wires!

I suppose I could see how some might perceive Luna Pier as a gaudy and garish midway populated by carnival barkers, each as grease laden as the plump frankfurters emerging beneath candy-striped canvas stalls. But then, I often saw things differently than most. Some might in fact say that I have The Sight. If you promise to keep it between us, I'll let you in on a little secret. Oh, I cannot do it. I apologize for leading you on, but a showman simply cannot divulge their tricks of the trade so early on in our adventure.

Let us proceed, shall we?

A voice echoed across the pungent primrose path that lay before me. I glanced toward the red and yellow striped awning bedecked with a hand painted sign that I elected not to read. Some mysteries are better left to the whims of anticipation until they reveal themselves in full, operatic splendor. I chose to embrace this aura of the unknown.

I thanked the gaslight gods for the overcast day, and pulled my veil tighter across my face to hide it from view. All will be revealed in time. Patience please, ladies and gentlemen. Let us see what awaits within this haughty hippodrome.

I paid my pittance in a small honor system box at the entrance and entered. I was not impressed. The floor of the tent was coated in sawdust that stuck to my shoes in an unpleasant fashion. A family of three accompanied me as the only other patrons, and the parents and small boy did not seem to pay much heed to the detritus on the floor. They were more entranced by the garish displays of tomfoolery set upon the small wooden platforms lining the interior. The displays created a path to funnel guests forward into a small antechamber at the end of the tent, currently blocked off from view by a large yellow length of canvas.

Before my bleary eyes lie the *"Indonesian Fish-man."* The mother withdrew in horror, but the young boy pressed forward, a salubrious spark of enchantment dancing in his eyes. Quite obviously, the taxidermized fiend presented was simply the mummified remains of an unfortunate simian hastily attached to the lower fins of a large game fish. Marvelous Wonders, indeed. Even the *"Mighty Hodag"* was naught more than another fanciful mockup of chimeric chicanery.

The next attempt to draw gasps of astonishment from the rubes was admittedly more interesting. It was another static display of what I suspected was a mannequin likely spirited away from a department store without consent. The man-sized figure's maw was pressed into a chitinous beak shape and frozen in a shriek of unbridled aggression. Greasy black feathers covered the shape like a downy decoupage, giving it the appearance of a hybrid that would only exist in the works of H.G. Wells.

The boy pressed forward at the behest of his mother, but the child's father, an unnaturally tall man, held up a reassuring hand. I tried my hardest to stifle a light chuckle as the feathery beast suddenly burst forward with a mediocre bellow. It was good enough to startle the child, who tumbled backward into the sawdust, coating his Sunday best in refuse.

A man in a red velvet jacket stepped out from behind the mannequin beast with a bright smile. I immediately detected the pain behind the wide, imperfect grin and the intrigue was quite palpable.

He spoke in a soft voice from behind golden capped teeth, his narrow mustachioed face beneath dark eyes, auburn hair, and a tilted red cap. "Young man, you mustn't touch *The Jackdaw*. He's been known to…bite." The man flashed his golden grin and chomped with all the theatricality of a trained showman.

The family remained silent, gazing back with widened eyes, undoubtedly wondering what they had gotten themselves into. The showman cast a quick gaze over his paltry parade of patrons and I smirked underneath my veil at the lingering gaze upon my form.

"I trust you all are here today to witness the most Wondrous Marvels to take place upon this Miracle Row. Surely you did not purchase a ticket to simply gaze at my *wunderkammen* of curiosities. Surely you have braved the unknown, set foot upon mysterious roads toward the most Marvelous Wonder your eyes ever did witness!" He suddenly coughed violently at the end of his histrionic hullabaloo and was greeted with silence. "Well?"

The family murmured their assent and I offered a kind nod. He stole one more glimpse toward me and I shifted in the sawdust. I shall let both our theatrical ringmaster and yourself decide whether it was a subtle motion of discomfort or intrigue. He grinned again, yet I detected the hint of confusion lurking within his youthful visage. Nevertheless, he led us toward the antechamber, and pulled back the yellow tarp with a grand flourish and self-composed musical accompaniment.

"Da-daa-da! I present to your wondering and most curious hearts, the unbridled spectacle of *Admiral Admirari's Flea Circus Extraordinaire!*"

A flea circus? I stifled a derisive sigh. Flea circuses were the apex of apathy, gilded gadgets and tiny mechanical trinkets glittering in the waste of their own self-satisfaction, powered by magnets and self-assured smirks that robbed patrons ("marks" more like) of their well-earned cash. Granted, I could not be one to speak against the fleecing facetiousness, but at least my act had some semblance of decorum.

"Come closer," the man beckoned. "All of—well, just you."

I glanced about and noticed the family had left, undoubtedly scrambling out of the tent with promises of nightmares and emptied wallets to boot. As the sole remaining patron, I took it upon myself to humor the chap, and I discovered with glee that his show was not in fact all illusions and misdirection.

The setup was simple. Tiny cars, cannons, trapeze towers, and even musical instruments crafted out of polished brass, awash in tiny switches and dials that human hands could not possibly hope to operate. Yet, they were all in motion and being operated by honest-to-Barnum minuscule creatures. The contraptions whirred and whizzed and sounded musically in the small chamber as the showman looked on proudly.

"You could get a better look, my dear, if you remove that stylish veil from your undoubtedly lovely eyes," he said.

"I can see just fine from here," I replied, ignoring his silver tongue and golden grin. "This is fascinating. Real creatures."

"You sound as though you expected otherwise. Come, see what Wonders my little friends can perform." He swept an arm closer to the display with a flourish. He stifled a cough, and I noted a tattoo on the back of his right hand: a pocket watch design as golden as his teeth, with an equally opulent chain trailing up his forearm. Prompted by some surely arcane emotion, I rubbed at the back of my own right hand, currently obscured by my long, black-sleeved blouse.

"They're all right here. In the flesh. Or the carapace, I suppose. My friends, my performers. My family," he said. His voice trailed off almost wistfully, and I lifted my eyes to meet his from beneath my veil.

"Your stage name is intricate," I confessed. "What do they call you when the lights are out and the curtains close?"

The young man glanced behind me to make sure there were no patrons in earshot. He removed his cap with a chivalrous bow, and I noted the quiver in his step. "Marcus Boverick, at your service, Miss—"

He trailed off again, obviously prompting me to reveal my own moniker. I ignored this and said, "Ironically, it is a service that I have come to offer, Mr. Boverick. I can respect one showman, but I was unimpressed with your show until I saw…this. I was unaware that fleas could be trained."

"If you treat them right and provide for them. One could only imagine what they are capable of."

"One could only imagine," I repeated. "Your imaginarium has potential, sir. I myself happen to be adept at igniting the imagination of the most seasoned mark." He bristled at this terminology, undoubtedly a man of honor who likely performed his show for the love of the craft, and not simply to fleece the rubes. "Oh, Admirable Admiral, I think we could help freshen up your show." I tapped a black lacquered nail to my shrouded temple. "Think about it."

"But, my dear, what are these gifts you claim to possess?" He coughed again.

I lifted my veil ever so slightly to offer one patented mysterious smile and no further response. I made sure to swirl my skirt in a theatrical fashion as I swept out of the showplace, leaving a perplexed ringmaster and his homunculi handymen to ponder my very presence.

One could only imagine…

MARCUS

Marcus Boverick was well-versed on being the one to invoke curiosity and confusion in others. He was not accustomed to finding the roles reversed. After the quiet family and mysterious woman in the black veil had left, he played host to only a few more pockets of patrons. The show was starting to stagnate, and he would need new attractions soon. It was part of what had made the woman's offer so enticing. He fully expected her to return and when she did, he vowed to extract more information and uncover her motives.

The sun had set over Luna Pier's Miracle Row. The midway games, the majestic Wonder Wheel, the rickety Luna Dipper roller coaster and the snack stands had all closed for the night. Marcus had more important matters to attend to during these twilight hours. He held his bare arm out to the flea circus, allowed his tiny partners to climb up, and stole to the back. There, he removed one more flap of canvas that led directly into his trailer.

Wordlessly, Marcus removed his cap and red jacket that he wore during showtime. He moved through a tin door shut off from the rest of the trailer, and sat himself in a reclining barber chair. He affixed one end of a clear plastic tube into a small glass jar and peeled back the pre-incised flesh of his forearm. The Fleas jumped in elation and swiftly marched up his arm, tucking themselves neatly beneath his skin as he affixed the other end of the hose to his exposed muscle. He folded the flap of flesh back over his partners, and allowed them to nourish themselves.

His flesh began to undulate, squirm, and shift. The golden chain tattoo swirled with the tiny forms shuffling around beneath. Within moments, the essence began to flow from the tube and into the empty jar. The golden liquid pooled forth, gleaming brightly beneath the single bare bulb that illuminated his workshop. Marcus closed his eyes as the Fleas did their work.

Then: fire, searing heat, and smoke ravaged screams. Sights he had imagined everyday within his mind. He remembered years spent after the fire, setting up shop to continue a lost legacy. He remembered the loose plank of wood under the boardwalk and the glowing, squirming beings that lived beneath. They had wasted no time leaping and clinging to his form. He could only imagine how long they had been there, but held no knowledge of what they truly were or if more of their kind existed. They had bitten swiftly, but did not take. Instead, the Fleas had given him Wonderous Marvels and Marvelous Wonders, truths unknown but now seen through the prismatic compound eyes of beings that were not meant to be in collusion with man.

He cried in his chair as the Fleas went to work. A bond had been established without words. A partnership, the discovery of something that lurked beyond science, yet dwelled deep within every living being. He called the luminous gold liquid flowing in his veins the "Oil," a fitting term from a dedicated snake oil salesman such as himself.

He thought about the exhibits on display in the main tent and the actions he had taken to acquire them. Actions he would have never committed without the Fleas insisting he do so. A show can only go on for so long before it grows tiresome. It was in his best interest to provide a good show, to keep the Boverick name on the lips of any respected entertainer. To endure his legacy. But he often wondered if his father, long lost to the flames, would really want his legacy tarnished in Oil and blood. Red upon gold, death unto legacy.

These were the tortured thoughts of Marcus Boverick, interrupted suddenly by an unfamiliar voice echoing from beyond his trailer. He sat up with a sniff, wiped his face, and removed the tubing from his arm. The Fleas crept out as he smoothed the flesh back, and he assured them he would make it up to them soon. Marcus stumbled out of his trailer, waiting in the doorway as he peeled back the strap of canvas that separated his mobile home from the antechamber.

A tall man was skulking about, peering at the cloth covered exhibits, reaching out with a gloved hand into the gloom and peering behind the curtains. Marcus cleared his throat loudly and the man turned to him, pointing at the showman with a swift, accusatory motion.

"My boy will not eat because of your flimflam show," the tall man snarled. He pressed closer. Marcus could smell the sour scent of cheap whiskey on his breath, and recognized one of the patrons from earlier in the day. "My wife is upset that we ever brought him here. I demand a—"

"No refunds, sir," Marcus cut in with a weary sigh.

"Excuse me?"

"My show is meant to shock and amuse. Emphasis on amusement, but there are times that the hideous appearance of my displays obscures all other emotions. I am...sorry that your boy did not appreciate the Marvels in my collection."

"He did not. My wife did not. She did not appreciate wasting our Sunday outing on this collection of claptraps. Give me my money back or I will go to the authorities."

"I assure you, sir, I have a license from the city. All is in order." Marcus took a moment to size up the angry father. Tall, slender. Interesting.

The man raised his gloved hand to his chin and seemed to think for a moment. "What if I burn it to the ground? Surely you cannot be financially stable. You have read the papers, no doubt. You have seen the bread lines forming and the stocks plunging. Surely you have insured your collection and are...growing desperate. A suspicious fire, indeed."

Marcus smirked and rubbed at his tattoo. "A threat, is it?"

The man shrugged. "A business proposition." He pulled a silver lighter out of his pocket, clicked on the flame, and pressed it close to Marcus. He recoiled from the heat, a flicker of fear piercing his dark eyes. Flames, screams, burning canvas, and smoke-filled lungs. He coughed involuntarily and the tall man shrunk back.

"Let us...discuss this like gentlemen," Marcus said. He beckoned with genial theatricality for the man to enter his chambers beyond the pied canvas.

It did not take long. Marcus had always kept the plank of wood in his workshop, the same sturdy chunk that had brought the Fleas to him. It still evoked a sense of eldritch power. Something from a world he did not understand—a hideaway for unknown travelers likely moving from locale to locale and seeking to impart their Wonders on the populace. To both take and give. They were so like him, and that is why Marcus believed they imbued their gifts upon him, and also why he took the plank of wood to the back of the tall man's head.

No words had been passed upon the tall man entering the trailer. Marcus had allowed him one brief glimpse at the setup and the jars of Oil, the sluicing essence imparted from his own willing body and others not so willing. He hated what he had become, but he knew better than to question the Fleas. There was only one method to reliably acquire new exhibits for the show.

After the man had fallen, Marcus picked up his limp body with a grunt, and slung him into the chair. He opened a singed tin toolbox filigreed with a tarnished brass "L.B."—his father, Louis Boverick, Master of Ceremonies and the first Admiral—and promised himself that it was all for him, for the legacy of the Admiral Admirari name. From within, he removed a small switchblade and a tiny clasped pocket watch. He flicked both open and allowed the Fleas to exit the watch interior. They clambered onto the blade of the knife, a parade of exquisite acquisitions, a troupe extraordinaire. Then, Marcus Boverick lowered the blade to the tall man and began to cut.

All for the legacy, for the Marvelous Wonders and Wondrous Marvels within.

After all, the show must go on.

CERRINA

It was an interesting piece. A bit rudimentary if I was being perfectly honest, but the proportions were appropriately unsettling. I had returned the next day as promised, and bore witness to the great Admiral Admirari fastening his new *Incan Mummy* exhibit to a display space alongside the *Mighty Hodag.* The wizened form was tall, slender. Interesting. Stripped of flesh, save for a few tattered wrappings, and withered into what could scarcely pass for what was once allegedly a human being. More likely, another store mannequin procured from the scrapyard and dressed with fittings and shoddy makeup work.

"A collector's piece, indeed." I smirked.

Boverick turned toward me, wiping a bead of sweat from his brow. With his sleeves rolled up, I had an uninhibited view of that fascinating piece of art on his forearm. The good Admiral coughed once, held up a hand to excuse himself, and stepped down off of the platform.

"My mysterious caller," he said. "To what do I owe this pleasure?"

"Madame Cerrina always keeps her word."

He flashed his golden grin. "Progress. So now that I know your name, Madame Cerrina, please inform a curious mind as to what services you could bring to our humble little show."

I squinted, took a quick pass from behind my veil and went to work. "Humble, yes. You lack the conviction of a seasoned showman. You work hard but are uncertain of your show's shelf life. I regret that your parent—father perchance—is not present to witness everything that you have established in his name. I should say though that—" I paused for dramatic effect and held a hand to my temple. *Wait. Let the anticipation build. Continue.* "He is most proud of what you have accomplished. He wishes to inform you that Madame Cerrina would be a boon to your operation and would bring in plenty of revenue as she communes with those long lost and past."

He paused, blinked, and I caught sight of a single tear. I had not counted on that and it caught me off guard, ever so slightly. "You have, uh, The Sight, I see."

I allowed a small smile to play from beneath the veil.

"Humbuggery," he stated. "I can respect that. Misdirection and deceit. Fairly accurate as well."

"Only fairly?"

He smirked back and gestured for me to follow him deeper into the show tent. I followed him to the back chamber with the flea circus set up and awaiting the day's first batch of marks. I watched with interest as he withdrew a small pocket watch from his pocket, not unlike his tattooed arm. He flicked it open, and the performers crept out. The tiny black mites immediately took their positions. The Admiral bent low and whispered something to the creatures, surely more as a sign of show than anything else, for obviously they could not understand him.

In an attempt to add more flair to the show, he produced a harmonica and performed an irritatingly jaunty tune as the fleas set about their tasks. I smiled and clapped along with the music, abhorring myself for allowing the mirth to overtake my good sense, but acknowledging the value in such a performance.

"You see, most flea circuses are archaic," he explained. "They either perform with automated contraptions that are too tiny for patrons to distinguish as simple mechanics, or the fleas are tortured with hot plates and glue traps. The poor things will do whatever they can to escape the discomfort, and it appears as though they are performing great feats of agility and talent."

"But not these?" I asked.

"Not at all. I have the good fortune to possess the only truly legitimate performing fleas in the world. I can even train them to dance." He broke into a little jig before me, and while I questioned his judgment in doing so, still, I laughed. He was charming in an eccentric way. I suspected that was why I took him up on his next offer to join him at the dance hall on the pier later that night to discuss our potential…partnership.

The Crystal Palace was a dirt-encrusted gem far removed from its opulent namesake. The dance hall was built of lacquered wood in a hexagonal shape with a peaked roof. It sat upon the pier itself and was a landmark in its heyday. However, due to the financial hardships that seemed to be gripping the populace, the hall had fallen into disrepair. It still pulled in a small batch of visitors, but nothing akin to its glittering, golden years of frolic. Our business meeting consisted of no dancing whatsoever, but we took it upon ourselves to retire to a bar built into the back wall. He procured a bottle of libations (and curiously enough, a light blue ice pop that he assured me was sea-salt flavor—which I declined) and sat upon the roughhewn benches built into the exterior side of the hall.

He wasted no time in bringing up my veil and questioned what I was attempting to hide. I decided if we were to become partners that he would uncover my scars sooner than later. I sighed and stared out across the water at the Miracle Row. On this misty night, the summer winds swept the haze inward to the midway, allowing the garish lights and the Wonder Wheel herself to sparkle like tainted gems against a dreary painted sky. It was beautiful in a damaged yet distinguished fashion. The fog grew thicker and I squinted to see the lights beyond the veil of mist.

"May I see?"

I blinked back to the here and now. Marcus was looking at me expectantly, his ice cream pop dripping down his hand and onto the warped wood below. I thought for only a moment and decided to show that which I had hidden from curious eyes.

I saw him make a vain attempt to stifle his gasp. Many would simply recoil in disgust. I grinned lightly through the scar tissue that I had grown accustomed to for so many years. Most were unwilling to afford any kindness regarding the damage the fire had cursed me with.

"Are you satisfied, Admiral?" I asked.

I glimpsed the flicker in his eyes, the subconscious touch of his inked hand to his own face, before I allowed him to touch mine. I should have noticed before. Without having to say a word, he knew. He knew exactly what had occurred, and I knew then and there that the pair of us were bound by a tragedy far too common to the performer ilk. Canvas and wood are easy to acquire, and they pair well with what the public expects of traveling freak shows and circus performances. But such assets were often harbingers of the errant spark, ready to ignite into a life destroying inferno. Flames to take lives, but also to imbue unforeseen passion.

"Your father?" I asked softly.

I saw him tremble, heard him cough involuntarily and smelled the salt of the ice pop as it dropped to the ground. He nodded. I held his hand closer to my face, knowing we had many secrets to reveal to each other and each other only.

MARCUS

Marcus Boverick's life changed once again that night. While before his innocence had been swept away in falling timbers and melted canvas, he found renewed vigor and life in the heat of his new relationship with Cerrina Bertolotto. The two of them workshopped her act, determining the best way she could contribute with her cold reading skills (the ability to determine events in one's life simply by careful observation of appearance and demeanor). He established an additional room for her act, within which they constructed a secreted and specialized projector box which they dubbed "the Fantoscope."

The Fantoscope was used to project eerie images and subtle shades which Cerrina used for great effect along with her mysterious presence. Many heavy hearts were joyously reunited with their departed loved ones under the guise of Madam Cerrina's *"Visions of the Past Grand Macabre,"* yet these specters existed solely in the realm of chicanery.

Word of the combined 3-in-1 show spread among the trolley park and pier, even as both financial downturn spread and the police presence began to increase in the light of a rash of missing persons. Cerrina and Marcus celebrated their newfound success with nights of drunken revelry and on two occasions, beneath starchy bed sheets tucked away within the confines of his trailer.

Yet as before and ever after, curious hearts tend to beckon, and Marcus felt that she was beginning to be drawn to the siren song that threatened their new salubrious life. He knew she had caught sight of him spiriting away while she entertained the masses and yet he chose not to act upon her encroaching curiosity. He would reveal in time. There was also the matter of the new exhibits, strange new artifacts and mummified beings arriving on a near weekly basis. He wondered just how far her acute sensibilities could carry her suspicion.

Marvelous Wonders, yes, but then sometimes mysteries are made to be uncovered when hollow hearts experience something new. The pair had been successful but they both felt the maw of guilt gnawing at their souls. Marcus seemed to experience it more intensely, becoming increasingly sullen and withdrawn each time he added a new exhibit to the menagerie. He was aloof when the police came to question about the rash of disappearances and became short with Cerrina.

Behind closed doors he was a broken man. Cerrina's inclusion into his life had held the darkness at bay but the brilliant popcorn bulbs were beginning to fade again. The Fleas had become more insistent to be fed and to extract Oil for a still unknown purpose and it was all he could do to keep them satiated. More and more he would beckon others into his workshop while Cerrina was tending to business or enthralling the masses. Each time the chunk of wood collided with an innocent skull and the Fleas set out to do their handiwork, he felt a sliver of soul dissipating into the grease laden wind, a miasma of guilt and regret.

The wooden plank felt solid in his hand and he remembered days past when burning wood had blackened his grip on reality and the weapon had found its first target. He was becoming what he had feared and all for what? Fame and fortune? A legacy that had already been stained and corrupted before he had even discovered the tiny beings? Marcus Boverick lay there as the Fleas drained him of Oil and he felt eternally empty.

CERRINA

Things had certainly changed over the past month or so. Our relationship had begun with the suddenness and ferocity of a cyclone, but had since dissipated into a gentle, weak-willed wind. The midway itself seemed less bright, instead dim and lacking the enchantment that it normally imparted upon my soul. Things felt...hollow.

True, Marcus and I had found success in combining my cold read act with his collection of curiosities and the flea circus, but even my specialized skills could not detect what machinations were greasing the gears of his enigmatic mind. He spent more time behind a locked door in the trailer than not, and he requested I never enter, but he would reveal it to me in time. Showman's trade and all, but I couldn't help but ponder what secrets he had left to tell beyond the humbuggery of the exhibits and the genuine Wonder of the flea circus. But I was determined to find out.

I had my opportunity one night in August as the warm summer winds blew wild and the midway rides closed early due to an impending storm approaching the coast. I was finishing securing down the tarp and fastening the tent while Marcus excused himself to go "balance the books." Given the particularly slow day, I had not expected this to take him too long to accomplish. After two hours passed, I became concerned, and ventured into the trailer to investigate.

Lo and behold, the door to his workshop was ajar—an unusual sight in and of itself. He always made sure to secure the showman's secrets contained therein, whatever they might actually be. I decided then and there that he owed me something beyond the companionship and partnership afforded thus far, and I carefully opened the door.

The workshop was a chamber of horrors, a sight which I might have partially anticipated, but had never truly prepared my mind for. My Marcus lay in a reclined leather chair, straps of rubber tubing fastened to his forearm. His beautiful, intriguing tattoo was smeared in blood and the red essence pooled into a jar on the floor. I gazed about, mind frozen at the rows and rows of bloodied jars lining the walls, some filled and others empty, but each with a strip of tape labeled with the date they were likely obtained.

I had seen horrors and sights that no person ought to see, but this was something that could pluck one's mind from the sanctity of sanity and plunge it steadfast into a raging maelstrom of madness. I had somehow stifled a scream until now, but it gave way into the stagnant, musky air as a flea leaped from my lover's flayed arm and onto my own.

Marcus stirred at the sudden sound even as I instinctively swatted at the creature, leaving a blood smeared remnant upon my sleeve. His eyes suddenly shot open, eyes that were once warm with a touch of melancholy, now replaced with something feral and unknown.

"What have you done?" he shrieked as he leaped from the chair.

The rubber tubing pooled loose, leaking red onto the bare tile floor. I looked at the slackening apparatus, past it and at a chunk of wood on a counter. Next to it lay a battered, singed toolbox. *What horrors lurked within? What Wonders and Marvels and further things to be shown that were held from prying eyes until you've paid your due. Admission is cheap, come see 3-for-1! What a deal! Murder, insanity, and bloodshed—all for one small token of your very soul! Come one, come all!*

The flap of skin hanging from his arm spun wildly as he gripped my forearm. The swinging motion caused me to giggle madly. Why not? It was all so absurd, *commedia dell'arte* here at its most satirical and extravagant. Tragedy and laughter and the barest, raw nerve of the Showman's trade exposed here for all to see. For me to see, only me, and what a lucky gal I was.

I wrenched out of his grasp as he circled around me, forcing me back toward the abattoir. "Marcus…" I began and did not know how to conclude.

Tears ran from his eyes, now softer, yet still lined with malicious intent. Not toward me, no, he could never harm me. I could see it in… everything he was. I have a sense for these things, you see? I have The Sight… don't I?

"I did not want you to find out yet, Cerrina," he whispered and coughed lightly. He tried to smooth the flap of skin back onto his arm but it refused to stay. "They need me and I need them."

"Who? Who, Marcus?"

"My friends. My little friends, my partners. You killed one of them, but there are still many left. Look around you and see how their gift glows. Sparkling like sunlight, the Oil and the essence that lives in us all. It's what fuels them, what compels them to put on their shows. But I never have enough. Never enough from me. So, I have to give them more." He held out his arm to me. "Look, look and see how they move." He traced the chain of his tattoo with his finger. "They're under there right now, moving about and taking what they wish. They take and they give, and I do the same for them. It's a beautiful partnership."

I wept for his frazzled mind and the sudden chaotic shattering of everything we had built. Golden Oil, the ichor of gods. Moving and rippling flesh. Justification for…I knew then, the exhibits and the missing people. I listened and I looked as he wished me to do. I saw the bottles and jars of blood, and witnessed nothing but a broken mind. No moving tattoos, no shining essence. And then I looked in his eyes and saw the same. Nothing.

He stood there and cried as the winds began to whip outside. I watched him twitch and cough, and knew he wanted to embrace me, but could not bring himself to do so. I held steadfast, and backed away toward the counter where the plank of wood and the toolbox sat. I caught a small glimpse of what lay within and shuddered at the fleas dancing upon the blood-encrusted pocket watch. Ordinary fleas, perhaps coaxed by him by the unruly methods he had described to me prior. No magic, no chicanery or supernatural mischief. I subtly reached in and pocketed something that would come in handy.

"I didn't mean to kill him," Marcus whispered. He fell into a hacking cough, and I reached out to him but pulled back just as quickly. "My father always drank with the Strongman and Boppo, the clown. Funny. He always drank with them after the show. But then...he'd be upset about the state of the show and I was the closest thing he could hit. So, I hit him back with his own baton. He was—and then—but if he burns then nobody would—"

Marcus trailed back into a sob, and I reached up to feel my own scars. Mine had been imparted purely by accident. By this tragedy we were connected, pied circus tents and carnival menageries fallen to flame. An errant spark here, a discarded ember there. All too easy. All too easy for a trapeze artist to fall, for a young child to brave the heat, and reach for flailing arms. All too easy for a shard to propel into a small face, and melt both flesh and innocence. All too easy for a young one with a scarred visage to seek out that which lies beyond this realm, and discover nothing there but blackness and empty pits, not unlike Marcus's own eyes. Where I found pain, others found solace by communication with the dead— even if it was mere trickery. But none of this mattered. My face had been scarred, but his mind had been singed beyond recognition. I knew this now and wondered how often in our relationship that he had been lucid. Did he dream of cutting my throat and feeding me to the fleas while I slept beside him?

He coughed once more from what I knew were smoke-ravaged lungs. I saw him shudder, and felt the remorse in his trembling hands and voice. I reached out to grasp him, determined for what I knew had to be done. Cleanse this hell with the very flames that had birthed it into our idyllic slice of cotton candy coated life.

"What Wonders you have shown me, good Admiral," I whispered, pulling him close. I could feel his eyes dart open with alarm as he heard the click of the lighter. I pushed away from him, grasped the chunk of wood and lit it aflame. It caught easily, a purging torch to eliminate the atrocities I had seen. I ran my hand along the rows of jars, smashing them upon the floor and coating everything in sight with a sheen of scarlet. I heard him cry in anguish, and I wept at the terror in his voice. But I also knew that this had to end.

Our foundation had been built upon a bedrock of butchery. I had already grown wary of bilking the marks out with false promises of beloved spiritual reunions. I could no longer be part of anything that brought pain, especially a den of depravity such as this.

He moaned wordlessly and flailed, pushing me aside and gathering up all that he could. I ran out of the trailer and into the tent where I touched the torch to the closest piece of canvas I could find. The flames ran quickly, as they so often do, and I swallowed the fear that arose; a bitter taste.

The Admiral appeared in the doorway of the tent, soaked in red that matched the jacket he so often wore. The flap of skin dangled from his forearm but the fleas were nowhere to be seen. Even still, he clutched the pocket watch in his hand as it shook feverishly.

I ducked past the smoldering flea circus, and past the exhibits— remnants of my love's unfortunate victims. I shuddered at the ruination I had unknowingly brought upon this beleaguered town. Nothing would ever be the same. But the flames would help. They took and they gave as so often occurs in life.

I pushed out of the tent as the flames spread behind me. The summer storm blew more fiercely now, wind shrieking into the night as the first spatter of rain upon my wretched form.

"I love you, Admiral," I called out to the flaming wreck. Present tense, for my feelings had developed into something unknown in our short time together. I wanted him to know before he succumbed to the fire.

He appeared in the doorway of the show tent as a burning shroud of yellow canvas fell across his shoulders. He did not flinch. He seemed perfectly calm among the element that had ruined his life and mind. In his hand, he grasped the pocket watch as it began to melt and coat his hands with liquid death, beautiful and gleaming gold, just as he had described.

As the flames cascaded and fell around him, Marcus Boverick spoke one sentence from within a golden grin. To this day, I have yet to determine my lover's last words on this plane of existence. Mysteries to be known but perhaps not, for a showman never reveals his secrets.

The rain poured more steadily and I knew it would snuff out the fire before it spread to the rest of the pier, but not before the Admiral, his show, and his den of death would be wiped from existence. Perhaps one day I could commune with his spirit and ask him things. Ask him if he truly knew what he was doing with his blood and the blood of his victims. Ask him if he really loved me.

But I knew better. Madame Cerrina Bertolotto could not really speak to the dead. It was tricks, illusions, or as P.T. Barnum would say, a display of "humbug." I laughed bitterly, and allowed the rain to caress my scars.

I had witnessed sights that should remain unseen and even more that I wished to purge from my addled mind. But as twisted as they were, they were Wondrous sights indeed.

One might say….

Wondrous Marvels.

Marvelous Wonders.

CHAPTER FOUR

SORRY

Fox Claret Hill

When Samantha was six, she watched her mother tend to her garden from her bay window reading nook. She'd pretend to study a book as she watched Cynthia lay a cheek to the parakeet-green grass and snip the strands into uniform with a sharp set of scissors. Then her mother would stand, dressed in a full-skirted tea-length dress, and wave a manicured hand at Samantha. Her bright white teeth, small in contrast to her low-set gums, shone from the garden's edge and illuminated the living room. Then she would flick her fiery curls behind her shoulder in a tangerine helix before crouching to tend to the delicate membranes of the candy-wrapper flowers. Samantha desperately wanted to join her mother outside, and place the petals in her mouth, convinced that the mosaic of purples, blues, and pinks would melt on her tongue.

However, Samantha was not allowed outside. Not because she wanted to bite the heads from her mother's flowers, but because Cynthia could not abide muddy knees nor dirt-speckled dresses, and Samantha was prone to both of these things and worse. Every day she was picked, pecked, and pinched, and her scalp was perpetually pink from the scraping fangs of Cynthia's comb. All bound up in lace and ribbons, Samantha was force-fed femininity and choked it down, until Cynthia met her fate in red, and Samantha regurgitated satin onto the floor.

Samantha, pretending to care about the princesses in her picture book, watched the whole event transpire, her baby teeth bared as her jaw dropped an inch. Cynthia, dressed in a blue checkered dress and a pair of yellow pumps, climbed a rickety ladder with a bucket of paint. After her husband traded her in for a younger doll, all her rage was harnessed into being house-proud, and she thought the gutters would look better in a vivid shade of crimson. However, no sooner had she dipped the brush in paint than she fell backward, clinging to the ladder with all her might. The first responders say she might have lived had the white picket fence not punctured her middle and the red can of paint not dented her skull. Samantha watched the paint mix with the blood, and as the two reds swirled together, the plants drank deeply, and the roses that followed had never been redder.

Life already achromatized by grief, Samantha was further subjected to a bleached and beige world when her father, Brian, moved her from suburb to city. He said it was for work, but Samantha theorized he couldn't stand the sight of flowers anymore. They rented an apartment in a building owned by rats, and Samantha would hear the fuzzy creatures tinkering late into the night, collecting thumbtacks and needles to wage the ever-losing war against hordes of armored cockroaches. She rooted for the rats, even on wet nights when her home smelled of wood shavings and rodent piss, and she couldn't sleep for their conversational squeaking.

Brian didn't last long in the city, but he didn't move them back to the suburbs. Instead, he took a handgun and clinked it against cheap veneers, pulled the trigger, and blasted rose petals against a motel wall. Nothing poetic grew from the splintered bone shards of his grief-assisted euthanasia, and the motel room was back up and running within twenty-four hours.

After that, Samantha was sent to St. John's Orphanage. Run by an unkindness of raven-faced women with long, gaunt faces and awful crooked teeth, who'd flap their cloth wings as Samantha ran past, bloodied and wild, an aggrieved child hot on her quick heels. The nuns snapped their beaks often, and Samantha has the scars to prove it. Amongst them is a thin pale slit on her right buttock, left by a swift stick and a firm grip. The nuns haunt her dreams more than her parents do; they appear as gargoyles on the roof of her home, waiting to snatch her non-existent children up and carry them away screaming into the night sky.

At sixteen, she fled God's house with a chocolate-haired girl named Anna, and together they stole a car and hit the road running. They didn't stop until the car ran out of gas and they found themselves in an arid small town surrounded by saguaro cacti and coyotes. Anna cut Samantha's hair that night with a knife sharper than Cynthia's prized scissors, and Samantha slicked it back with grease and sweat. After planting a kiss on Anna's chapped lips, she looked in the cracked rear-view mirror, and kept slicing until the suffix 'antha' was severed from her name forever.

At twenty-six, Anna and Sam were married—not legally, but they had the rings and the love, and that was good enough at the time. They shared a small suburban house, and, whilst Sam worked daily on their garden, it never grew right, and the petals only made her sick. Nothing grew in Anna's womb either, and Sam refused to use her own, so their bed expanded its reach until they could no longer see each other under the covers.

By thirty-six, Anna had moved Betsey into the house that Sam had painted, and Sam moved into a lonely single-wide outside of town. Betsey was bigger, butcher, and richer than Sam, and together, she and Anna planted seed after seed until their house was swarming with babies. Sam watched from afar as she drove back and forth to her job at the local auto shop in a Mustang older than she was. All the children looked like Anna and Sam couldn't help but wonder if she'd cursed her when they were together, or if it was just bad luck.

At forty-six, she let the hum of the generator lull her to sleep like the snores of a lover, and tried to not let the night-time eat her alive.

Today, she awoke to thunder and an unfamiliar sound, and found that she'd fallen asleep with a gun and bottle of Jack, and wondered what she'd been planning to do before she blacked out. She listens intently and deduces that the sound is the roar of tires on a dirt road. She peers out of her grime-caked window and watches a van approach in a plume of desert smoke. A young man, dressed in a mailman's uniform, hops out with a letter in hand. He pushes the envelope through the veil of spider web covering her mailbox slot, and Sam opens the door, dressed in a t-shirt and worn boxers, and waves, but he's gone before she can strike up conversation.

She retrieves the letter from the sticky strands and finds it scarred with glassy patches of damp and stale coffee rings. She brings it inside, and leaves the door open to air out her home. After taking a sip from the bottle, she tears into the envelope. Keys fall out with the letter, three of them on a rusted rung. She puts them to the side and begins to read.

Dear Samantha,

If you're reading this, I am dead, or very nearly there. A few days ago, I was admitted into hospice and I know it can't be long now. Frankly, I hope Death hurries the hell up. I can't stand the look on everyone's faces. It's cancer, of course. Bowel cancer, initially, which spread rapidly to just about everywhere else. Which means, given your age, you should get yourself checked, as it's often genetic, and as I'm the one who gave birth to you, there's a decent chance you've inherited my shortcomings. I know that's burying the lede and I'm sorry for that. I'm sorry for a lot of things.

Sam squints at the legible handwriting as if it's difficult to understand and re-reads the passage. She reads it five more times, attempting to understand, but the information sits, a pool of tar atop a blocked drain, and she has no choice but to keep reading.

I'm sorry I didn't keep you. When I became pregnant with you, I knew I had no choice. I couldn't let you grow up in this house, in this family. I thought by giving you away, you'd escape the curse, but it wants blood, not proximity. My cancer has weakened it, and I thought it might kill it, but as Death begins to pace my porch, the curse begins to resurrect, and I know that it has latched on to you. I'm sorry to have not lived longer, and I'm sorry to introduce you to Sorry.

Sam finds herself winded, and after regaining her breath, she fills her glass to its rounded edge and collapses on the couch with the letter still in hand. As the blankets swallow her into plush-recess and morning rain patters the windows, she continues to read.

Sorry is a clown, though not of the human variety, which I know will be hard for you to understand. I grew up with him, so I don't know quite how to explain.

He was given to my great-great-grandmother, Mildred, in 1907 as a gift, and though he entertained her for a time, Mildred eventually grew tired of him. Her toying turned to cruelty, and in turn, molded Sorry into a monster. He snapped and killed her mother that same year, and the blood he drank from her body has bound our family to him ever since. So, let me present to you an offer. I leave to you my house, my fortune, my land, and in exchange, you will look after Sorry until your dying day, at which point, the bloodline will end, and so will he. Let our family tree burn, but enjoy the warmth while you can.

If you choose to accept my offer—which I urge you to do, lest another family obtain the house and Sorry with it—please read the following carefully:

The large key is for the front door, the medium is for the back door, and the smallest one is for Sorry's door. Unlock it upon arrival and lock it again if you leave the house. He will not bother you and is harmless during the day. All you need to do is supply him with milk and meat, and he'll be the sweetest pet.

However, at night, he changes.

So, you will find that in every bedroom there is a door bolt. Whatever room you choose, I advise you use the lock as soon as the sun sets and do not emerge until it rises. Good luck, my darling daughter, I'm sorry we never met.

Eternal love,

Beatrice Webb.

Sam sips at her drink and feels the liquid slosh in sync with the sickening rock of her trailer in the now-furious winds. Lightning strikes again, and for a moment, she sees a man in the middle-distance, posed and frozen, watching her through the window. When the secondary flicker arrives, she realizes it's only a strange-shaped rock, but she shuts the blinds anyways before flipping over the letter. There's an address on the back and Sam looks out at the inky black sky, imagining what it'll look like in the Lone Star State.

In the following weeks, she makes the necessary arrangements to start again in Texas, and once the trailer is sold and her belongings are packed, she hits the road, trying to ignore the thought of clowns. Her biological mother was clearly not in her right mind when she wrote the letter, so Sam dismisses Sorry as a fever dream and death-wrought delusion.

When she arrives at the house—which is taller than it is wide—she notices that it leans to the left on half-sunken foundations, and cranes her neck to get a good look at it through the rusty gate. Its white, like sun-bleached bone picked clean by desert-dwelling wildlife, and though it's a beautiful corpse, its carapace is ramshackle and in need of more than a lick of paint. She hops out of the still-running car and opens the gate. It screams as she forces it, its flaky russet dermis raw from decades of misuse.

As she continues to drive, the wheels crunch over the grass, dried out from drought after a heatwave. The surrounding trees are in a similar state, as are the vines that climb the columns and face of the building.

Once parked, she approaches the house and uses one of the slender pillars that support the drooping portico to heave her leaden body onto the porch. The two days of twelve-hour drives had not been kind to her long-suffering knees, and as she shuffles towards the double doors, the painted white porch floorboards depress like piano keys. The doors, made of oak, each sport an iron door knocker shaped like a bull's head. As Sam had discovered in her brief trip to the library to use the internet, the Webbs were meat-money rich, or they were before Beatrice had to sell most of the land and all of the cattle to afford maintaining the enormous house.

Consequently, though Beatrice had been faithful to her word about leaving everything to Sam, Beatrice and her daughter had very different interpretations of the word 'fortune.' Sam envisioned swimming through gold and sleeping in sheets made of filthy dollar bills, but when the check came, what she got was $23,000.

And as she steps into the house, she realizes every drop of it will be spent on repairs. The windows are boarded up, so only the open doorway illuminates the ancient vestibule ahead. The pale light from the overcast sky sketches her, long and thin, across the warped floors.

She enters and the door swings shut behind her as she fumbles for a light switch. Her fingers quickly find one next to a patch of peeling wallpaper, but the bulb flickers on, shorts out with a *pop*. She sighs, wishing she'd remembered a flashlight. Her phone, being a relic itself, is not a valid option, and she prays the problem is the bulb, not the fuse.

As her eyes adjust, she spots a side table to the left side of the room. It's occupied by a fringe-shaded lamp and piled high with unread letters belonging to her mother. Sam presses the toggle on its brass throat, and its failure to ignite confirms the worst. So, she resorts to plucking a dusty sconce—complete with skinny pillar candle—from the console, and with a satisfying clink from her Zippo, the wick takes to the flame and casts a warm glow across its cadaverous surroundings.

Sam holds the candle to the artwork above the side table and admires the oil-painted cattle, white and red, grazing in the fields. The herd meanders through the grass and she can almost hear their distant bellows. Sam closes her eyes, enjoying their happy song, before a thump from upstairs silences the animals. She starts, reopening her eyes, and finds the figures petrified in paint once again, and while the sound from above does not repeat itself, it unnerves her all the same, no matter how much she brushes it off as the building clicking its joints.

She turns about the room, noticing that every painting is of animals, primarily cattle, but some horses and a few dogs. The dogs are all English Setters with straight backs, speckled coats, and floppy ears, surrounded by game birds of all kinds; ducks, geese, coots, rails, snipe, woodcocks, and doves, glassy-eyed and broken, dead from bullets before the dogs could wrap their maws around their breakable necks.

As she turns back to the open door, she gasps, drops the candle, and nearly burns the house down in the process. She bends, her knees creaking as she does, and retrieves the extinguished stick. *Clink, woosh,* warmth.

A blackened mirror, framed with chipped faux-gold, reveals a spectral twin to her. A ghastly pale face with no eyes, underlit by the flame in her hand. She chuckles as she approaches it, and the raspy intonation echoes up the threadbare stairs. The closer she gets, the more she recognizes herself, and she slicks the escaped strands of her short gray hair back into place at her temples. The knots of her knuckles are cracked, and her nails filthy with oil and grease. She adjusts her white tank top and silver chain with arthritic fingers.

Sam faces the stairs on the right side of the room. She had ignored them thus far due to the dark pooling on their landing. As she fiddles with the keys—precisely the littlest one—her heart pangs outside of regular rhythm, and she decides to continue ignoring their unlit presence, staying in the comfort zone that the first floor provides. Pulling herself away from the impenetrable black, she turns left, through an oak door with a calloused metal handle, and finds herself in a dining room. The candlestick sends light through the slatted chairs and projects jail-cell bars onto the white-washed walls.

It's sparsely decorated and, like the vestibule, is predominantly white with umber-colored accents. The mahogany table and chairs are lacquered in dust, except for the polished spot at the end closest to the door. The place where Beatrice must've enjoyed her solitary meals. The chair sits at an angle, as if occupied by her ghost. Sam thinks, later, she'll sit in the chair next to the haunted one and have a first and final meal with her birth mother, and then, gently, she'll push the chair back into place.

Above the mantle of a boarded-up fireplace is a painting—again encapsulated in flaking gold—of a severe-looking woman dressed in a conservative brown dress with a lace collar. Her hair is parted sharply down the middle, a flash of white scalp demonstrating the thinness of the chestnut strands, and pulled into a braided bun. Sam knows who it is before she reads the name; Mildred Webb, the petulant curse-bringer.

A handful of photographs sit beneath the portrait that Sam can't bear to look at for long. They're not much older than she is, and set in free-standing frames. Most of them are of Beatrice; her slender figure, sometimes pregnant, draped in peasant dresses, her charcoal hair nearly waist-length. She had high-cheekbones and foxlike features, and Sam sees much of her own face reflected in the developed film. Some of the photos are of Sam's grandparents, who appear in stark contrast to their flower child. Wrinkled and deadpan, they stand in the fields surrounding the house. To Sam, they resemble *American Gothic*, with their farming tools and cross-bearing necklaces, and she can't decide whether this amuses or frightens her.

Sam moves away from them but lingers in the room, admiring the fine china in their glass-covered cases. Yet, the longer she stays, the more Mildred's eyes burn into her exposed skin, and she moves into the next room to escape the penetrating gaze.

The attached room is the kitchen and the orange bulb of the candle multiplies in the white-tiled walls. Sam feels relief as the illumination points out a spattering of mod-cons throughout. As she approaches the refrigerator, the stench of rotting meat hits her, even through the closed door. Getting the electricity back up and running jumps to the top of her list of priorities as she finds trash bags and moves the rotting off-cuts into the black plastic membrane.

She holds it at arm's length as she stalks back through the kitchen and dining room and the yet-unopened passageway, searching for more trash to expunge from the ancient beast's guts. The door opens into a drawing-room, half-concealed by white sheet ghosts in the shape of old furniture. Sam soon finds something else to throw away; rotten peonies reduced to mush in an antique vase. They melt between her fingers as she throws the putrid flowers in with the rest of the organic matter.

Sam places the candle on a corner table and looks around the room. It's spacious and empty like all the others, and Beatrice's ghost manifests in the form of a worn salmon-pink armchair with its seat dented to the shape of a bony backside, a half-eaten packet of crackers on the table, and an empty mug of coffee beside it. Sam adds the former to the bag with slight hesitation, and watches her mother's limpid form move from plush surface to open doorway, bare feet grazing splinters as she shuffles. Sam can feel the weight of the tumor in her own belly, the arches in her feet flattening into flippers as she mimics Beatrice's path around the furniture.

When her mind can focus past the spirit of her mother, she begins to notice the clowns. The porcelain clowns, dressed in black and white—more Pierrot than Circus—crowd most surfaces. Over the mantlepiece is a portrait. His innocent face pushes Sam back towards the far wall, his sadness tangible. Sorry stares at her as if he wants something, but she has nothing to give the pathetic oil amalgamation of Beatrice's imagination, and with aching ankles, she takes her candle and the bag of trash and leaves the room behind.

She dumps the latter on the porch, swaps it for a suitcase, and as she heaves the clunky thing with its broken wheel towards the door, she spots a man on the other side of the age-old gates.

He's young and wiry, dressed in a wife-beater and denim, and his cowboy hat shields his face from the sun and Sam's vision. All she can make out from the shadows is a deeply dimpled chin and a golden canine tooth. He spits in the bushes as he waves. "Hey there," he calls out, his accent thick. "Here I was thinking this place was abandoned."

"Nope," she replies, "It was my mom's, and now it's mine."

"Your momma's? Well, I didn't think Beatrice had any kids."

"She didn't raise me," Sam says, tone terse. "But she left everything to me."

"All right, I didn't mean no offense," the man says, spitting again. "What's your name?"

"Sam."

"You live alone, Sam?"

She thinks to lie but finds herself shrugging and saying, "Nope, just me." A hush falls between them, and Sam excuses herself. "I gotta get going. Lots of work to do on this old place."

The man laughs wryly. "Well, I bet there is. I'll be seeing you, Sam."

He doesn't move from his perch, and she slips away and locks the front door behind her. Luggage in hand, she moves her mind from the man and decides to ascend to the next level of her new home.

The dust that plumes under her boots smells ancestral, and when she thinks about it, she realizes it is. If dust is made of skin, then she's living in an ancestral urn. *It's going to be hard to clean,* she thinks as she pulls her graying palm from the handrail, literally and emotionally.

At the top of the stairs, she faces a wall and a window hidden by heavy drapes, and when she turns around, a hallway unfolds before her, long and dark, with innumerable doors leading to innumerable rooms. Pressed close to the right-hand side is another, steeper staircase, and she stands at the foot of it with the candle. An ornate door sits at the top of the gradually thinning flight; painted Sacramento green, the carved faces in the primordial pea soup whisper to her, and the keyhole calls for the little silver key in her pocket.

When she snaps out of it, she finds herself six steps closer to the door and quickly turns around, extinguishing the candle in her haste. The whispers get louder as footsteps walk up to the other side of the green door.

Sam hurries back down, her suitcase knocking into knees and cleaving into calf. Fumbling with candlestick and doorknob, she flings herself into one of the rooms at random, and seeks refuge on the other side. Dropping her suitcase, she forces her hands steady and relights the candle. She finds herself in a large bedroom with an iron bed frame covered by a familial quilt, and in the far corner, next to the dresser, is a narrow white door. An ensuite reveals itself on the other side, complete with a clawfoot tub and floral floor tiles, and not being one to reject luxury, she decides that this will be her room.

Her suitcase finds a temporary home on its back, a makeshift wardrobe until she can bring herself to unpack, and the candle sits atop the dresser. It guides her as she opens the trunk at the foot of the bed and changes the lived-in sheets that cover the sweat-stained mattress. She perches on its edge to rest her body while changing pillowcases, and the springs groan beneath her weight. She'd give anything to lean back and sleep for a day, or a week, or forever, but she changes the pillowcases and gets back up. She starts tucking the fitted sheet, and as she reaches the cold metal headboard, she notices the bedside table's drawer is ajar. Abandoning her task, she opens it all the way, revealing a journal, which Sam handles with intrigue.

The cover is tan, and the texture makes her think of pigskin rather than the typically used cattle leather. The pages inside are clumped together, as if it has sat out in the rain, but a few pull away from the wad and are legible despite the intricate cursive. Written atop the first page is, 'The Diary of Mildred Webb,' and the date below reads, 'The 4th of January 1907.'

As Sam's eyes flit about the page, Mildred peels herself away from her sullen dining-room portrait, and slivers slickly from the shelf and onto the floor. Her hooped-skirt and corseted-waist turn her silhouette into an oddly portioned marionette as she glides from room to room and susurrates up the stairs. Eventually, she finds a resting place in the corner of

Sam's bedroom, looming over her, illuminated by the bioluminescence of her spectral ectoplasm. She's uglier in person, Sam thinks, the oil painting having concealed rotten teeth and a hollow-eyed expression.

When she speaks, her tongue is black and pointed like a leech, and her lifeless eyes stare through Sam's corporeal form and focus on the damp spot on the ceiling. "Beloved, betrothed, blue," she whispers, the strain in her voice made visible by the taught tendons in her throat. She continues to speak via Sam's morbid curiosity, though as the vision becomes more real, Sam resents her imagination.

My storybook romance was punctuated by an untimely death at the hands of cholera. Our wedding day was supposed to be tomorrow. For weeks, my wedding dress has hung in the wardrobe in my bedroom, and at night, the door opens, and I see it dance in the wind, the bodice filled out by my own merry, married ghost. Sometimes I rise from bed and join her in dance, and we whisper in delight at the idea of becoming one. She needed a body, and I needed to be married. How silly of us, so unaware that it would never come to pass. When I next see my ghost, I don't suppose she'll be dancing in the dress. I think she'll just be hanging.

When he died, his mother took me to his room. I didn't remember his room being so large, nor his bed so tall, and him so tiny. His mouth was agape, eyes wide, all framed by the skin of silverfish. Bedding wrapped around his frail body like a chrysalis from which he will never hatch. That bony creature was not my Edward, and with nothing left to say goodbye to, I turned my back on him and ran from the room.

The funeral occurred a few days later. It was a rainy, outdoors affair. As they lowered Edward—all wrapped up in linen and pitch—into the ground, I begged to be buried with him. At night, I dream of lying naked in Edward's coffin and being devoured by the same maggots currently eating him. I want our flesh entangled in the bellies of insects.

Sam wants her to stop, but her hand turns the page, and Mildred keeps speaking, despite the flesh on her delicate bones coming loose and her eye sockets struggling to keep the eyeballs contained.

Today, Father called for me from the bottom of the stairs. He'd just returned from a trip to the city, and as I stared down at his mustachioed face, I knew that he had a surprise for me, and I descended the stairs in my stinking undergarments with vigor.

I rounded the corner into the drawing-room and froze in shock. Standing in the middle of the room was a clown. He looked more like a doll than a person. Dressed in all white, he wore a tall pointed hat and a frilly outfit complete with puffy pantaloons, knee-high stockings, and bells on his collar.

His delicate face was painted white, smooth as porcelain, and his eyebrows were painted as thin lines, bowed with sadness. His mouth was black; the painted lips, rounded at the edges, were drawn into a permanent semi-circular smile, though I could see that the man behind the makeup's mouth was held in a severe line. His impossibly dark eyes, framed by small triangles, were filled with the vulnerability of an infant. It made me want to kick him.

Father announced loudly that he'd bought me a clown. I informed my father that one cannot just buy a clown. Father shook his head and said that I was wrong, that this clown was all mine for as long as I would have him. All I would have to do is name him, which would seal the deal.

"Fine. I will name him Sorry because I'm sorry that he's here," I said, and Papa sighed at my choice of name, but Sorry began to do a jig, kicking his feet up, swinging his arms back and forth, jingling all the while. However, his face remained utterly emotionless, the painted smile doing all the work for him.

He danced for an extraordinarily long time, and when I became unsettled, I snapped. "Sorry, sit," I screamed, and he did as I asked, immediately dropping to the floor and crossing his legs like a schoolchild. It was then that I realized Sorry would do anything that I asked.

Mildred recites another entry with a childish glee. Sam's had enough, but the tulpa in the room keeps talking, keeps her hands turning.

Sorry is a delight. Never have I felt so attended to or entertained. He will not speak nor sing, though he does almost anything else I desire. He's a sweet little creature, and in exchange for his services, I leave him a bowl of food scraps before bed; I never see him eat, but the plate is always licked clean in the morning. Even the bones and gristle disappear!

Mama doesn't like Sorry, no matter how happy he makes me. She's uncomfortable in his presence, whether he's with me or alone. She says she sometimes walks up the stairs only to find him at the top, staring down at her, and that his night-time wanderings fill her with terror.

Today, she told me she wanted him gone, and when I screamed at her, she slapped me, as she has so many times before. When I ran out into the hallway, Sorry scampered after me. I raised a hand to him in my upset, but thought better of it and turned away. As I did so, he reached for my wrist, I believe in an act of kindness, so I turned back to him and said, "Sorry, hit yourself." He raised a slender hand and smacked himself hard, harder than I was able, across the cheek. He flinched at the impact, confused by what he had done.

Mildred falls silent as the rest of the entries' words become illegible where the ink blooms across the page in blue-rimmed puddles. As soon as the final period meets Sam's pupil, Mildred begins to melt. Blue crystalline flesh degloved and skeleton exposed, Mildred offers a bony smile before turning to dust and slipping through the gaps in the floorboard.

Sam slams the journal shut and puts it back in the drawer; she's read enough and this is one work of fiction she doesn't care for.

She leaves the room and book behind, trying to rid Mildred's cruel visage from her mind, and trying not to think about Sorry the clown. She turns to face the window at the top of the first flight of stairs, wanting to grab the rest of her luggage before it starts to rain, but she stops in her tracks when she looks at the thick drapes, made from rich plum-colored velvet. At first, she thinks she's imagined it, but the fabric moves ever so slightly. When it settles, she gasps and reaches for a gun holster that isn't there.

Somebody is standing on the other side of the curtains.

From their imprint, she'd guess that the person is a man of short stature and slender build. The description of the clown from Mildred's diary obscures her mind's eye, and she can almost see the painted man through the opaque curtains. It's ridiculous, but like watching a horror movie and then being afraid to close your eyes in the shower, she knows she's being silly, but she can't simply dismiss the fear.

Life in the Nevada desert has given Sam a leathered hide and a quick tongue, so even without her gun, she takes a heavy step forward and growls, "Come out from there with your hands up. I know this house has been sitting empty for a while, but it's mine now, and I don't like unexpected guests."

The person behind the curtains doesn't move or speak, so she raises her voice. "Come on now, I can see you. I know you're there. If you come out now, I'll consider not calling the cops on you." She takes another step forward. "If you're hungry, I've got food. If you're broke, I've got cash. But I cannot have you hiding out in my house." The fabric-covered shape twitches but doesn't reply. Her face grows hot from fear and anger, and she grabs a loose skirting board and wields it like a bat. "You've got till the count of ten before I'm coming in there after you," she rumbles in a forcibly low register.

The intruder falls still again, and the count begins. One, two, three, four, five, six, seven, no response or movement. She draws the last numbers of the count out as she gets closer and closer. She realizes by the time she calls out a slow-motion nine that she really will have to drag this person out by force. Bracing herself for impact, she takes another step forwards, and reaches out a hand, fingertips brushing velvet.

"Ten," she hisses and draws the curtain to the side in a sharp, sweeping movement. She yelps instinctively, but there's nobody there, only a nest of daddy long legs and blooming black spores. She shakes her head and laughs as she draws the curtain closed again. Except, as the material settles into a flatness that no longer resembles a person, the laugh catches in her throat, and she backs away from the window.

Hearing a sudden sound above her, she looks up at the gappy boards. Footsteps run along creaking floorboards. "What the hell?" she whispers, and as she turns to the green door, she knows she can no longer ignore it.

The staircase acts as an escalator, and carries her up the passage in a fugue. Once she reaches the top, not having remembered moving her limbs at all, she teeters precariously on the top step, pressed against the door.

She fishes the keys from her pocket, and as metal finds metal, a rush of light-treading feet and jingling bells run at the door. The person stops before they collide with it, and Sam nearly falls back as if they ran into her instead. She takes a deep breath and looks at the shadow of their feet, mirroring her own boots. Exhaling, she turns the key until it clicks, and pushes the door open. Whoever is in the room follows its arc and hides behind it, keeping a slab of wood between their two bodies.

Sam glances at the cot pressed against the left wall and the chamber pot beside it. It reeks of rot, and the room feels like a prison cell.

The person, still hiding behind the door, drops to their knees, and Sam feels the vibrations of their shakes in the floorboards. Fighting every instinct that she possesses, Sam steps into the room and, from a respectable distance, looks behind the door.

"No fucking way," she wheezes, as if sucker-punched. "No, this isn't possible."

A clown is hunched over on the floor, his pointed hat wilted and his clothes filthy. Sorry cocks his head at Sam, the permanent smile painted on his face contrasting harshly with his sad, puppy-dog eyes. In a springy moment, he jumps to his feet and hops from one foot to the other, his hand outstretched, wishing to grasp but not wanting to shake.

"Hello, Sorry," she murmurs. "I guess I'm your new caretaker." At this, he looks upset, his angular and pretty face screwed up in a confusion that Sam isn't sure he's equipped to handle. "Beatrice is gone. I'm Sam."

Sorry steps forward into the yellow light, and Sam gasps. Covering his painted flesh are a plethora of century-old wounds of varying severity. Breaks are evident in badly healed bone, and his ancient clothes indicate stabbings where slender slits are caked in century-old blood. She considers Mildred's words, *It was then that I realized Sorry would do anything that I asked,* and a penny of thunderous proportions drops to the ground. Sam wonders which came first? The enforced self-mutilation or compelling him to murder her mother?

"What did that monster do to you?" she asks, feeling his wounds on her own flesh, invisible but tangible. "Would you like to come downstairs?" Sorry gives no indication of having understood the question. "Can I have your hat? I can fix it," Sam asks, trying to smile and forcing adrenaline-infused bile down her constricting gullet. At this, Sorry shakes his head in a frantic jingling, and Sam steps back with hands raised in surrender. "I'm going to leave the door open," she whispers, "and I'll bring you some food and drink. You must be hungry." Keeping her eyes on him, she retreats out of the room and moves slowly down the stairs, being careful not to run though her body begs her to.

Once in the only familiar room, she bolts the door shut and collapses on the half-made bed. She shakes violently, her mind sending her body into shock rather than trying to process what she's seen. All the while, she listens out for Sorry, more animal than human, expecting him to creak down the stairs, but he doesn't budge. So, after a while, she unlocks the door and continues about her day as best she is able.

In the kitchen, she pulls a gas station sandwich from her backpack and plates it, carries it up the stairs, and leaves it on the landing outside Sorry's room. He watches her reproachfully from his cot, like a rescue dog at the pound, and like those mistreated mutts, once she turns her back, he scampers across the floor, grabs the plate, and demolishes the offerings gratefully.

She locks his door as she heads to the store. Sorry needs milk and meat, and she needs groceries for herself too. When she returns with everything they need, including cleaning supplies, she unlocks his door again. She leaves his door shut but lets him know it's unlocked and goes back downstairs to prepare them both dinner.

When she rounds the corner to the narrow stairwell with a plate of steak and a glass of semi-skimmed, she screams, and both go smashing to the ground. Sorry is perched on the landing, illuminated by the many candles lit throughout the vicinity. At incredible velocity, he flees in terror back up to his floor, and Sam gets the dustpan and brush.

After making sure there's no glass in his steak, she tries again, this time steeling herself against another possible sighting. Neither can be blamed. Cohabitation takes time, especially between two such different beasts. Not wanting to bother him, she leaves the new plate and glass at the bottom of his stairs and retreats back to the dining room to enjoy her own meal. The steak is the same, but she opts for wine instead of milk.

When the sun begins to set, she takes the bottle and herself to bed. Beatrice was honest about everything else, so she locks the door and hunkers down for the night. She burrows under the comforter and quilt, and reads one of the many books she brought with her while getting progressively drunk.

After a while, she hears Sorry slurp at his glass of milk through the walls, and she raises her own glass in cheers. When he starts in on the steak, she makes a mental note to buy earplugs. His wet tongue slathers over the rare meat, and teeth tear into it in large chunks.

That's when she hears a different noise. A smashing of a window from downstairs. *The kitchen,* she thinks, before hearing more smashing and thumping as someone climbs inside the house. Sorry skitters down the hall on all fours before she can even put her book aside. Sam's heart pangs. *What if the intruder has a gun?*

"What the fuck is that?" A man yells. She recognizes his voice.

There's silence for a moment. She can barely hear anything over her pounding heart. The crack of breaking bone rings clear throughout the house, and Sam shudders violently. The snaps are followed by the thump of a heavy body hitting the ground. And then the bites, rips, tears, and guttural screams start. Sam is glad she doesn't have neighbors, and she covers her ears, though it doesn't seem to help.

When it all goes quiet, she swings her legs from her bed and pads across the room. Undoing the bolt, she peers out into the hallway and covers her mouth in horror as she sees Sorry, still on all fours, hunched at the top of the stairs. The intruder's shoulder is trapped in Sorry's unhinged jaw, and his razor-sharp teeth—of which there are hundreds—are hooked deep into the trapezius.

Sorry drops the man she'd encountered earlier, the one who'd asked if she lived alone. He's reduced to a twisted pile of protruding bone and minced meat. His face is twisted into a permanent scream, and his eyes know only fear.

Sorry glances at Sam, his painted smile now an upside-down frown. He opens his mouth and hisses before latching once more and dragging the man towards the second staircase. Sam closes her door as he passes. The man's head bumps on each wooden step, and after twenty-or-so knocks, Sorry begins his feast.

Sam climbs back into bed, realizing she lied to the corpse in the attic; she doesn't live alone, and never will again. Sleep consumes her, and when she wakes, she's more refreshed than she has been in years.

When she opens her door, she finds Sorry's drooping, pointed hat on the floor, speckled with blood, and she carries it tenderly downstairs, excited to repair it for him.

CHAPTER FIVE

PENNY FOR YOUR FORTUNE

Katerini Koraki

The boardwalk never changed; the city simply grew around it. Like a tumor, it clung to the shoreline by the docks, the half-rotten boards of black wood somehow managing to avoid collapse year after year. Sailing into town, the rickety old rollercoaster out on the pier was the first sight to peek over the horizon, followed shortly by the Ferris wheel, and then the EMPIRE BOARDWALK sign in its flickering electric glory. A squat line of shops, two thirds of them abandoned, hung off the pier like a row of decaying teeth. To the east, all that remained of the second pier was a line of pilings and the rusted metal skeleton of what was once the largest greenhouse in the world.

Residents of the city never went to the boardwalk, save the rite of passage of a trip or two as children. Tourists wandered over on occasion, drawn in by the tinkling music of the carousel or the smell of cotton candy. But, as soon as they arrived, the charming vintage facade faded, and the dilapidated structures and stink of the sea drove them back downtown to their hotels. Surely, the corporation that owned the place wasn't turning a profit on it. Surely, the city didn't want the health and safety hazard driving down beachfront property values. Still, with every proposal to tear the place down, the proprietor or the mayor would give some long speech about history and preservation, but the truth was it would have cost more to tear down the eyesore than to leave it and pray a hurricane would push it into the sea for good.

It wasn't always that way. Once upon a time, in another century, the boardwalk was the most wonderful place in the world.

On a deep blue June day, long before the rust and water and decay, the boardwalk had a ribbon-cutting—not just a perfunctory gesture, but a ceremony. Half of the city stood shoulder-to-shoulder down the blocks by the shore, jostling each other and standing up on their tiptoes to see farther ahead. Up near the ribbon, a troupe of tap dancers from a nearby dance school were finishing up their performance. The music barely carried to the back of the crowd, but the metallic clang of their shoes on the impromptu platform stage did. In the very last row, Lena Marchetti stood between her sister, Louisa, and Louisa's newest boyfriend, Gerald, trying not to think about the way her own dress clung to her with static electricity and other people's sweat. A dull ache blossomed at her temples and she shifted her weight between her sore legs. She looked over at her sister's lit-up face and mentally calculated the minutes until they could go home.

The dance troupe finished their set to a sea of riotous applause before making their way off the stage. Replacing them entered the mayor: a short, stout man wearing a top hat and a suit two decades out of fashion. Even though he stood with his face right in the microphone, no one beyond the first row could hear what he was saying over the rabble of the crowd.

"Just get on with it already, I want to go in!" a woman a few rows ahead called out.

Gerald scoffed and took off his cap to wipe the sweat from his brow. "Get comfortable. It'll be a long while before we're anywhere near the entrance."

After the mayor snipped the red ribbon wrapped around the iron gates loose, Gerald's prophecy came true; those near the front flooded inside, packing themselves into every last square foot of the boardwalk, while those near the back hardly moved a step. All they could do was stand and watch the Ferris wheel spin round and round and the cars on the rollercoaster crest and fall. As morning gave way to afternoon, the temperature only increased, magnified by the body heat of the buzzing crowd.

Louisa stepped over an abandoned, trampled tent on the ground as the group shuffled forward. "I told you we should have camped out last night."

"We shouldn't have come at all," Lena grumbled. "The boardwalk's not going anywhere. We could have come in a few weeks when the excitement would have died down."

Louisa shot her sister a glare. "That's the whole point. We're here when it's all happening." She then looked down at the red velvet frock that had cost half her paycheck. "And I didn't break out my glad rags just to sit around."

Lena rolled her eyes and decided she was too hot to respond.

The sun dipped low on the horizon as revelers poured in and out. What seemed like eons later, they made it close enough to smell the taffy and the cotton candy. More than anything, Lena's sore legs and sunburnt skin called for a place to sit. All scowling, the trio soldiered on. Jaunty music from the carousel seemed to lift Louisa's spirits, but even that soured as the fifth chorus of "By the Beautiful Sea" began to play. The only thing stopping them from going home was the stubborn determination of having waited so long.

By the time they reached the gates, blue twilight had fallen over the ocean, the crowd inside was thin, and the ticket-taker was waving everyone through without making them pay.

Gerald rolled the sleeves of his sweat-soaked shirt back down. "This better be the best goddamn boardwalk on God's green Earth, Louisa."

"It will be. Trust me. Now take me on the carousel!" She dragged him off to the ride before he could get a word in. "Meet us back at the popcorn stand in two hours!"

Lena stood alone. All at once, the electric lights around her illuminated, bathing the boardwalk in a soft orange glow. The shops stood on her left and the rides on the right, perched out on the pier. Just looking at the rollercoaster made her sick, so Lena decided on the shops. She thumbed the coin purse in the pocket of her skirt and figured her meager savings would buy her, at the very least, a souvenir for all the time she spent waiting.

Taffy made Lena's stomach sick, so the first store was out. And she felt much too old for a turn at the penny arcade, so she kept walking past the second. Not enough money for a summer frock. No need for a bathing suit. Excuse after excuse to avoid the other stores and keep walking until, finally, she reached the end.

Lena looked around. Almost no one milled about that patch of the boardwalk. The evening air cooled her skin and cleared her head. Then, she noticed: in the darkness, between the streetlamp and the electric signs of the other storefronts, stood the very last building. Flaky green lettering curled around the curtained glass window, announcing the place's name: 'Wright's Emporium of Curiosities.'

Why not?

She pushed the door open and stepped inside. Dim gas lights reflected off rows and rows of glass displays. The interior was just as deserted as the space outside. After a few hesitant steps, Lena realized that no one was coming to take her money and show her around. She couldn't help but feel like she wasn't meant to be there—like she was breaking in, and someone would soon come chase her away. From the opposite wall, the dead glass eyes of stuffed elk heads watched over her. Lena clenched her fist around the coin purse in her pocket and walked down the ratty red carpet to see the displays.

First was what the Emporium called a mermaid. It wasn't one of the long-haired, giggling princesses she saw when she went to the pictures. No, it was an animal—a brown, desiccated husk of a thing. A mermaid, the sign claimed, but it was obviously just two mummified corpses bound together with crude staples. Lena recognized the tail as that of a catfish, but the upper body was harder to identify. A monkey, maybe, with its face twisted into a permanent scream that nestled itself into Lena's imagination. Looking at the creature turned her stomach sour, but she could barely look away. With effort, she tore herself from the mermaid and moved on to the other exhibits.

Rows of shrunken heads hung by their tufted hair, skirting the line between surely leather-crafted and surely real. A glimmering silver chalice that supposedly bore the curse of some cult on the other side of the world. A taxidermy hawk extracting the intestines from the split carcass of a prairie dog. A bone china doll with beetle's wings glued on its back labeled as a fairy skeleton. Hypnotized, Lena made her way through the rows of exhibits, one by one.

Unable to see out the window, she had no idea how long it had been since she entered. Stiffness in her legs and lower back told her it had probably been a while. Still, the thought of leaving, of returning to the screaming children and incessant music and body heat, made her want to weep. She decided to stay, at least until Louisa and Gerald came to find her. At least until then.

It was only on her second turn about the room that Lena saw the door—tucked into the shadow of the displays with its deep mahogany blending into the crimson wallpaper. No sign hung on its frame warning visitors to keep out or drawing them in to the wonders inside. When Lena turned the tarnished brass knob and pushed, it swung open with ease to reveal a bare, steep staircase down to a basement. Another exhibit, perhaps? One Lena certainly couldn't miss. Careful not to fall, she lowered herself step by step.

Down there, the only light was from a single candle burning on a wall sconce. Once she reached the foot of the stairs, Lena kept her hand on the wall until her eyes adjusted to the dark. As they did, her heart sank. All she could see was the hard dirt floor, four unfinished walls, and a tall wooden box in the corner. Closer inspection revealed the box to be a display cabinet, same as the ones upstairs, with the glass panel facing the wall. For a few seconds, she just stared.

I've come this far. Why not?

Rational mind silenced, Lena braced her hands on either side of the cabinet and jimmied it out until it faced the adjacent wall. She took a moment to catch her breath, wondering what could be so heavy, then walked around to see what the box held.

Inside the cabinet sat a woman. 'MADAME ESMÉE,' the sign read, 'PENNY FOR YOUR FORTUNE.'

The fortune teller's porcelain skin stood out against her patchwork dress and the jet-black wig falling limp down her shoulders. Her face was so detailed that she almost looked like a mummy herself—like the body of a maiden dipped in porcelain to keep her youth forever. Not quite real, but too real to be a simple dummy. Her hands sat poised over a crystal ball and, on her face, a permanent smile was tattooed in red paint. But her most striking feature was her eyes. Lena thought back to the dead, dull eyes of her dolls as a girl and marveled at the intricate detail of the fortune teller's. Even though her stare was fixated down at the crystal ball, Madame Esmée's green irises caught the light of the gas lamps with a gentle glow.

Before she realized what she was doing, Lena was reaching out to slot a penny into the machine. It dropped in with a satisfying thwack, and the machine whirred to life. Tinny, flat music played from somewhere deep inside the box, and deep violet light emanated from the crystal ball as the fortune teller's hands moved around it in jerky, robotic circles. The automaton's overwrought ministrations were distracting, but Lena kept her focus on the fortune teller's eyes.

Madame Esmée's face snapped up to look straight at her client. It sounded like the gears were grinding and breaking. Lena jumped back and screwed her eyes shut, afraid that the fortune teller would break through the glass. When she lowered her arms and looked a moment later, Madame Esmée was back in her original position. A bellowing buzz rang from deep inside the cabinet's gears, then a strip of yellow paper printed from a slot below the glass. Without taking her eyes off the machine, Lena took a few hesitant steps forward and snatched the paper before shoving it into her pocket and bounding up the stairs.

She didn't look back as she sprinted out of the emporium and back to the crowd. By then, the sky was black, and all the children were gone. All that was left were couples, performers, and gaggles of men leering at girls and smoking pipes of hash. Weaving through the sea of people, ignoring the catcalls and hawking street vendors, Lena wondered if she would ever find her sister. Thankfully, as she rounded the corner to the popcorn stand, Louisa's red velvet dress stood out like a lighthouse beacon guiding her home.

Unfortunately, Louisa wasn't so comforted by the sight of her younger sister. "Where the hell have you been? It's an hour after we agreed to meet. You know how much I hate the fuzz, but I was about to report you missing. You know what they say about these carnival types. Father would have my head if anything happened to you, especially after Mama—"

"Nothing like that." Lena masked the adrenaline still pumping through her with a sweet, calm voice. "I just got caught up in…a game. A stupid boardwalk game. Silly me! Let's scram."

Gerald and Louisa shot each other a look, but Lena was already halfway to the new subway stop, so they just followed. Subway platforms were so hot that they were like little portals to Hell, but Lena welcomed it with open arms. Already, Wright's Emporium and Madame Esmée felt like a dream. Lena decided it had been a sort of heatstroke fantasy crafted by her mind after reading one too many of her sister's pulp magazines. She decided not to think about it ever again—to stay as far from the boardwalk as she could for the rest of her life.

Her resolution stayed strong until, sitting in the train, her hand glanced across the paper in her pocket. While Louisa and Gerald whispered in each other's ears, giggling in the way new lovers do, Lena lifted it to her lap and squinted at the letters printed in swirling, uneven font. Holding the fortune up to the light, she was able to make it out.

AN ACQUAINTANCE WILL SOON BECOME A TREASURED FRIEND.

Chills wracked through her body. It must have been a coincidence. A canned line printed out at random to convince fools like her to part with their pennies. She was about to ball the fortune up and throw it out the train door—when she caught a glimpse of a word printed on the back.

MAGDALENA.

Using every ounce of her energy, Lena gripped the edge of her seat to stop herself from collapsing, crushing the fortune. When she felt strong enough to sit upright, she tucked the slip of paper back into her skirt. Next to her, Louisa swatted Gerald's shoulder as she laughed at a joke. To Lena, it felt surreal, like watching characters in the pictures. Her blood felt thin as water. MAGDALENA, in the calligraphic font of the fortune, burned in white heat whenever she closed her eyes.

At long last, the train screeched to a halt at Gerald's stop. "Are you sure you don't want to come back to my place? There's a juice joint down the road that's delightful this time of night."

Louisa smoothed out her dress. "No. Lena and I are career girls now. We've got to get up for work tomorrow."

Gerald smiled as he leapt out of the train. "I'll call you! How's Wednesday?"

Louisa examined her nails. "I'll see if there's room in my calendar."

The doors slammed shut, and the train continued puttering along its route. On any other night, Lena would have started needling her sister about her boyfriend as soon as Gerald was out of earshot. Tonight, though, she sat silent. The paper in her skirt weighed a thousand pounds. Luckily, Louisa was babbling about her crush and wouldn't stop until she went to bed. Lena moved through the tiny apartment like a wind-up doll, going through the motions of washing and brushing her hair and slipping on her nightgown, without really thinking about them. For two hours, she stared at the dark ceiling, waiting for a sleep she knew would not come.

Once she'd had enough, she slipped out of her bed and plucked the fortune from her skirt. Careful not to wake Louisa, Lena tiptoed into the kitchenette. Holding the thin paper up, she watched the shadows of the moon and streetlights pass over it. Then she reached into the nearest drawer, struck a match, and watched the fire lick and consume the paper.

Once the fortune was just a few scraps of blonde ash, Lena left the kitchen and tucked herself back into bed.

That night, she dreamt of green eyes too alive to be made of glass.

Life felt a little more tangible when the alarm clock woke her up at six. After checking that the ash was still in the wastebasket and downing a cup of coffee, Lena almost felt back to normal. Whenever she found her mind wandering to the basement at the boardwalk, she pinched her hand until the sharp pain snapped her back to reality. The gray, cool sky that greeted her when she walked outside was a comfort; summer sun would have been too much to handle.

Walking into the library felt like diving in a pool of cool water on a hot day—hushed tones and dark, overstuffed stacks offered a sweet relief to the loud, bright memories of the boardwalk. Antsy nerves still bit their way up her ankles and palms, a hangover from the night before. When the head librarian peered over her glasses to assign Lena to shelf stocking duty, gratitude flowed through her. Mindless, manual work—exactly what she needed. Quickly, she fell into the rhythm of slipping the worn-out hardbacks onto their respective shelves. Nothing out of place, nothing that shouldn't be there, no tricks of the eye. Lena walked back to her desk with the serenity of repetition and a book of poetry tucked under her arm.

On her desk, everything was as it should have been: two sharp pencils, a fountain pen, and an inkwell. Standard issue, they all were, from the stationery store down the road. The last two items on the desk were not so generic: a pair of glass paperweights shaped like sparrows. She swiped them from her mother's bedroom before the funeral. Every day, she would run her fingertips over the bumps of their feathers and look at how the glass warped and magnified the view of her beige maple desktop. Not that day.

On that day, the sparrows sat on top of a thin yellow paper. Through the glass, she could make out the words *FOR LENA. MY LENA.*

Nausea rolled through her like a wave. She screwed her eyes shut and counted to three but, when she looked, the fortune was still there. More than anything, she needed to leave. So, she turned and headed straight out.

The head librarian caught her just before she reached the door. "Miss Marchetti, your shift doesn't end for at least another three hours."

"I know. I'm sorry, Mrs. Stanwick, but I'm having…I don't feel well." Flashing lights appeared in Lena's vision. She swayed on her feet, and the head librarian caught her.

To Lena's surprise, her supervisor patted her on the shoulder. "Alright, dear. Do you need me to call an ambulance?"

"No, no, no. I'm fine. I just need to go home and rest. I'll be back tomorrow at eight." One step at a time, Lena made her way out of the library.

The world swayed around her as she walked, as though she were aboard a ship on a choppy sea. At the same time, everything felt hazy. Surreal. As if, any minute now, she would wake up to her alarm clock and start the day all over again. She didn't remember the trip home. One minute, she was on the curb in front of the library and, the next, she was climbing the steps to her apartment. She supposed that she took the streetcar, like she did every day, but the shivers that wracked her body indicated she may have walked through the unseasonable cold. It didn't matter. All that mattered was dragging herself through the apartment and into bed. She wondered if she felt the way her mother had in those last days—if the dizziness and auras and churning stomach was just the madness setting in. Sleep came as soon as her head hit the pillow. As she drifted off, Lena prayed for a dark and dreamless sleep that she would wake up from laughing at her own silliness.

Instead, she found herself in a dream, lying on her side in the soft grass of an alpine valley. Birdsong lilted through the meadow, and clear air filled her lungs. A strange sensation blossomed on her scalp—something hard pressing up against her skin. Somehow, before she turned, she already knew what she would see. Madame Esmée, with her painted smile and green, green eyes, ran her porcelain hands through the tresses of Lena's curls. Equal parts comfort and fear bubbled inside her. It made her feel like a little girl again.

Lena shot awake, panting, disoriented at the stuffy, familiar air of her apartment. Her heart beat a thready hummingbird beat for a full minute and her vision blurred at the edges. Once the panic subsided, she looked down at her lap.

Dozens of thin yellow fortunes blanketed the bed.

LENA COME AND SEE ME. DON'T YOU MISS ME LENA? WE ARE VERY BEST FRIENDS. DON'T KEEP ME WAITING FOR MUCH LONGER. I DREAM ABOUT YOU TOO.

There were so many that she couldn't possibly read them all. The sick, migraine-like feeling crashed over her again. Haze filled her field of vision and, when it cleared, she was walking onto the train, coin purse in hand.

I'm either going to the boardwalk or the asylum.

Whichever it was, she swore to herself that she wouldn't go home until the whole ordeal was sorted. Lena picked a seat far from the only other person in the car and leaned her head back against the window. South, she calculated that the train was headed as it pulled into the next stop. South to the boardwalk. What choice was there but to go along for the ride?

Shivering, she climbed the stairs of the subway stop into the overcast day. With that weather, the boardwalk seemed a completely different place. Sunday's crowds had been replaced with dope fiends stumbling through the blustery winds to beg for spare change, and only the most dedicated vendors lined the streets. Empty rollercoaster cars rose and fell on their predetermined paths. Underneath the howl of the wind, the same saccharine carnival music as the day before played on a loop from the carousel, echoing through the empty boardwalk. Lena kept her head down and made a beeline for Wright's Emporium.

Again, no usher stood by the door to charge her for entry. She walked right in, alone again, and headed straight for the basement door. At the head of the stairs, she paused and asked herself whether she'd made the whole thing up—whether she should turn on her heels and telephone one of those analysts who could interpret her dreams. She pictured it: an old man with a beard and glasses, tutting and jotting notes in a leather-bound book. *Miss Marchetti, I think this fixation on the fortune-telling automaton represents your inability to grieve the death of your mother.* Anger boiled in her stomach at the mere thought, so she squared her shoulders and marched down the stairs.

The fortune teller's cabinet stood right where it had the day before. Each step towards it brushed aside the dirt at Lena's feet. Dread dropped like a weight in her chest as she moved closer, but a hysterical voice in her head declaring it was all a dream crowed louder than the fear. Then she was face-to-face with Madame Esmée again, staring at the green eyes trained on the crystal ball.

"I got your messages, and here I am," she announced, voice quivering. PENNY FOR YOUR FORTUNE, the sign on the cabinet replied.

Lena reached into her purse and pulled out a penny. Gently, she pushed the coin into the slot and waited. Just like before, the crystal ball lit up violet, the music played, and Madame Esmée's hands were set in motion. Except, then, everything was different. The crystal ball went from tacky and too bright to an otherworldly glow. Wonky, discordant music that was obviously from a warped piano roll became a clear performance, as if from a wandering band of folk musicians. And Madame Esmée herself moved her arms with the fluidity and clarity of a real person as her inky hair cascaded down her back. Even her skin took on a radiance beyond cracked paint over porcelain. Finally, Lena understood how the girls in her fairytales felt, in the midst of magic they could not understand. She walked so close to the cabinet that her breath made condensation on the glass.

After the fortune was printed out, nothing turned off. The crystal ball kept shining. The music grew even louder. Madame Esmée's hands moved from the ball to the table. She used them to push herself forward until she was right up against the window. A thin pane of glass was the only separation between the two women. Lena would have been happy to stare at the green of Madame Esmée's eyes all day, but the fortune teller broke the spell by tapping on the glass and pointing down. Down to the fortune, of course. Lena crouched and plucked it out of the machine, cradling the fortune in the bed of her hands. That time, there was only writing on one side.

MY MAGDALENA. I KNEW YOU'D COME BACK.

The train ride where she resolved to banish the fortune teller from her life felt like a million years in the past. How stupid she was! What was it that the first fortune had said? A treasured friend. Yes, that was it exactly— that was the warmth radiating through her body like a burst of sunlight.

Inside the cabinet, Madame Esmée moved again. This time, she lifted her hand to the glass. Up close, Lena could tell her skin was still porcelain. Her hand was too small, her fingers fused together in a hard web. And yet, her eyes remained as real as anything and trained on her visitor. Heart wrenching at the thought of her fortune teller, her friend, alone in the box, Lena lifted her hand to Madame Esmée's. Slowly, her fingertips touched the glass.

Vertigo slammed into her as though she'd just stepped off the rollercoaster. Disoriented, she tried to stumble away, but she couldn't move her legs, like they weren't even there. Coming to, her vision never quite cleared. It took on a warped, scratched, yellowed pallor. No longer was she standing in the basement, staring at the Madame Esmée machine.

She was inside the cabinet, looking through the glass at a girl with long black hair and eyes like emeralds.

Sharp pain knifed its way up the ridges of her fingers to her shoulders and head. Looking down, she saw the porcelain replacing her young skin like a spreading rash. She felt every cell as it ossified and turned. Within the span of a minute, her mouth, hair, and face had hardened to a shell. She tried to cry, to scream, but her glass eyes could not produce tears and there was only porcelain where her vocal cords had been.

Meanwhile, on the outside, the girl who had been Madame Esmée sank to her knees, shoulders shaking. She was a pale, pitiful slip of a thing—a feral animal with unwashed black hair and a tattered patchwork dress. A dry, painful screech tore through her emaciated body, turning into a frenzied laugh as it rang out. Time seemed to pass differently for Lena. She couldn't estimate how long the girl lay on the floor like a beggar.

Eventually, though, Esmée picked herself up, wiped the tears from her eyes, and faced her victim. "I can't be sorry, Magdalena. You'll understand soon enough."

Enormous mental effort allowed Lena to cause the machine to spit a fortune out. Five simple words: *HELP ME. FIND A WAY.*

Dark circles stood out below the girl's guarded green eyes. "I make no promises."

Shaking steps carried her out of Lena's line of sight. Every creaking stair echoed through the basement, as did the click of the lock on the stairway door.

Madame Magda sat alone.

Dreams cannot come where there is no sleep. What Lena had was the sight of the bare wall, the sound of distant music from the carousel above, and her own thoughts. She imagined Esmée visiting some witchy woman in the woods somewhere who knew how to return things to normal. She imagined Louisa waiting by the door for her to come home, finally marching down to the police station in tears and demanding a search. But what would a search find? No one would think to scour the boardwalk, and even if they did, all they would see was a porcelain fortune teller with eerily real brown eyes.

Hours passed, then days, then decades. Lena sat and waited, underneath the spectacle and excitement up above. Hope of seeing anyone she knew ever again dissolved as the years passed. Eventually, she started praying for the boardwalk to be torn down. That, she reasoned, was the only way anyone would find her.

But the boardwalk will never change or be torn down. So, the carousel's music plays on and on, and all Lena can do is listen.

CHAPTER SIX

TAMAN SHUD

Eddins Sinclair

Alexandria Drinkwater (the name she has chosen this time) settles in the lee of the hurly burly and spreads her thick, unfashionable gown across her bony knees. She faces the pond, and places *The Rubaiyat* in her lap in preparation. Her bonnet does not quite keep the pinch of the vernal sun from her eyes, so she picks at the hem irritably, adjusting, fussing. There are so many things these poor weak creatures have wrong about her kind, yet the sun is a bother among bothers, one had to admit. So many bothers. She will not be disturbed by the ugly mechanical sounds, braying of animals, and profanities of humans drowning out the call and response of the tide.

Unfortunately, these ugly creatures of daylight must be tolerated to be consumed.

She will not be disturbed by boys throwing rocks at the swan drifting peacefully at the water's edge. *Beastly children. Where are their parents?*

Yes! … Where are their parents? She pauses her preparations.

Alexandria scans the still, black water's edge. Wind stunted pines sway in the oceanic breath. Gulls gyre and laugh harshly at the victim swan. Or are they crying? Struck by a pebble, the swan raises her wings in alarm and squawks. What an unpretty noise. Another tiny projectile splashes on the swan's port side and another strikes the poor animal on the back of her head. The bird flaps hard, flaps, flaps and ponderously gains speed. She trails her large feet along the smooth surface of the pond so they send rippling Vs of light toward the shores, cleaving it, splitting the only calm thing in sight or sound. The swan sails a short distance before gliding back to the water's surface on the far side of the pond. She shuffles her wings into place. Probably, she is used to the cruelty of little boys.

Where are the parents? A mother or father?

Ah, there. On the far side. Tipping back her parasol, a pretty young woman furrows her brow and yells from under the shadow, "Ambrose! Ruben! Stop that immediately!"

Ambrose.

Ruben.

"Both of you," the young mother scolds, "come here this instant!"

Immediately. Instantly. Oh these warm, weak, silly creatures. Time means so much to them because they have so little of it.

She will remember those names.

Ambrose.

Ruben.

A name is like a scent, like a banner on a hill. A name leaves a trail if one knows how to follow it. The trail begins with the sulky children—Ambrose, Ruben—who kick the sand, stick their hands in their pockets, and tread up the bank to the trail that encircles the pond. The young mother walks quickly, kicking the skirts of her dress, and extends her hand so the children must follow by command. "Your father would be very disappointed," the mother says. "Christ weeps when little boys are cruel."

"Mother?" One of the boys (Ambrose or Ruben, Alexandria does not know which) points towards her. "What is that lady wearing on her head?"

"Ruben!" Mother grabs his hand.

Mother pulls her boys and the trio turns toward the road to town. Mother clutches her parasol. The winds know. They disappear behind a copse of shore pines. Undoubtedly, they will attend the carnival which traveled up the coast from California, teasing Alexandria with hunger. Probably they have come to the coast for this very reason.

Alexandria closes her eyes and breaths in the moist, salty air: *Ambrose, Ruben.*

Yes. When the wind is right it whispers. Later she will follow that whisper. Follow its trail of promise and renewal…

The crash of some great wooden contraption startles her, and the uncouth words in a harsh workman's voice— "Idiot foozler! Watch what'yer doin', son. You're likely to bring the whole mess down on our heads! And then we won't have heads to swear by, now will we?"—disturbs Alexandria's reverie.

With a sigh, Alexandria opens her eyes. This is the first time she has heard the British insult, *foozler*, on this side of the Atlantic. And on the far side of the New World, no less. Funny how language travels, pulling its power to hurt and heal with it.

It is time for the sunlight prayer.

She opens *The Rubaiyat* and begins to read. Alexandria intones quietly:

> *Ah, my Belovéd, fill the Cup that clears*
> *To-day of past Regrets and future Fears—*
> *To-morrow?—Why, To-morrow I may be*
> *Myself with Yesterday's Sev'n Thousand Years.*

No, not seven thousand yet, but someday. The humans have no idea of the incantations of their own words. She will be singing this for generations.

A knot of fishermen stand idly by, watching as the hot air balloon swells like a monstrous jellyfish in the meadow. "Saw one of these in Frisco," one of them says.

"My brother took a ride in one," another announced loudly. "Said it was grand, but I ain't sure man was meant to fly."

They look up as Alexandria comes down the path beneath the shadow of her parasol, limping on her cane, and respectfully step out of her way.

"Ma'am." Several tip their hats like cowboys.

Alexandria dips her bonnet soberly back at them. *No*, she thinks, *man is not meant to fly*. She eyes the canvas behemoth with its empty varnished-soaked guts filling with superheated air. It shrugs like a great blister forming on the earth, and Alexandria snorts again behind the safety of her bonnet. No, that thick bubble is not what one who knows the sky would call flying.

"You wouldn't get me up in one of those contraptions," yet another fisherman says. "I'll take my chances on the open sea."

There is less chance in life than any poor man expects, Alexandria thinks. More predation.

Alexandria limps past the men until she is sure that the turn in the trail hides her from view, then she snaps the cane into the air and swipes at the weeds like a naughty little girl (something she has not been for a very, very long time), beheading many of them, although she is careful to keep her parasol pointed toward the sun. She walks fast now, strong, wanting to cover the distance as quickly as possible to avoid the bright afternoon. It was important to be seen every day—long experience had taught her that much. A harmless old spinster with family money generates little conversation; a rich old woman lurking alone in a mansion is an object of dangerous curiosity. Decorum is particularly potent in a bustling coastal town with its odd assortment of wanderers, laborers, and oceanic adventurers. These humans imbibe. Despite the beaches and the beckoning forest, their children drink as much as their parents and seek fun in mischief. A wretched cluster of warm-blooded biology—they must "beneath the Couch of Earth Descend," she thinks.

It is the low hanging fruit of the nascent tourist trade that keeps her there.

Ambrose.

Ruben.

Of course, she could do what many of her kind have chosen to do and hide in abandoned houses and cold caves, in the nooks of dense forests and dank sewers, in ancient factories and derelict barns, in ruins and abandoned wells—all the inhospitable and lonely places that bipedal lower vertebrates instinctively fear—but that is to court filth and discomfort. Or she could wander the countryside as she did as a youth, a forever nomad. But such freedom is tiresome. *Better,* she thinks, *to hide in plain sight, comfortable, and never far from her food supply.*

A horse clops on the close side of the hedge, and Alexandria drops her cane back into position and resumes her limp. She rounds another bend and Godwin Harbor drops into view. The town has a hundred or so weathered rooftops lining two dozen gravel roads and the margins of the bay. The farms lie beyond the meager coastal range. Already the inhabitants have started to congregate. She limps, limps, limps...

Gaudy carnival posters have been plastered along the wooden fence next to the saw mill. They repeat their ridiculous exaggerations, their promises that cannot be kept, shoulder-to-shoulder, the same five-foot posters over and over, in the manner that the advanced advertising team is trained to do. There is no escaping the bright technology of their printing. "West Coast Carnival & Fair," the gothic letters proclaim. The first posters are sedate and blue. Giant figures dancing alongside a happy child carrying…things. Candy? A pennant? Yes, a teddy bear. How quaint. Then two posters with a robust woman grinning stupidly and doing the can-can as she exposes both her legs up to the thighs. "Dollymop," Alexandria mutters. And next to the whore of the dancing stage, eye-catching bright yellow, white, and red posters—three in a row. These are even bigger, as tall as a full-length mirror.

Alexandria stops cold.

So they will have a freak show like a circus. A bilious-looking fat lady sits atop a tiny stool; she also has a mighty beard—so they have combined the grotesque and the ridiculous in this one character. A gigantic Chinese man in a Xiezhi Guan and a gorgeous golden robe holds a tiny Caucasian infant in his massive bronzed hands. His proportions in the poster, if true, would make him eleven-foot tall. A stern-looking strong man in tights and inappropriately tight red shorts crosses his arms to show off his biceps. The loggers will mock the Bearded Fat Lady, ask the Chinese giant stupid questions about why he talks so funny, and challenge the Strong Man to fight…

But it is "The Wonder of the Miniature World" that stops Alexandria cold.

If there were anyone here at this moment to witness, they would see Alexandria's irises turn from gray-blue-green to fiery blood-red. They would see her sclera fill with blood, and the pupils wobble and reform as upside-down crescent moons. They would watch, horrified, as her shoulders arch to peaks and her hands (which look much more like claws at the moment) extend. Her jaw unhinges like a snake's and her tongue whips out, splits, and extends a stinger, white and slippery as wet bone.

"Mergildo Navarrete!" she hisses. "So you and your moonchild brother still live!"

Who knows what would have happened next if Alexandria had not heard the voices coming her direction from the street. Suddenly she is a bent old woman in a bonnet again, a Mother Goose staring at the grotesque illustration of a two-headed man of childlike proportions dressed like a Biblical king. One head grins as if he too is in on the joke, while the other, smaller head reposes in gentle slumber. "Babylonian Princes Seth and

Osiris," the black subtext reads. "One Speaks. One Sleeps. One Mother. Two Fathers."

Ha! These philistines. Seth and Osiris indeed! If they only knew what they let crawl into their cradles…

"'Scuse me, missus," a polite man's voice says, "but are you awright?"

Alexandria turns to see a small man with a round face leaning into her. His wife and two big-eyed children, all dressed in their Sunday best even though it is Thursday, lean around him to look at her.

"Oh!" she says in her best Gilded Era English. "Dear me, I seem to have…"

"You dropped your cane and your bumpershoot," he says, and gently lifts her parasol and cane back into her hands.

"Thank you very kindly, sir," Alexandria says.

"Sure you will be awright, missus?"

"Oh yes, quite fine, thank you."

"Then we shall let you pass…"

"And don't forget this," his plump wife says. She steps around her husband and lifts *The Rubaiyat* from the grass, brushes it off, and fits it into Alexandria's hand holding the parasol.

"Awright, let the missus pass," the round-faced man says, smiling and shooing his family out of the way.

Nodding to each other, bowing, nodding, thanking, Alexandria hobbles past the plump wife and the big-eyed children with their dirty fingers and wet faces.

What a disgusting species these humans are. Alexandria would prefer to hunt all sorts of other animals. But, as the great poet says, "Ah, make the most of what we yet may spend, Before we too into the Dust descend." *We are given what we are given,* Alexandria thinks, *spend it now.*

Mergildo would have to be dealt with somehow, his presence on this side of the continent could not be ignored. For now, however, she must keep up appearances. Alexandria buys a small loaf of bread, a bit of cheese, a side of cod, and an apple at the bustling market. The food makes her nauseated. She will bury it all in the sandy backyard after sundown.

"Here lady," a rude lad yells at her, "it will be big fun!" He thrusts a flier into the wrapping around her fish. It has a picture of the two-headed homunculus. The artist drew the vestigial arm of the sleeping head reaching toward the viewer.

"We will see," Alexandria whispers. She crumples her enemies and drops them on the ground.

Alexandria watches the back of the yowling child as he wanders away, thrusting his fliers at men and women already heading for the fair. She whispers softly:

And much as Wine has play'd the Infidel,
And robb'd me of my Robe of Honour—well,
I often wonder what the Vintners buy
One half so precious as the Goods they sell.

Oh, he will have terrible dreams from now till the end of his days. Yes, he will. Insolent lout.

The night overlooking the ocean is very dark. Pacific waves tolerate only the weakest light, and then only grudgingly, only faintly, as the new electric torches glow along Main Street. Even the moon has little sway over Sedna's demesne.

Alexandria waits as the rude jumble and music of the fair and the honking motor cars die down.

She waits as the drunken men stagger from the taverns, singing obscene songs hoarsely and off-key.

She slides up the walls of her house as a shadow. She slips through keyholes and cracks in the walls. She is an unlikely shape in the attic. She fills the basement with cold mist. In the backyard, she claws a hole in the earth in seconds and dedicates the foul human nutrients to the Chthonic gods so much closer to the surface than anyone imagines. She sings:

Into this Universe, and why not knowing,
Nor whence, like Water willy-nilly flowing:
And out of it, as Wind along the Waste,
I know not whither, willy-nilly blowing.

She zips through the dark salty air as light as a zephyr, flies up the shingles, and swirls down the chimney. In the ancient house, Alexandria Drinkwater (a silly name, certainly, and one of many names among many) climbs the dusty bookshelves with many a quaint and curious volume of forgotten lore in the gloom. Up by the ceiling, she pauses.

What meets her pointy bat ears is the complaints of the house on its moorings. The ocean wind will pry them all from the land eventually, Alexandria thinks happily, but not tonight. The creature that calls herself Alexandria whispers to the wind: "Ambrose. Ruben." The wind is a friend. Outside, the spirits chortle.

Ambrose.

Ruben.

Yes! The wind whispers back.

And Alexandria sings:

That ev'n my buried Ashes such a Snare
Of Perfume shall fling up into the Air,
As not a True Believer passing by
But shall be overtaken unaware

The hunt has begun. She stalks in beauty, like the night of cloudy climes and windy skies.

Far below her feet, the tips of the wind-tormented pine trees dance a gig. She sniffs the air. The carnival sprawls a short way beyond in the meadow—small as these things go, the castoffs of greater enterprises. Alexandria had seen the first Ferris Wheel in Chicago, but its roll was too cumbrously slow to be of any interest. This Wheel beneath her has a truncated revolution, barely twenty feet off the ground at its apex. Godwin Harbor has no nearby railway, so whatever comes in must be delivered by horse or truck. A watchman walks through the tightly closed tents and stalls, swinging a lantern in his left hand. He is cold, and slaps his torso and left shoulder repeatedly with his right hand. He is lonely (or nervous) and sings a ballad badly and loudly:

"... They parried and thrust, they side-stepped and cussed,
Of blood they spilled a great part;
The philologist blokes, who seldom crack jokes,
Say that hash was first made on the spot..."

One such as this, making such a noise, would be an easy victim. Unlike her animalistic European forebearers, however, Alexandria knows not to overharvest the herd. She knows not to risk exposure through ravenous abandon. These humans are helpless when alone but, like all lower lifeforms, can be dangerous in a pack. Besides, one need not gorge oneself if one knows the best nutrients.

Ambrose.

Ruben.

The gusting wind responds, *This way…this way…*

Just then—like a giant beetle or one of those infernally loud buzzing bugs that climb from the mud every seven years in corn country—a dark shape whizzes past her head, knocking her off true so she flounders for a moment in flight. It halts midair and she hears jeering laughter.

Alexandria snarls. "Mergildo Navarrete! You foulness! You aberration! You monstrous birth!"

Mergildo laughs and bobs. "*Buenas noches!*" His two heads are there, one awake and one sleeping, but he has chosen the form of the forest god Pan for the lower parts. His hairy torso and goat feet are ruffled by the high wind. The spirits also giggle. "So good to see you also, madam," he says in his English heavily accented with Spanish aspirants and softened vowel-sounds. "You are looking well, I can see. Imagine our finding one another in a lonely place like this."

"The master of panic and forest keeps will not look kindly—"

"Eh, madame," Mergildo says, rocking back on the pressing sea-breath, "this creature you fear stays many leagues away from a new land such as we find ourselves in, no? Though he would be much enriched by—" The tiny creature waved his long-nailed hand at the drowsing carnival structures.

"You should leave, Mergildo Navarrete!" Alexandria scolds. "This ground is where I hunt. You are not wanted here."

The sleeping head awakens suddenly. Its eyes flick wide and it gibbers at her; what a horrid grin full of shark's teeth. Just like in the advertisement, it reaches its weak vestigial arm out to her.

"Which of you is Seth and which is Osiris? Babylonian princes, indeed! They are not even Babylonian, you realize."

"Egypt? Babylonia? What do these *patáns* know of the world beyond their own noses? It is all the same to them." Mergildo floats toward her as the wind blows; the spirits are pushing them together for their own amusement.

"Keep your distance, foul brothers!" Alexandria says. "The ancient gods of the Nile will not laugh at the obscenity you have made of their names."

"Ah *señorita*, you do so wound me. No such wounds as this will be delivered tonight." Mergildo laughs and the idiot head chitters reflexively like an echo. "Nor do you threaten me with the warning of greater beings. Osiris only worries about his floods and flowers, and Seth fears these new machines of war. Both are ancient and thick with pollution, anyway. Old deities hold no fear here. Their power does not stretch past their own waters. The storms are too fierce along the hem of the great goddess. Even the gods sink into the bosom of Gaia as the meek inherit the earth."

Alexandria snorts. She must try a new attack. "I suppose you are still using that bit of confabulation about ocean-going birds by Coleridge to weave your spells?" she challenges. "Or are you summing up the cheap trickery of Kubla's pleasure dome? Keats's *Lamia?* Or one of your countrymen? A little Calderón, perhaps?"

Everything seems to amuse the little vampire, and he chuckles merrily. It is not a pretty sight or sound. "Oh, no, I have found something far more powerful from within these very shores." The brainless second head bobbles on its weak stalk of a neck. It gibbers nonsense. Language will never give it power. It is truly a parasite.

"Pray, do tell," Alexandria says. "What is this new incantation?"

"The 'Conqueror Worm.' Perhaps you have heard of it?"

Alexandria snorts. "Cheap colonial filth."

"And you?" Mergildo challenges back. "Are you still summoning Anglo-Saxon dragons? Or perhaps the blankness of ponderous blank verse epics that calls the queen of death an incestuous birth? Blasphemy that."

Alexandria stiffens as she hovers. "I have found great power in *The Rubaiyat.*"

Her Spanish antagonist blinks at her in what appears to be honest surprise. Even his idiot brother-head stops and stares. Then they both laugh. "That British confection? The misprision of ancient Persian quatrains? No, *hermana de la muerte,* you jest—hahahaha!"

"Fly," Alexandria shouts, her exasperation causing her to dart about like an angry fairy princess. "There are towns and houses. Seek along the coast. They are drunkards and wastrels. They will be easy prey. Go inland. The mountains here are low, easy to surmount. There are cities beyond. Take your filthy withered grape of a brother with you and depart!"

"*Hssssst!*" the idiot head says.

Mergildo follows with a snarl. "You have not the power to tell us where we might feed, *madre de diablo*."

Alexandria's eyes blaze like a tiger's, and her jaws open wide so that her stinger-tongue might snap and probe like a scorpion's tail. The two-headed brother does the same, their deadly, snapping tongues a nightmare version of children miserably insulting each other. From the ground, their hissing and snarling sounds like a storm warning.

Then, from below:

"...Hello my baby, hello my honey
Hello my ragtime, summertime gal
Send me a kiss by wire, by wire
Baby, my heart's on fire, on fire
If you refuse me, honey, you lose me..."

Both creatures of the night stop, listen. Mergildo smiles slowly. Beneath them, the watchman strolls back through the quad of the carnival grounds, singing stupidly.

"He is a local," Mergildo says, "employed for the two nights that inhabit your charming little town. He is not one of us."

"One of us! One of us!" the idiot gibbers, perhaps the only words it knows. "Soon you will be one of us!"

"Don't you dare!" Alexandria warns.

"Sorry, madame, but we, the proud brothers Navarrete, dare." With that, Mergildo chants, summoning his powers from the words of the air:

A blood-red thing that writhes from out
The scenic solitude!
It writhes!—it writhes!—with mortal pangs
The mimes become its food,
And seraphs sob at vermin fangs
In human gore imbued.

The two-headed brother dives like a stooping hawk toward the lonely man who, just now, suspects something is in the night, high above him. It is far too late.

Angry as a hornet in a fire, Alexandria buzzes into the mouth of the laughing wind. No matter the insults, she too must feed, as all things which suffer life-in-death must feed by finding a living thing. The watchman screams once, and his cry is carried away by the wind.

Ambrose.

Ruben.

Follow…follow…

Yes. There in the rickety cabins which line the northern shore of the bay. Tourist housing. Here today, gone tomorrow, and taking their nightmares with them. Windy voices direct her. If their sixth sense prickles their dreams in a wave like electricity, the boys will awake. If they turn to the window, they will see an elderly woman with frightening eyes in an antique Edwardian dress. Wild white hair fans around her head. She will be holding the window frame. Her mouth will move as she urges them to invite her in. Like her prey, her kind has solved a great many problems and can do a great many things with its own version of technology. Yet at this point, the Lamia (among other names for them) must still be invited to cross the threshold. For a moment, frozen in instinctive fear, the children will realize the horror, comprehend that they sleep on the second floor and thus, no human should be standing outside their window. They will scream and save themselves. But Alexandria knows her business, and neither child awakes as she softly reconstitutes from a shadow. She gazes for a moment. Hunkered deep in their pile of blankets, Ambrose and Ruben look like cherubim. Alexandria salivates. Softly, weaving her song into the wind, she sings:

> *…Came stealing through the Dusk an Angel Shape*
> *Bearing a Vessel on his Shoulder; and*
> *He bid me taste of it…*

The eldest child stirs, slowly kicks himself free of the blankets, and sleepwalks to the window.

> *While the Rose blows along the River Brink,*
> *With old Khayyám the Ruby Vintage drink:*
> *And when the Angel with his darker Draught*
> *Draws up to Thee—take that, and do not shrink.*

"Granny?" the child says from sleep.

"Yes, my love," Alexandria responds, and she repeats, "*take that, and do not shrink.*"

"Will you sing 'The Muffin Man?'"

"Of course, my sweet." But she would do no such thing. The nursery rhyme contains a powerful incantation against evil.

"Amen…" the child mumbles, and unlocks the window. He climbs back into the big bed with his younger brother.

They say the Lion and the Lizard keep
The Courts where Jamshýd gloried and drank deep;
And Bahrám, that great Hunter—the Wild Ass
Stamps o'er his Head, and he lies fast asleep.

Now the children will sleep through anything.

She kneels by the bed, and slowly uncovers their feet. The boys have plump, soft, pink feet. They lead soft lives. Alexandria's jaws unhinge. Her long tongue slithers out, splits, and a crystalline globule, like a drop of dew, forms on the end of the stinger. It falls tear-like to the elder boy's foot (Ambrose?) She gives it a moment. Now that part of him is numb. The stinger is white and clean as ivory as she stabs the sleeping child between the big and second toe, and drinks.

Other Nosferatu (as they are sometimes known) are careless and jeopardize their society. The essence of a child is pure. She only needs a little to persevere, even though it will not quite be enough to quench her pangs. Tourists are always young lovers or young parents, and both are good hunting.

Alexandria repeats the procedure with the other child.

She thinks, *I have grown nervous in this quiet life among the beasts.* The humans will find the watchman in the morning, certainly. His throat will be rent yet bloodless, and cries of "murder" will fill the air. Perhaps they will not even have the carnival at all. Or the man will simply disappear and some will be concerned, some not. Whatever the scenario, she will show the proper shock if need be. Life and life-in-death will go on like before. Let that nasty little ape with his withered pocket-monkey travel

111

with his mongrel thespians. The little devil can do what he will. In the end, it will not affect her at all.

Alexandria folds the blankets back in place so the cold air will not disturb the children.

The boys shuffle and moan in their sleep. They will dream about her throughout their lives. She will appear at the window, they will feel cold, and they will wake to the sound of poetry. Alexandria has not bitten enough to turn them. This is also part of her craft. She keeps the pack small.

Downstairs, Alexandria hears the mother mew. Curious, and still hungry, she slips down the stairs as a shadow. The mother lies curled on the daybed. She is a pretty young thing, soft and pink like her boys.

"Who is she, George?" she mutters in her sleep. "Who is she?"

Alexandria wonders if her sixth sense warns the mother of the dangerous supernatural creature hovering incorporeal in the night air. Or perhaps George is the husband who is not there at the moment. Perhaps he is visiting the mistress that the mother intuits, but is too afraid to admit exists when she is in the light.

Lord, what fools these mortals be. Alexandria looks about, spies the mother's purse, pulls it through the air, and opens it. She pauses a moment, recites, *"At once the silken Tassel of my Purse Tear, and its Treasure on the Garden throw,"* and plucks out the neat bundle of bank notes.

I sometimes think that never blows so red
The Rose as where some buried Cæsar bled;
That every Hyacinth the Garden wears
Dropt in its Lap from some once lovely Head.

Now I have been paid, Alexandria thinks, *this little bit of confection will be paid too.* Sometime in the near future, the pink mother will have a moment of power and grace. The Lamia-sting can bestow gifts as well as receive blood. George will have much to answer for.

The vampire's jaw unhinges, and a crystal droplet forms on the point of the stinger...

Alexandria is unhappily surprised to find Mergildo and his idiot brother seated on a shattered tree trunk outside the cabin. The two-headed brother's small body fits easily in the contours of the ruin. He smiles unpleasantly. His parasite-double slumps on his shoulder in sleep. The idiot's mouth is smeared with blood.

"*Hssst!*" Alexandria says. "Get thee gone, abomination."

"That is no way to speak to a boon companion," Mergildo replies.

"You are a filthy carnie and will be gone two morrows from now."

"Perhaps we two have grown tired of the wandering life. I like it here. The houses—they have empty faces, some of them, no? And there are trees and boats that sail in and out, in and out, in and out—" Mergildo makes a florid gesture with his hand as if conducting an orchestra. "Much to feed upon. Many spots to hide."

"You will frighten them. They will panic."

"Certainly a woman of the world such as yourself cannot plan to stay in this forsaken hamlet forever. Someday, they will see that you age so, so slow." He shrugs. "They will be frightened then, no?"

"That is for me to decide."

"Aye. It is. I would decide soon. Maybe—" He looks up at the moon just breaking through the cloud cover. "We shall travel together?"

"Never!"

"Such a shame, this lonesome life we lead." And then the abomination vanishes in the moonlight.

At dawn, she begins the prayer that launches the day as she always does. Sunrise, and the onset of pain, must be met:

Awake! for Morning in the Bowl of Night
Has flung the Stone that puts the Stars to Flight:
And Lo! the Hunter of the East has caught
The Sultán's Turret in a Noose of Light.

The pain will wax and wane as her body adjusts to the charm of daylight. Today, she will stay inside, however. They need not see her every day. Still, she must watch...

It is early. From behind the shutters, she can see between the trees to the main street and its tiny market. Men have congregated there in a clump. Two women walk hurriedly past. Alexandria is wise in the ways of the herd; she knows how to read the text of human behavior: a body has been discovered. A curse has fallen on the land. They are afraid.

The ancient mistress retreats to the inner sanctum of the house. All she needs is a single pine seed to tell the powers that she wants renewal from the earth. She places it between the candles on the table:

> *Up from Earth's Centre through the Seventh Gate*
> *I rose, and on the Throne of Saturn sate,*
> *And many Knots unravel'd by the Road;*
> *But not the Knot of Human Death and Fate.*

The candles burst into flame.

> *Then to the rolling Heav'n itself I cried,*
> *Asking, "What Lamp had Destiny to guide*
> *Her little Children stumbling in the Dark?"*

One flame turns red, leaps, and trembles…takes shape. An elderly man in a turban sits cross-legged in the air. His beard is neatly trimmed. His robe is likewise composed of neat lines and smooth tucks and hems. Omar Khayyam bows hello from his head and shoulders.

The other flame turns blue, shrugs, and settles…into an elderly English country gentleman in a heavy frock coat. His bald scalp gleams with fire, as does his ragged hair and furry mutton chops. Edward FitzGerald stands stiffly in midair and bows his head in recognition.

"Masters," Alexandria says. "Forgive your servant for calling you, but I must know how…" Alexandria explains that a two-headed mooncalf has begun killing the villagers of her little home. She speaks in medieval Persian. Edward is traveling through the dimensions of time with the Persian mathematician, and slowly, over the seventy years since the first edition, has learned the ancient language that he transmogrified into magic. These two are also supernatural twins kept alive by the power of words. There is much she will never tell the two poets of *The Rubaiyat*. Sometimes, when she swoons during the day and has one of the sunstroke dreams of her tribe, Alexandria wonders how much Omar and Edward know about her. Do they actually know she is not a gentle enchantress like the kind found in children's story books?

The two ghosts talk. Their lips move in their world, but she cannot hear them.

Finally, Omar turns to her. His face shimmers with fire. "Ruba'i thirty-eight," is all he says in English heavily accented by the ancient Persian tongue.

Of course. It was there all the time in front of her. She always feels just a bit humiliated by the masters.

Their flames flicker and go out, bringing back the darkness.

Alexandria braves the afternoon sunlight. The herd is agitated.

"—murder—"

She hears it repeatedly as she passes the flustered humans. Yes, murder most foul. *Well, my little fruit baskets,* she thinks, *soon the wyrm will go to ground.*

"Did'ya hear?" a rough looking logger says to his rough-looking friend. "There was a note in his pocket?"

Alexandria's preternaturally strong hearing perks up.

"Naw. What's it say?"

"Some nonsense syllables, I hear," the logger says. "'*Taman shud.*' Lord knows what that means."

"It means, *is finished,*" Alexandria whispers under her breath, "in ancient Persian." These are the last two words of *The Rubaiyat*. Mergildo, the double-faced rat, is mocking her. Their time has come: THEY are Taman Shud!

The herd gives her little mind as she passes. She pays a nickel at the booth and hobbles into the carnival quad. A pile of wildflowers sits in the middle where the watchman was found. A minister is preaching ("...for the devil is always in the wind..."). Alexandria averts eyes already stinging from the sun. The sheriff is there, warily scanning the crowd as children romp and the young people dance to the fiddler on the green. If anything, the murdered watchman has increased business. She had assumed they would shut the entertainment down, but if there is money to be made, humans will do almost anything. And horror and the occult somehow attracts these creatures who are so vulnerable to these very forces.

To wit: the tent with "Human Freaks" above the flap has a line. They are men and women of all ages, and are all giddy. They are given sanction to openly mock the strangers in their midst. Alexandria has no intention of waiting. She could, of course, knock every one of them off their rockers with back-and-forth swipes of her hand…but the sheriff is here and humans can be very dangerous when engaged as a mob. So she falls back on an old trick.

"Oh forgive me, forgive me, please," she whines, "but I have lost my little Mittens." She cries plaintively, "Mittens? Mittens?" Tears build in the corners of her eyes. "Has anyone seen my little Mittens? She did not come home last night—" Alexandria limps past their idiotically compassionate gazes.

"Sorry, mother," one young man says, "what does Mittens look like?"

Alexandria ignores him. "Mittens? Please, Mittens?" She has reached the head of the line. A young man scrawny as a strip of beef jerky slumps atop a tall stool. He is unkempt and long-haired beneath his backward painter's beret, and he is perfectly blank with boredom. His eyes raise dully to meet hers. "I've lost my Mittens," she pleads, letting her shoulders sag. "May I see if she is hiding in your abode?"

"Five cents, lady," the empty-eyed man says.

An older man in back of her speaks up. "Let'er in, son. She's lost her cat." He is echoed by a number of voices and whistles.

The scrawny man shrugs and tips his head toward the flap.

"Thank you, thank you," Alexandria gasps.

It is exactly what she expects. Ugly confabulations float in brine-filled mason jars—a calf embryo with a doll's head sewn onto it; a wax carving of a devil baby draped with what looks like seaweed—and various animal skulls painted reddish shades. A long feather sits in a whiskey jar: "Genuine Indian Magic Feather." Illumination is a single kerosene lantern dangling from the frame high above, so everything is vague and haunted. "Very Dangerous! Do Not Touch!" a sign above the assembly reads. Alexandria snorts. Stupid animals. These faux-oddities are clearly the castoffs of a Midwest traveling show. Stupid, stupid.

Within the big tent, each freak has their own tableau. It is a small and unimpressive display as these things go. The Bearded Fat Woman sits licking a lollypop before a painted backdrop of a candy store (some of her [his] hairs have stuck to the sticky sweet); the Giant Chinese Man appears to be casting some sort of spell while standing over a brass bowl filled with smoking, sickly-sweet incense—he looks quite tired and sad (she can see the outline of the stilts beneath his tattered golden robe); the Strong Man is nowhere in attendance (probably sleeping off too much sleep). At the far end sits a miniature tent made from black canvas. It is closed off.

"See the Devil Double Spawn!" is emblazoned in red above the tent flap. "Women and Children Are Warned NOT to See!"

The space is packed with humans slowly threading toward the main attraction. They mutter and laugh awkwardly. She would have to wriggle through them and decides instead to take a chance. Alexandria glances back at the slice of light at the entrance, then folds and drops her parasol, and melts into a shadow that shoots along the grass-floor of the display. Her shadow slips easy as smoke into Mergildo's domain. In the dark lit by a circle of candles, he is delicately nibbling on an apple (forbidden fruit for their kind—abomination!) and taking questions as the nameless idiot sleeps and drools on his shoulder. "No, Mr. Mayor," he says, exaggerating his accent, "my dear brother has never been in love. And, so you all may know, neither have I. No madrone has imprisoned my heart. I am thus so hard to please."

For some reason this is funny and the tiny crowd chuckles.

"Do you know who killed the poor watchman?" someone calls out.

A murmur runs through the tiny assembly.

"Ah, so tragic, so horrifying! A terrible, terrible thing. It is against God Himself!" Mergildo calls back, pointing at Heaven and rocking slightly so the idiot brother appears to sway. "Was he a friend or lover to any of you?"

Throats clear and feet shuffle.

Mergildo's eyes grow large and luminous. "Did his mother cry?"

This has gone far enough. Alexandria materializes from a column of black smoke, a genie appearance. The crowd catches its collective breath, stares for a moment, then begins to applaud. They think it is an act.

"Madrone! *Mujer hermosa!*" Mergildo screams. There is a definite note of fear in his voice. The pale eyes of the idiot brother flick open.

The crowd gasps.

Alexandria extends the *mano cornuto* with her left hand—the horns of Satan, pinky and index extended, middle and ring tucked under the thumb—and sends Ruba'i thirty-eight screaming across time and space:

One Moment in Annihilation's Waste,
One Moment, of the Well of Life to taste—
The Stars are setting and the Caravan
Starts for the Dawn of Nothing—Oh, make haste!

For a moment, the two-headed brother stares stupidly. Then the candles whip out. The crowd gasps again and more applaud. Mergildo mews strangely in the dark (or is it the idiot brother?)

"Hello?" some human says.

The two-headed brother screams horrifically. Sparks swirl toward the canvas ceiling, which catches fire immediately. Flames in a ravel of red and yellow crawl up the walls from below as well, and all can be seen in the blazing light. In the midst is Mergildo and the creature on his shoulder—they flail, they melt, they burn, they scream. The humans scream in turn and stampede. Several are knocked to the ground and trod upon. In the big tent outside, more humans scream as the fire spreads.

Alexandria steps back and laughs. She will wait just as long as she needs, then return to her shadow form. The sunlight will torture her, certainly, but if she can make the shade of the trees, she can flit back through the forest to the protective gloom of her house. There she will seek a verse from *The Rubaiyat* for healing. A young man stumbles into her and she strikes him savagely across the face, breaking his neck. Another falls over his corpse.

What fools…

She looks down at herself. Sparks climb along the hem of her long gown.

What is this?

The sparks unite, give birth, grow. They leap into blooms of fire, tiny castles of heat and light.

Now it is Alexandria's turn to scream.

The Masters! How foolish, how stupid of her! Of course. They were never fooled. Frantically, she searches her mind for a verse to counteract the spell.

How long, how long, in definite Pursuit…
Divorced old barren Reason from my Bed…
The Two-and-Seventy jarring Sects confute:
The subtle Alchemist that in a Trice…
And still a Garden by the Water blows…

It makes no difference. The spell is moving too fast and is too certain of its purpose. She feels the ancient body that she knows and loves engulfed in flame. Flames whirl in and out of her, coursing through the dry cavities that contain the crystals of blood, old and new, as Alexandria tries to fight the fire demon quenching its hunger on her bones. The canvas burns away, letting in the sun through the boiling smoke. Briefly, before the lights flare permanently out, Alexandria wonders if vampires have an afterlife…

About suffering they were never wrong, the old masters…

And then: Taman Shud

In a garden overlooking the golden grain and the distant Sultan's palace, beneath a flowering bough, Omar Khayyam passes Edward FitzGerald a jug of wine and a loaf of bread. The ancient Persian recites happily from their book of verse:

The Moving Finger writes; and, having writ,
Moves on: nor all thy Piety nor Wit
Shall lure it back to cancel half a Line,
Nor all thy Tears wash out a Word of it.

The staid Victorian responds:

Ah, Moon of my Delight, who know'st no wane,
The Moon of Heav'n is rising once again:
How oft hereafter rising shall she look
Through this same Garden after me—in vain!

Then the poets toast each other and drink.

GOBLIN MARKET

Valerie Alexander

I

I come out of the forest at dusk. I find him where I find all my guests; at the river, the border between shadowy wilderness and the serenity of a summer evening. He eyes me with cautious interest at first. He could go home, this big, athletic, black-haired boy who looks to be nineteen or twenty. But I'm a pretty thing, with my satin dress and practiced wiles, and like so many humans, he responds to my song.

Come buy, come buy, I sing in a voice smooth as honey.

A pearly blue mist hangs over the summer fields as he weighs his options. He's curious about the carnival tickets in my hand. Curious about my invitation. And the golden-red fruit I'm eating—he wants to know where it's from, how it tastes.

Oh, better than he could imagine, I promise. Sweeter, rarer, more addictive.

If he had been born a century or two ago, his grandmother would have warned him to never eat what the Fae offer, particularly the goblins who sell their wares by the river. But such sensible wisdom isn't taught in the modern age, and anyhow, I'm too human to make anyone think of the grotesque creatures who once said, *come buy, come buy* to girls like me. That's my worth to the Fae.

Night is falling. He could retreat to his friends, to his college parties. But I can see the enchantment in his eyes as I promise, "I will show you mysteries more incredible than any found in your world."

And so, he naively comes forward, as I did once.

Just a sheltered prairie girl, easily tricked. That's how the goblins saw me that first time, no doubt. That evening in 1869, all my mother's warnings fell from memory at my first sighting of goblins, glamoured to look like normal folk, and their market of exotic fruits.

Everyone in town had whispered about foolish Jeannie, wasting away when she could no longer find them to buy the fruit a second time; she'd been buried on her parents' farm, no grass growing over her grave.

Intrigued, I'd gone to the river myself and found the goblins. Off I went with the goblins to their carnival, to the music and lights I could see through the forest, with that golden fruit sweetening my mouth.

This evening, the young man crosses the river to me, wearing the crude, loose shirt and jeans men wear these days—fashion seems to change so quickly, though, of course, time runs differently here.

"Come," I tell him. "Just through these boughs here."

"Boughs?" His voice is suspicious.

Hard for me to sound modern enough sometimes. The old prairie accent they can forgive. My long loose hair and satin dress convince the men easily enough. But words are subtle. And I can't afford to spend enough time in their world—my world, once—to study and master the changes since I lived there as a sheltered, well-bred daughter of seventeen.

Luckily, my new guest can already hear the music. His eyes change, filling with curiosity and reverence. And as he moves through the cool, ferny scent of the forest, I know he is scarcely aware of the intricate green webs brushing his face and the slight tugging on his clothes from the thick, twisting trees exactly a human's height. Odd trees, and maybe he'd think about that if his senses weren't prickling from a different and more vivid novelty:

The strangest, sweetest music.

The smell of flowers and fruits he's never known.

Laughter that isn't quite human, but more inviting for it.

And then, visible through the treetops, the tents of violet-gold and rose-green, lifting its head above the trees; a glittering, grinning dragon. My guest bursts through the bordering trees—who perhaps were warning him to stay with them, who perhaps once looked more like him than he would believe—and into the carnival of his most ominous fantasies.

One of the Fae sweeps by in her gown of green and purple light, glamoured—as they all are—to look human. I cannot compete with their magicked beauty, but still, I try to guide him to the money-making ventures, the most expensive tents. That's how I earn my keep. There's a price to pay for the humans who stay too long, who can't resist the fruits and nectars. For me, that's serving as the Fae's doorman, inviting others into a luscious and addictive hell.

My handsome black-haired guest looks everywhere for the dragon, but like everything here, it's an illusion. The real dragons stopped dealing with Unseelie long ago, and they stay in their own world now. Still, there's plenty here to captivate him; flickering spirits and ominous fortunes and broken dolls and poisoned wines. He won't remember the details tomorrow, but he'll never forget the fascination he feels tonight, which will make the rest of his life dull by comparison.

"Step right up, ladies and gents, come one, come all, to the finest show in town and some of the wildest and wickedest tricks on earth." The master of ceremonies is tall and broad, his exuberant white mane and mustache giving him the look of an elderly walrus. Dressed in a tuxedo, he gestures to various parts of the carnival with a silver-tipped cane. "Visit the amazing, the one and only, King of Pain! Gamble your heart's desire in the gallery of games and win more than you ever imagined! Visit the Haunted Castle, the Doll Maker, and don't forget to learn your fate, as told by the talented Lady Zena!"

Dozens of humans mill around the attractions, all with drinks in hand. There is no joy or fun at this dark festival, and no children, but there is novelty enough to distract anyone. They watch a large, bald goblin roll on a bed of nails for their horrified delight. Nearby, to a hellishly merry tune, three small Unseelie in their natural tusked and furry forms dance for the crowd, while a fourth extends a cup for donations. One of the servers places a glass of nectar in my guest's hand.

I escort him to the fortune teller, where Lady Zena awaits him in a purple cloak. She doesn't require any glamouring at all; she's a changeling, a human stolen from her cradle and reared in the Unseelie world. "Come and let me tell your future," she cajoles him. "I see all. Love, money, betrayal… Learn your fate…" He pays and provides his hand and she hisses. "I see cancer. I see death. I see suffering."

He laughs, not easily taken in by all this. I admire that. So, Zena unveils the crystal ball. A small version of himself appears within, with what appears to be black mold growing from his skin. A jot of realism penetrates his amusement. "That's sick."

He pulls me away, toward the dusty scent of old books. That's the Library Tent, thick with the smell of incense and herbs and dried flowers and old paper. Some carnival guests love to do nothing more than take a table and read. But every page is written to coax them further into a story of utter despair, one that leaves them hopeless and weeping by the time their friends fetch them. To my relief, he bypasses it for the second-most expensive tent—the Hall of Curiosities—and pays more at my urging. He's persuaded by the three-headed fox who guards the door of the tent and bursts inside. It's my job to listen to his incredulous, crowing delight as he marvels at the gryphon stretching its claws, the shrunken heads that greet him by name, and the mermaid who swims up to her tank and kisses the glass.

But I can't let him dawdle. The night is young and I must bring in more people to increase my reward. So, I push him toward the Tinies, a case of small jelly-like creatures with no mouths. Their human eyes meet his.

"This is unreal!" he says with glee.

It could all be too real for you, I long to tell him. *Run before something monstrous swallows you and you learn what reality is.* But of course the Fae would detect my treachery in an instant; they seem to hear and see all.

My guest straightens as he sees the most macabre—and somehow the most gratifying—curiosity; the corpses. They're mostly skeletons, bits of hair and flesh clinging to bone, and yet they move and speak so easily. *Have some wine,* they say with rotted tongues. He gasps before veering out of the tent.

"I-I think it's time to go home." He blinks, recovering his focus. Then he does something unexpected; he looks at me. "You keep shivering. Are you okay?"

I'm merely thirsty for my nightly dose. Last night's fell short. "Just hungry."

"So, call out sick and we'll go get something to eat."

How sweet. The guests used to court me when I first arrived, but that occurs less and less these days. And it's risky to leave; the Fae world meets the human world along rivers, but time functions differently and many nights, I emerge from the forest to find myself at a different river. The carnival is always moving. Even if I could leave without permission, they would detect my absence and possibly sentence me to serve as a Tiny. And I can't have him leave yet. "Oh, but you haven't visited the most beautiful tent of all."

It's time for the expensive delights that need none of my sales services.

The huge purple Bordello tent glows in the summer night. Soft lanterns light a curving path to the entrance. Inside, a slow song winds around the room as half a dozen dancers perform onstage. Like the food and drink here, their dance is enchanted. He can't see their eyes glowing with thirst, can't understand they will drain him of his energies, and his ability to love another woman ever again. A blue-skinned beauty with violet eyes saunters toward him. He falls into a chair with a stunned expression and I know he is now blind to me. He has found his destiny for the night.

I return to the grounds, searching for unescorted guests to lead to the most expensive tents. The Witch Doctor—seller of ointments, potions, and elixirs—is convincing a group of women they can regain the dewy complexions of their youth. "My most popular elixir," he promises. "Allow me to apply it to your visage, my ladies, and watch the miracle appear. Who is my first volunteer?"

The women cry out with disbelief as their faces soften and smooth in the mirror.

I glance back at the Bordello tent. The three-headed fox grins and laughs at me. My earlier guest will stagger home in the wee hours, in a daze. Or perhaps he won't, and he'll awake cold and cramped on the forest floor. Either way, it will be naught but a haze of delight and regret, the taste of debauchery, a sense of the impossible, and his wallet well-emptied.

The other servants and I never talk about how long we've been here. Time has little meaning here, and I count it only by the increasing ache in my limbs, the decreasing compliments from male guests, and my dimming hopes. But we've all learned by now exactly how much the Fae detest humanity. They complain that we poison the earth, from whence they draw their magic. They recall those long-ago days when their worlds mingled and the humans hunted them, exhibited them in cages, or burned them as monsters. They would capture the least magically endowed and parade them in freak shows, blaming them for their own crimes. Centuries later, the Fae are just a legend to them, but the Fae have forgotten nothing. They love to trick humans now, drain their money and energy, then send them home with confused brains, numb hearts, and an unshakeable sense of despair.

Or rather, the Unseelie do—the kingdom of uglier, crueler Fae who run the carnival. The Seelie, the Shining Ones, tend to ignore humans, but they do forbid the Unseelie to kill us outright. They dislike violence. And so it goes on; the Unseelie torment the carnival guests, the Seelie step in when they must, and the humans keep showing up for the fortune teller, the Haunted Castle, the Bordello. The carnival servants whisper that one day the Seelie will intervene and liberate us all. But I've seen no sign of that.

And all of us stay of our own accord. You might think no nectar is addictive enough to make you forsake your own world and give yourself over to a species that deplores you, to an arrangement where you debase yourself each night for the pleasures of oblivion. But you might choose the same, were you to hear captivating music and see the carnival radiance on a black prairie night.

The carnival is closed for the night. The Fae have reverted to their true forms, bewhiskered, furred and hoofed and horned, some tentacled; their variety is astounding. They bark orders at those of us who sweep up the trash left by humans. Tonight, it's my job to clean the most sinister tent with the most innocent name; the Doll House. As always, the 'dolls' are scattered about; an arm here, a shoe there, hair hacked off for fun, an eye gouged out, an ugly red mark where scissors were used. Dismembering the dolls is a popular pastime with the crueler guests, who delight in mutilating something that looks and feels human. I gather the correct pieces as much as I can so the goblins can repair them; eyes restored, skin smoothed, feet reattached. And do it—hopefully—before the dolls fulfill their contract and turn fully human again.

"Don't bother with the rest of it." It's Samael, one of the demi-Fae.

I don't look at him as I clean. "I have to. You know they put the wrong parts on the wrong people."

"It speaks well of you that you still feel compassion, Laura."

Demi-Fae like Samael play a specific role, with Fae deliberately impregnating human women to increase their influence on human society. It never goes to plan, as far as I can see. The demi-Fae always pick a side. Samael's visits seem to be motivated by loneliness. In the Fae world, he is repelled by the brutality and the callous eagerness to humiliate humans. I suspect most of his carnival visits are merely to ensure the exploitation doesn't go too far, though it's difficult to imagine how much worse it could get. But in the human world, he says no one agrees with his environmental passions, he doesn't age as the others do, and secrecy is a burden. The other human servants suspect him of being a Seelie spy. He is too beautiful to look truly Unseelie, with soft, dusky skin, luminous amber eyes, and a tangle of dark curls.

"How is everything back home?" I ask. The human world is no longer my home but I always ask. While my perception is that I've only been here a year or so, I know more than a century has passed back home. My few ventures back to distribute carnival leaflets have shown me a coldly foreign and mechanical world.

"If you came with me for a visit, I could show you," Samael says. "It's not as terrible as you think, Laura."

It's a tempting offer, but not for the reason he thinks. Samael is irresistible company, not only as an ambassador to the world I lost but as the only person who speaks my language. Most of the other servants are too deteriorated by their addiction to be stimulating company.

"I know you think I can"—I try to think of the right word— "retreat from this, but I've seen what happens to those who stop."

"Don't be frightened by others' failures. I could help you wean yourself off." Then he adds, cruelly in my opinion, "You're a pretty girl, but I can already see its effects on you. One day, you will wear out entirely."

The Fae aren't known for their tact. Stung, I leave him without a reply and go to the Hall of Curiosities.

At this hour, the attractions have also reverted to their real forms. All the freaks and wonders, who pay for their addiction by serving as monstrosities every night, are human again. It's a painful transformation, bones and muscles screaming in agony. Some cradle their naked bodies on the dirt floor, moaning in pain. The gryphon is a bearded man much older than me, the mermaid, a woman named Carol who says she was an attorney when she came here in 1982. The corpses don't transform into anything; they made the mistake of returning to the human world to quit, and deteriorated for too long before crawling back to the river in rabid thirst. They usually continue to decay, despite pushing the fruit into their skeletal mouths each night.

I help Carol out of her tank. She vomits dirty water on the floor as I wrap a curtain around her heaving, naked form. "Come. It's time for relief."

Before we go, I check on the Tinies. They never transform, not until they complete their punishment. They can't move, but they're very much alive. Inside each little oddity is a thinking, screaming soul. This is the fate of anyone who angers the Fae. "You can't help them," Carol says tiredly.

Their eyes plead with me.

We make our way to the burning lights of the market tent. The goblins look us over with contempt, but provide the nectar we've earned, along with figs, melons, damson plums, and fresh cool water. The nectar varies from night to night—sometimes it's more of a juice, sometimes more of a wine, migrating from dark pinkish-green to scarlet to a reddened black. At the river, we gorge ourselves and it's divine; fruit that grew in a fairy earth, as they say, from different soil, with roots that drank a different water.

Next to me on the grass, in the starlight, Carol weeps with delirious joy as she crams her mouth. These are the moments we suffer for.

If you don't know the fever of addiction, I'll tell it to you now. Others sneer at you for being bound, enslaved, but you feel so free in the dark violet waters of oblivion, floating in a private dream that feels cosmic, seven million stars glittering in your narcotic queendom. *I'm in love* turns to *I am love*. I feel more than free, I feel nonexistent.

Emancipated.

I'm gone.

II

Now it's a summer afternoon. Thunder booms across an overcast day, intensifying the electric ions shimmering in the air. Dark purplish clouds clot the sky. Nearby cornfields rustle as the smell of ozone fills the air. The mounting storm makes me think of Samael's offer; I think of returning to live in the human world, with its technology and ugly clothing and freedoms. A strange energy fills my skin like hot, prickling light. The wind rises suddenly, shaking the trees, and thunder rumbles again, closer.

I did go home once. I'd been with the carnival three or four days, I estimated, and I knew I would be ruined when I returned, but thoughts of my parents' anguish haunted me. So, I crossed the river and made my way across the prairie. To my surprise, the fields were now farmed. But our house was still there, surrounded by strangers. Someone played a banjo; it was a party. I stared from behind the birch tree in shock, and realized the woman holding a baby was my older sister Lizzie. Another child pushed his face in her skirts. She looked far older than nineteen years. And the gray-haired lady taking the baby was my mother. I'd been gone years— at least eight or nine. That was when I learned the Fae world ran on a different clock, or no clock at all.

Cold terror sliced me as I realized the carnival might leave me behind, for they'd told me it moved from town to town. At the thought of never tasting the nectar again, I ran back to the river as fast as I could without speaking to my family.

Beyond the trees, the sun's fading glow lights the riverside dandelions and wild violets. The evening melts into a cool, odiferous summer night. I walk the river until I find two couples on a blanket with a bottle of wine and their curious smoke.

One of the men squints at my dress. "Is this some renaissance thing?" They laugh and ignore the tickets I hold out, but then the distant music and screams and laughter reach their ears. So, it's into the forest and past the trees trying to reach them in warning. Like everyone else, they move toward the gold and purple tents.

A fire-eater amazes a rapt crowd as they enter. The redheaded girl is suspicious. "What are you, our guide? We can do this by ourselves."

Not with her cynicism potentially guiding them out of here. "This is not a conventional carnival. They prefer a guide until you adjust."

"Adjust to what?" someone mutters, but soon enough, one of the Fae extends goblets of the nectar. *Dark magic; drink it up like a poisoned fairy buttercup.* And with that, they belong to the Carnival.

The other girl is distracted by one of the Fae, who is glamoured like a masculine angel. If only she knew what he really looked like. Lucky for her, she won't find out. He'll coax her on and on into spending her money and her time, draining her, severing her from her man, but he'll never mate with her. The Unseelie are revolted by most human women. Her boyfriend walks barefoot across shards of smashed green and purple bottles, so bewitched, he doesn't realize his feet are bleeding. Around them, the Fae are laughing.

The redhead watches her boyfriend drift toward the Bordello tent. She's not affected by the nectar; how I envy her. She calls his name but he ignores her. "Come," I say, and lead her toward the Castle of Spirits.

"Come, ladies and gentlemen, for the terror of your life!" the carny calls. "Experience the shades of serial killers, the most murderous ghosts of history!"

She looks troubled. I personally loathe the Castle of Spirits, but I force a smile and she pays. Into the dark vestibule of a gothic castle we go, moans of pain filling the dark. A white, filmy shape becomes visible. "Help me," it gasps. "Help me!" The girl flinches as another shape, that of a blood-spattered woman with an axe in her head drifts toward us. A third ghost, a small child, suddenly appears next to her and she screams.

We move into a faux cemetery, one lit by a false moon. Diaphanous shapes rise from the fake grass, but she refuses to look, hiding her eyes and crying. "Where are my friends? Why is everything here so evil?"

Why are you so impenetrable? I think. But really, it's admirable. She would never get trapped here, betraying her own kind for a drink at the end of the night. But that means it's time for her to go, for the few humans who can resist the carnival dream tend to remember far too much and raise a fuss.

As we emerge from the Castle of Spirits, the clashing organ music and fire-eaters and satyrs inviting women to stroke their backs sound like chaos. Then I see him by the Apothecary, paying for more nectar—my handsome black-haired guest from last night. His blue eyes are dazed and fixed on the cup extended to him, which he immediately takes and gulps down. Dark juice runs down his jaw. I recognize that avarice, that thirst.

"Laura. You look distressed." Samael. He's not merely concerned; he's warning me to change my expression, for the Fae want the servants to look joyful at all times around guests. "She's uncharmed," I tell him.

To my vast relief, he offers to escort us home. Samael is safe to travel with as he can always get me back to the carnival, no matter where it has moved on to. We escort the redhead across the river and into her town. It's everything I detest in modern life, from the ugly automobiles to the crude stares of men. At the same time, it's a relief to be away from the carnival. Away from the ever-present monitoring and looming punishments.

"It's not like it used to be, you know," Samael says on the walk home. "The carnival needs to be careful. Someone who goes missing today can be viewed with cameras, tracked, and found."

"They can only track them as far as the river." But he's right, and the Fae don't want bad reports that could scare off visitors. "Do you think they'll ever lose interest in the torment?" It's a relief to speak freely.

"You know that they don't feel as we do."

'We' is an interesting way to connect us. But 'we' are not the same. He has a freedom I never will. The nectar doesn't affect the Fae or the demi-Fae; it's just a drink to them. "I know that to them, it's as if their suffering happened yesterday."

"The freak shows may be over," he says. "Humans may no longer capture the goblins and parade them, starve them, hurt them. But now, they poison the earth and its waters and air and soil. They aren't blameless."

The river looks black in the starlight. I wish our journey was longer; the summer night is peaceful, and here, I am no one's slave. I think of the black-haired guest who could still be wandering the carnival right now.

We sit on the grass. "I love the smell of summer," Samael says.

"What does it smell of to you?" Nothing smells as intoxicating to me as the world of the Fae. Strawberries in spring, a bough dripping with melting snow, the spices of the Cuisine tent; everything is richer and more elegant to my nose there.

"Possibilities. Freedom." He smiles. "You don't have to go back tonight, you know. I'll create an excuse for you."

It sounds so appealing. A night on my own, no hideous goblins to jeer at me or threaten me for not bringing enough guests in. But that would mean skipping my nightly nectar.

When I don't answer, he says, "It hasn't been that long for you. You could still adjust to going home." He reaches for my hand. "You can't do this forever; your human body won't last."

"It isn't a choice." I wish that, just once, he felt the thirst, the ecstasy.

"I will get you identification, money, a solid start. We'll go back and forth, get you acclimated to living here. The independence, the variety of things to do, will appeal to you."

Then I know the rumors are true. Samael is not Unseelie, he's a half-Seelie spy to monitor and intervene in the Unseelie's cruelty. "What a savior you are. But I don't want that life." I rise, because the itch is building in my dry throat. "I must go back."

He doesn't follow.

The fairgrounds are especially filthy tonight. Spilled blood and discarded prizes litter the dirt. Some of the dolls in the Doll House have reverted to human, their dismembered limbs and scattered teeth and eyes twitching in the dirt. It's grotesque but it's also a sure ticket to an extra dose tonight, so I begin to clean it up.

Carol the mermaid never appears. Perhaps she angered them and is serving time as a Tiny. Alone, I take my fruit and nectar into the forest so I don't see Samael. And soon, I'm lost in a lavender-blue cloud, euphoria raining down like light. Senseless, animal joy fills me, like invisible fingertips running up my spine and sending glowing demonic atoms into my blood. *Love me, love me*, narcotic me says to the imaginary friends and lovers I'll never have, and then I'm drenched in an ecstasy worth all the pain of gray daylight.

The next day, I wake on the ground in a cold rain. I vomit onto the forest floor, my bones pulsing with pain.

There's a whispering in the trees. They are agitated. I gently push aside their branches, for I try to respect who they once were, and see blood soaking the soil. Something pale is in the dirt; the rain-washed body of the redhead's boyfriend. He must have become aggressive with one of the Fae. He's not dead. The Unseelie insist they preserve the life of every human who enters their carnival, and it's true. The few who accost them are never killed, merely transformed after beatings they can't survive.

One of his swollen eyes opens enough to look at me. His broken jaw moves but there's no help I can give him; the transmutation has begun. His feet are twisting, sinking into the forest floor. His pallid skin is rippling in shades of brown and green. Fresh green shoots burst from his eyes and mouth, muffling his screams, and grow over his skull until he stiffens and rises as another twisted tree.

You might ask me if I feel especially guilty when it's a guest I've brought in who ends like this. But today all it means to me, to all of us, is another missing man. Samael's warning of last night returns to me. The carnival will have to move again.

III

Another river, another town. Into humanity I go on a cool fall night. No *come buy, come buy;* my errand is to leave their painted signs on doorsteps, in mailboxes. Fleet of foot I am, not only for fear of being apprehended—to be detained could sever me from the carnival permanently—but from fear of the strangers around me.

The night is crisp and dry, a crescent moon glowing in the east. Dry leaves crunch under my boots, and the October breeze nips at my thighs.

A familiar face appears from behind a tree. She's wearing a leather coat and heavy makeup, but after a few moments, I recognize Carol. She stopped appearing as the mermaid in the Hall of Curiosities and I never knew why. I didn't ask the others, afraid of the answer.

"You can leave the goblins, Laura," she says. "I did it. You can do it too."

My first impulse is to retort about the others who've left, who've faded on their deathbeds. To remind her of the corpses she worked alongside, who came back for that nectar when it was too late to stop their decay. But she will only speak of Samael's suggestions to wean me from it.

So I say, "I despise your dull and mediocre new life."

Carol does not flinch. "Nothing is worth servitude, Laura. Let us help you. It will be worth it."

That's when I see Samael sitting in a tree. I become conscious of his beauty, her polish, and my own aching limbs, my thinning hair.

"Don't come to me again," I say, and move past them to place a flyer on a house's front steps.

Back at the carnival, there are no guests. It's a night for repair and rejuvenation. The Fae spend their powers on creating flawless attractions, and shaping mesmerizing beasts and small monsters. The other servants, spared the pain of transmutation tonight, tidy the tents and grounds.

I'm cleaning the Doll House when I see a familiar doll; a black-haired man, with bright blue, unblinking eyes and a forced smile. My stomach turns as I imagine how he will be broken and disassembled and rearranged tomorrow night and every night until he fulfills his agreement. But as I've learned to do, I drop the tent curtains and go on the hunt for new guests. It doesn't matter. If it wasn't him, it would be someone else. Just as one evening by the river, it won't be me singing *come buy, come buy,* but another girl. A girl looking weaker and thinner in her satin dress, the light slowly dying in her eyes, but determined to make it to the end of the night.

CHAPTER EIGHT

THE SECRET SHOWING ON THE MIDWAY OF DREAMS

Daniel R. Robichaud

J ack Willoughby stumbled down the road from the bus stop, swinging his valise in one hand, with half a bottle of rye in his coat pocket and the rest sitting uncomfortably in his gut. The heavens hid themselves behind a dark blanket, but lights and sounds of merriment filled the night ahead of him. Jack smiled to himself when he saw big posters announcing the attractions. To see those garish affairs, you might not know there was a war to end all wars being waged in Europe at that very moment. The smells of sawdust, greasepaint, and gunpowder were especially intoxicating that night, and beneath them was another, subtler aroma. By their powers combined, they accomplished a miracle—washing away the reek of burning gasoline stuck in his nostrils since leaving No Man's Land and making his slow boat return to New York City and then south, back home to Shumble, Texas and finally out here to the panhandle.

Jack walked on the enchanting fumes, following them beneath the sign welcoming one and all to the Gambini Brothers' Midway of Dreams and down the way, past the colorful stalls and shouting barkers, where three balls or three shots with a .22 rifle might be had for a pair of bits. Where a kewpie doll was yours for the taking, if you were a man of skill or deadeye aim or steely will. They were all the same, those dudded up barkers and the comely temptresses adorned with enough decorative plumage to keep out of the hoosegow should the local law poke their noses around for decency's sake.

Briefly, the moon peeked from behind those clouds like an exhausted man peering one heavily lidded eye at the chaotic world before pulling the blankets back up over his head. A distant rumble might have been thunder or a locomotive.

The smell led Jack deep into the carnival, past the geeks and freaks, past the tent promising miracles and damnations in the form of various pickled punks, to a dark building. There, an overweight man in a red and white checked jacket and similarly colored striped pants, like some crazy barber's pole, chatted with a stogie-chomping midget. They paid Jack no mind until he coughed into his palm, making them glance his way wearing expressions that castigated him for disturbing the calm and implored him to make his interruption worthwhile.

Jack decided not to waste any time. "Name's Willoughby; Jack to my friends. I can swing a hammer for rigging up and down. Had some experience with traveling shows, but I find myself, well, down on my luck. You moving soon? Need an extra hand to help get on the road? I'm your—"

"Hey Mooney," said the man in the checked jacket, talking to his companion without taking his eyes off Jack. His jacket swept open, revealing a large belly and broad chest squeezed into a delicately embroidered vest. "Looks like we've got ourselves an applicant for work."

"Tell him to hit the bricks, Chauncy," the little guy said, his voice far deeper than Jack had expected. "We'll be lucky to break even in these sticks."

It was a familiar tactic, of course; Jack had been serious about his previous work. All traveling shows pretended to be barely breaking even when new help showed up. If they offered him the geek's slot, Jack told himself he would sternly refuse. He was low, sure, but not rock bottom. If they let him roughneck, he'd go for it. Hard work for a meager wage was more his speed than roof, straw bedding, all the chicken heads he could eat, and all the doped hootch necessary to make them appetizing.

"I got my own tools," Jack said, shaking the valise to let the hammer and screwdrivers clink together. "I can maybe cut your rig-down time for just two, three dollars. Only two, three dollars, mind."

The larger man laughed, one hand moving to rub his belly the way some men did a pregnant woman's tummy for luck. "First time I ever seen someone bark for manual labor."

"Send him away, Chauncy," Mooney, the little man, said. His wide, white face fit his name to a T. "We got problems of our own."

Chauncy's hand paused mid-rub, and the man stared intently at the newcomer, the intruder, the interloper. "You got a shake to you, friend. You on the sauce or the needle?"

"Coming off a snort of sauce," Jack said.

"Don't believe him, Chauncy. He's got the junk sick look."

"No sir," Jack said. "Just a little high. Got half a bottle in my pocket, if you've an interest."

"Mooney here doesn't drink," said Chauncy. "And I can't. Not anymore." He appraised Jack again. "We don't pull up stakes tonight, it being Saturday, our biggest day." He elbowed Mooney, who didn't yuck-yuck it up with him.

Was it Saturday? The week was a blur. Jack wondered how many empty bottles he might've left across the country, in trash cans at this bus stop or that train station. Saturday. He could've sworn it was Tuesday. Maybe Wednesday.

"However, we do pull up tomorrow morning," continued Chauncy. "Need to get on the road by noon, you see. You lay off the sauce for the rest of tonight, you ought to be dry as the Mojave when the rubes wake up for first mass. Swing by, and you got yourself some work."

The little man yanked the stogie out of his mouth and pointed it at Jack like a spear. "You come by wet, and you can take your troubles and blow. Got it?"

Jack's head bobbed. "For two, three dollars, I'll be dry as California."

"For a dollar and a half, you will," Chauncy said. "As well as a place to bunk. Maybe a square or two."

Jack brightened. It was better than he'd expected. The thing about carnies? They did not care who you were, where you came from, or what demons followed you. So long as you kept your troubles from blowing back on the show and could do the day's work, you were fine.

Jack found a hitch in his throat that made *thank you* far more difficult to say than two simple words.

The rumble came again, closer. Chauncy glanced toward the heavens, cussing under his breath about, "Of course there'd be rain tonight, probably all day tomorrow, too." Mooney rolled the stogie between his fingers as he toked, eyes never leaving Jack. "You a weatherman?" Chauncy asked.

"No, sir."

"Well, neither am I," Chauncy said with a single laugh. "But I tell you what, the old Gambini Brothers set up their show for a month, then the last weekend will turn wetter than a fish's keester." He patted Mooney's arm, who stopped staring through Jack to glance the other man's way.

"It's bad business is what it is," Mooney said, though Jack wasn't sure if he meant the weather or hiring a drunk. Chauncy said something under his breath, which passed Jack right on by.

Mooney considered and then shrugged. "Go ahead, then." The small fella plugged the stogie right back in his yap, giving Chauncy his blessing.

"Hold up, Willoughby," Chauncy said. He dug a half dollar out of his pocket and tossed it to Jack. Not coin of the realm, but a poker chip painted with a funny Egyptian-looking eyeball shape. "That'll get you a bite of chow."

The two men started talking, voices low but impassioned. Jack could have spontaneously vanished for all the attention they were giving him.

Jack was about to turn away and find a place to feed his face, but the allure of that dark structure called to him. "Sirs?"

The two men stopped talking again, glancing his way. Chauncy was inscrutable, but Mooney's expression told him he was treading close to losing the offer they'd made.

"Why isn't that attraction up and running?" Jack asked. He indicated the dark setup behind them.

It was a house of some kind, crested with leering, peering gargoyle faces. They looked like some sort of lacquered papier-mâché, not stone. A spook-house, maybe? A screamer for the rubes to yowl in fright and grope one another in the dark?

"That?" Chauncy asked, glancing back to the building and then once more Jack's way in a theatrical fashion. "That there is the Secret Showing."

"Sir?"

"A midnight-only gig," Mooney explained. The little man produced a turnip-shaped pocket watch, studying the face for almost two seconds before snapping it shut. "An hour before it gets the chance to dazzle the rubes."

138

"You say you're in the business, Willoughby. But you're curious, right?" Chauncy showed his yellowed teeth in a snarling grin, swept a hand to indicate the milling masses losing their money at fixed games of chance, cheap rides, cheaper attractions, and smiling at the opportunity to do so. "Then, think about how curious *they* are."

Jack bobbed his head like he understood.

"You want to see for yourself, come by at midnight," Mooney said. "We let you in the same as the rubes, you got the dimes to see."

A wind blew from behind the building, ruffling Jack's hair and giving him a fresh opportunity to smell that subtle, enchanting scent.

Jack asked, "It a *cootch* or something?"

Looked like no façade for a *cootch* show Jack had ever seen before. If a place like that did feature dancing girls in little to no costuming, then he supposed the girls would have to get themselves all made up in greasepaint and ashes, to look especially cadaverous as they peeled away their few flimsy layers. That line of thought brought back his time in the trenches, and he broke out in a cold sweat.

"It's something, all right," Chauncy said. He and Mooney traded knowing glances and grinned, baring tiny teeth and long, yellow ones. Again, the thunder rumbled, setting the earth to shaking beneath his feet.

Jack shivered, but he tried not to show them he was disturbed. "Maybe I will come back."

"You could learn a thing or two," Mooney said.

Chauncy dropped into his bark to add, "All it costs…is your *immortal soul*." Then they laughed like a couple of contented hyenas.

Jack shivered as if a goose had walked over his grave. But he turned and headed off to follow his nose in search of the grub tent this time around. Finding it would have been easier if he'd been able to rely on his nose, but his time overseas had robbed him of that. Still, his search eventually yielded success.

They had corned beef hash and coffee. Jack showed the poker chip in exchange for a plateful and a mug. The cook was a one-eyed man in his mid-forties, head as hairless as a cue ball and almost as pale—not just bald, the man had no eyebrows or even eyelashes. Burned flesh decorated the backs of his hands. When Jack said his thanks, the cook peered at him as though trying to look into his soul. "You're not a local boy," he said, his accent familiar.

Jack shook his head. "Not an Okie, no."

"What part of Texas?"

"Around Houston."

The cook grinned. "You're not so far from my people, then, by gum," he said, and finally Jack recognized the strong accent.

"You're Creole."

"Cajun," the cook corrected.

"What the difference?" Jack asked.

The smile vanished. "You have to ask, then there's no helping you." He should've noticed it straight away.

"Willoughby," Jack said with an open hand. "Jack to my friends."

"They calling me Lafayette here. But it's Richelieu. Rich." They each offered hands. Rich squeezed and shook with confidence.

"Good to know you, Rich."

"Good to know you, Jack. You eat up, and then come back, we chew the fat some. Ain't no one from my neck of the woods hereabouts."

"I'm not Creole. Cajun, I mean."

"You remind me of home, and sometimes that's enough, yeah?"

Jack took his food and ate up. The hash was a little too greasy, but there was a healthy dose of butter. The cup of joe was a far bitterer mud than expected, all the sugar in the world would not help it, and Rich the cook had milk halfway on its journey to cream. But a full belly was better than an empty one, so Jack did not complain. He ate and swallowed the way he had learned to do in basic. While he ate, the horizon glowed with lightning. The heat had not diminished since he arrived. On the plus side, he was sweating out the booze.

By the time he finished his victuals, he was sweaty, shaky, and sober. Then, with the food and coffee churning in his belly, Jack headed back to chat the night away with Rich. The man could spin a yarn just as good as most of the swamp folk raconteurs Jack had known. Eventually, he got round to asking, "You know anything about the Secret Showing?"

As soon as the name was out of his gob, Rich's merriment shut down. "I know enough to keep well away. Bad *juju* there."

Jack thought he was pitching a gag, but he couldn't see the punchline unless the name of the game was Goof on the New Guy. "You're kidding, yeah?"

"This isn't some kind of hazing ritual, by gum. It the God's honest truth. Don't put your nose in a place like that."

"Putting my nose anywhere can't be helped," Jack muttered.

"What's that, then?" When Jack made no reply, Rich said, "Sorry to hit a nerve."

"It's an injury, is all. I don't like to talk about it." *Or think about it, even.* However, his dreams were filled with labyrinths of wood and mud, the trenches and the trickle of gasoline pouring down the wall into the ankle-deep water he was standing in. The sound and stink of a burning bomb as it came over the trench wall. The rush of the flames and the effort to outrun them. He always woke to that new friend, the smell of the gasoline and burnt meat.

The cook held his hands up, showing off the scarred backs. "We all carry something old and scarred. I got these when I worked stir a few years back. Cooking for twenty is bad enough, but two hundred? And some of those men the screws let in my kitchen were tough, tough customers. Refused to back down when someone stoked their ire." He sighed and looked at the old wounds. "I got mixed in a fight I had no stake in."

"Me too," Jack said, "and I can't leave it behind."

Rich studied the man for a good long moment, then nodded. "Well, ain't no matter. Don't be going to that Secret Showing. It cost you more than the two dimes you shell out."

A two-dime attraction in a park that's only got nickel shots? "It's got to be some kind of *cootch*, then."

"Ain't no girls in that place," Rich said. "None you'd want to dream about dancing with, anyway." He was done talking then, having to get some more food for his charges. When Jack offered to help, Rich waved him off saying, "No Texan ever did touch a Cajun's kitchen without losing fingers, by gum." It was said with a smile though, and Jack took no offense.

The hours passed, and Jack wandered the grounds, getting an eyeful of the place and the different amusements and distractions. Because of the threat of rain, the rubes huddled up; because of the threat of lightning, the Ferris wheel shut down. The merry-go-round carried on though, its tinny calliope music adding a strangeness to the night.

Everywhere he went, he heard whispers about the Secret Showing. Never to the more proper looking members of the Okie community, but to the hungry adults with a younger and wilder disposition. The barkers offered little in the way of details when asked. "It has to be seen to be believed," was the answer the rubes got, along with winks and knowing sneers. Jack had to admit it was a pretty fine way to work up a crowd's curiosity—make them feel like they got wind of something special, don't reveal too much, let them dream up something really interesting.

As the midnight hour approached, the crowds thinned. Families with kids threw in the towel, headed on home; so too, the older set. Soon enough, only folks in their twenties and thirties remained, a mix of loners or those on dates with no place else to go. The clouds were still thick across the heavens, offering the moon no holes to peer through.

Chauncy walked the midway, yowling for attention with a megaphone. "Step right up, ladies and gents. Step right up. As the witching hour approaches, step right on up to the rear of the Midway of Dreams, where the Secret Showing is now open for business. Please, step right up, ladies and gents. This way to the finest attraction you'll likely ever see. Step right up. Only two little dimes for your ride through the veil. Just twenty cents for a glimpse of heavenly blessing and maybe a little hellish damnation. Step right up, ladies and gents. Step right up."

Again, Jack had to admire the showmanship. The places he'd run with, before being called overseas to a wholly horrific other carnival sideshow, were nowhere near as classy. They'd been joints geared toward relieving change from chumps' pockets and purses too. However, they were sleazy affairs, grubby and cheap. This Gambini Brothers setup? It had a queer kind of class.

Jack found himself spirited along with the crowds, heading toward that dark attraction—toward the watching eyes and toothy grins of the gargoyles overhead. It was no longer dark, however. Flickering lights in the second-floor windows lent the place a creepy kind of holiness. And my oh my, how the flickering lights gave those leering creatures a proper stony aspect. Or maybe a rough sort of flesh, ready to come alive at any minute.

Wee Mooney was at the door, trading dimes for tickets, handling the crowd like the professional he was. "Come one, come all, but only if you're over eighteen. And the Gambini Brothers do not recommend the Secret Showing for folks what suffer from bum tickers or bedwetting."

That only intensified the crowd's curiosity; they were happy to hand over their coins for a glimpse. Jack knew it was being built up, sort of like the old gag about the man-eating chicken, which was exactly as advertised—not an oversized bird eating human flesh, but a guy in a chair with a plate of fried fowl. A good barker could turn a crowd's ire by appealing to their inherent hatred of their neighbors—telling them that, no matter how foolish they felt at that moment, wouldn't it be better to see that uppity gent down the way or that catty missus from across the lane taken in just the same? Most places, such tactics worked nicely. No one could appeal to mankind's worst impulses better than a barker, a reader of the human condition and the human spirit, a stoker of both curiosities and cruelties.

Jack didn't need a reliable sense of smell to know something was fishy there. Still, he handed over two dimes, and Mooney held onto his ticket just a little longer than the others, so he could ask, "You sure you want to see for yourself, shakes?"

"Haven't had a drop since I got here," Jack said. "I'm dried out, now. You want to hold my bottle for me to make sure?"

"No sirree," Mooney said. "If the Chaunce takes a chance, then who is Mooney to say, 'no way'?" He handed the ticket over and softened his voice so only Jack could hear. "Word to the wise, though. I'd not go through the third door if'n I was you. Might be more than you want to take, if you understand what I'm trying to say."

Jack did not, but he bobbed his head anyway, and followed the crowd through the doors.

The first room was big enough for the crowd of not-quite forty, and it was done up in spook-house finery. It could have been a grand ballroom from some old money house back east, but for the sawdust on the floor and the earth visible through the gaps in the floorboards. The walls were done up in wood treated with some kind of brine mixture to maximize the illusion of age and exposure. Here and there, painted faces in reds and oozing greens grinned through cobwebs. Disembodied eyes gazed from the corners. A pair of chandeliers remained dark overhead, though Jack expected them to flicker to life any moment.

Mooney came in with the last of the customers. "When she was young, Amanda Tremblay was the most desirable woman in Worcester, Massachusetts; a pretty thing with a sizable dowry and a love for dance. However, none of the gentlemen who came to waltz with her could woo her, and she died a spinster. It was in the ballroom she fell, and it was in the ballroom she rose. Haunted that room for twenty years, enticing menfolk to dance with her and then devouring them before the song was done. Sent herself twenty odd souls to the devil. When the last of her local family died, the house turned over to a Boston relation, who had no need for the place. He set the house for demolition, but the Gambini Brothers bought up everything they could of that haunted room, hoping to catch that one piece that served as her prison, her fetter to this plane. She can't leave this room, you see, so the Gambinis are giving her a change of scenery, if you will." Mooney's chuckle was downright sinister before he added, "And a fresh crop of prospective dancers."

A haunting melody filled the room. It was a scratchy-sounding music, which skipped a few times. One of those wax cylinder phonograph recordings, Jack supposed. Spooky, all right.

Mooney cocked his head to one side and cupped his ear. "It seems that the specter of Miss Tremblay is here, even now. Sees herself a possible partner." He grinned at the crowd. "Only young men with no attachments, please. Miss Tremblay's happy to play heartbreaker, but the Gambini Brothers prefer not to get their midway showmen involved in such dramas."

This was met with a ripple of tittering laughter. A gasp interrupted it, and then another.

"Why, here she is, ladies and gents."

A shape appeared behind Mooney, materializing from the air itself. A feminine figure, wearing a dress and veil the pale gray of a grave shroud. Her hands were clasped before her in a prayer directed toward the floorboards.

Mooney asked, "Is there one among you brave enough to take a turn with this lady? Her preference was for gentleman while she yet lived, but the grave robs us of our preferences. These days, anyone will do."

"I will," said a gawky looking rube. His Adam's apple was much too large and his chin much too small, his eyes and teeth too prominent for his wide face. He might have tried combing that brown mop of hair before he left whatever farmhouse he called home, but the wind had set it loose and wild. A little pomade would help with that. However, only a canvas flour sack would help him charm girls.

"Well, sir, you are the brave one," Mooney said. "Have your spin around the dance floor with this wan creature." As he stepped forward, she took his hands and guided him through a ballroom dance lesson.

The crowd watched, rapt, as the two glided around the room's perimeter. A door opened, and the two passed in. It shut behind them, and the gawky rube screamed. There was a pelting sound of feet racing off, and the rube wailing, "*Oh, hideous horror!*"

"Alas," Mooney said, "she must've offered him a kiss. The grave offers no benefit for a peaches-and-cream complexion." This found a gentle laugh and eased some of the tension.

Jack noticed how the couples clung a little closer than before. A good fright would do that, making the sting of forty cents entry fee for the two of them all the easier to bear.

"Now, this is but the first of the offerings in the Secret Showing," Mooney said. "And it might be enough for some of you. I want anyone who's seen enough the opportunity to bow out gracefully. Yon door leads to the side of the attraction, and some helpful folks from Gambini Brothers' Midway of Dreams will be pleased to guide you back to the comfortable lights of the world you know."

To Jack's surprise, the crowd shed off several couples and a couple of lone visitors. Not everyone had the stomach, the stones, or the desire to test their bravery. After they'd gone and the door clapped shut, Jack tallied twenty-five or so bodies remaining.

Mooney said, "Now that we're lighter a few pounds of chicken feathers, shall we see what awaits us next?"

The next room was filled with mirrors. Warped glass offering up humorous or terrifying alterations of those who gazed into them. Jack knew these things from his time running with a show. He was not alone in that knowledge, either, from the few sighs and giggles of the rubes. A simple enough trick, Jack thought, but what was the Secret Showing angle?

"Now, just about everyone and their uncle has heard about the funny mirrors," Mooney said. "Makes a thin lady look fat, a fat man look thin, a shortie into a giant and a tall 'un into a little fella maybe even smaller than *me*." That was met with several chuckles. "But this is the Gambini Brothers' Midway of Dreams, and there has to be a wrinkle on the familiar, yeah?"

Jack found himself bobbing his head, too. It was quite a magic spell the little man worked with his words.

"Well, you might've wondered about that moniker when you came in. Just what is a Midway of Dreams?" Mooney waved his hands around the room. "This room holds some evidence for your perusal. These mirrors are not simple carnival tricks. They each belonged to someone who died in near proximity to them, the narcissists who could not help but gaze upon themselves one last time before the reaper came, the infants rudely stolen from their beds by death's icy grip—the young, the old, the infirm, and the ought to've been healthier."

The crowd's interest was piqued. Jack knew his was. It was an unusual angle, all right. Cleverly playing on the traveling show's name.

"Now, the mirrors did not catch the souls of those who went on to their final reward," Mooney said, offering a dramatic pause before adding, "or their endless punishment." He bared those small teeth in another eerie, manic grin. "No siree. These mirrors caught the *dreams* of them what strayed a little too close in their final moments. Now, there are some smarty-pants doctors who will try to tell you that dreams are nothing more than the belches of a slumbering mind, a random assortment of pictures and sensations. But we know different, don't we ladies and gents?

"We know that dreams are something far more valuable and powerful, windows into other worlds. So I invite each of you to find a mirror. Double up, if you wish. I know some fellers here might not want to stray too far from their gals, and likewise some gals from their fellers. Find yourself a mirror to look in, and stare with me. There's a trick, of course, a little trifle of words, and when we say them together, we'll stop seeing our own reflections and see the dreams of the long dead. Maybe we will catch a little something personal to us. Who knows? The ways of the dead and their sleeping in the everlasting arms or the eternal torment are a mystery to even me, ladies and gents. Even to me…"

The crowd split, finding their own mirrors to look through. Jack found himself standing before a three-foot-tall piece, something that had been set in a freestanding frame, judging by the holes on its sides, not something secured to a wall as it was there. Glass was a slow-moving liquid, and the stuff in that particular frame had run a little much, making his lower section wider than his upper. A distortion in the upper side lent a hazy quality to both his face and the air around him. Aside from those flaws, the mirrors seemed to be nothing more than reflective surfaces.

"Now, everyone, repeat after me," Mooney said before intoning, "*O mortua, monstra mihi somnia tua terras.*" He spoke slowly, allowing the crowd to keep up with him. It sounded like Latin, but Jack had no appreciation for what the words might mean. Still, he spoke along with the rest, not expecting anything particularly dramatic.

Jack almost choked up his hash when his reflection shimmered like the surface of a pool disturbed by a tossed stone. He gaped as another image materialized in those waves. It was incomplete. A patchwork of jigsaw pieces interspersed with the familiar. But he saw narrow, muddy walls supported by wood planks and sandbags, and a dark sky disturbed by the flickering light of an incoming fiery—

Jack wheeled around, his heart hammering away like some trapped miner yearning for freedom and fresh air. He wept and clutched his breast with his right hand, massaging the shirt and skin over his racing heart. His other hand patted at the pocket where the half-full bottle waited, yearning for the rush of a soothing quaff from the next best thing to the River Lethe.

He did not draw the bottle out, however. The tears flowed down his cheeks, and his heart refused to quit its race, but he finally decided to reassure himself he could not have seen what he thought he did and turned back to the mirror. The dreamy vision had vanished. The ripples were gone. Once interrupted, his ability to glimpse into the otherworldly via whatever dark magic filled the mirror had ended. He tried to remember the words, but they were gone, wiped away as though his mind dared not recall them. Only his reflection remained, haggard and blurred around the face. The hand that teased the bottle in his pocket moved up to his scratchy cheeks and chin. Around him, sounds of distress and heartbreak. He dared not look.

Mooney said, "And there are some among us who are not satisfied with windows. Their hearts yearn for something else, but what if the windows were to suddenly transform into doors?"

A series of startled cries and gasps filled the area. Jack glanced aside seeing limbs pushing through a couple of the mirrors, distorting the glass into shimmering gloves, allowing the long fingers within to flex and clutch, the arms to stretch as far out as possible.

"Such fancies are nonsense, of course," Mooney finished. Suddenly, the hands all snapped back into their mirrors and the surfaces restored. Nervous laughter caught like wildfire, accompanied by some weeping, some chattering teeth, some shivers, and other evidence of intense fright.

The gag made itself clear; have some mirrors be real and others be some kind of theatrical material stretched over a hole. Carnies waiting on the other side of the wall could reach through at the prescribed moment. That did not explain what Jack saw, but he supposed the lighting and the atmosphere had opened his mind to suggestion, a type of mesmerism. He saw what he had wanted to see…the same as everyone else. It was the only answer that made sense. Why else would he see the trenches from which he'd barely escaped? Those were not the dreams of some dead man, woman, or child. They were his own fearful recollections.

Mooney said, "There is one more space left to visit, one more showing to reveal. This last has made some of weaker constitution swoon and some weak hearts stop cold. I implore you, ladies and gents, not to take this offer lightly. If you have any doubts about your capacity or interest, then I invite you to venture out through the exit to your left. The rest of us shall wait here for three minutes before moving on." He produced that turnip watch from his pocket and studied its face.

As the seconds ticked by and the rubes lost their nerve, Mooney did not glance up. Twenty-five dwindled to fifteen in the first minute, six in the second, and three in the last. One of these was Jack. The others were a pair of men in their twenties, Okies with stout shoulders and gritted teeth. Under those shirts, they would sport farmers' tans, brown arms and lily-white chests. One of them chewed on a piece of wild grass, while the other chomped on bubble gum.

Jack wondered if Mooney would try to talk him out of continuing. If he did, Jack decided he would back out. Curiosity killed the cat, but would satisfaction really bring him back? He doubted it. He was about to hike through the doors himself when Mooney snapped his turnip watch shut and said, "Gentlemen, if you'll follow me?"

He led the way to a set of creaking double doors into the final space. A dual line of tea light candles formed a path beyond—flickering flames guiding them toward a circle. "Don't stray," Mooney said. "Just stay close and keep your hands at your sides if you please."

The doors banged shut behind them, robbing the room of whatever glow might've come from the mirror space.

The little man leaned down to fetch a tea light candle and used it to set a small lamp glowing. In the sudden flush of light, Jack saw a modest-sized room, for perhaps ten or twelve people. The walls were bare planks. Fully half the room remained dark because of the way Mooney held the lamp. His shadow was a giant stain. He returned the candle to the floor and adjusted the lamp's glow to the intimate level reserved for spinning ghost stories.

"There are marvels and miracles in God's country, but there are also terrors here on the earth that have no truck with the kingdom beyond pearly gates. This is not a room for the former. This is not a venue for the miraculous, it is strictly reserved for the latter. You might look upon me and think there's one such ignoble specimen. But there's nothing terrifying about me. What I refer to are things you've never seen. Even more outlandish than the lobster lad or the other offerings for your entertainment in the freak tent. Even more otherworldly than the defects found floating in the Mr. Pikel's jars of wonder."

A soft clinking came from the darkness behind the small man. Jack thought of all the tales he'd heard of about spooks rattling the chains of perdition.

"In this room is one of the gravest secrets, one of the direst terrors ever to claw its way to this horrible world," Mooney continued. "Here you've come, bravest of the lot, the most curious for our Secret Showing. The road here has passed you through the shadow world just to the left of the one where your little town and farmlands sit. The Midway from the gates has guided you into a realm that's removed from normal—a place where the shadows manifest without need of a body standing or moving too close to a light source. It's into the realm of nocturnal wanderings you've entered, gents, and you're about to learn how quickly such a jaunt can shift into something else. From Dream to Nightmare. There are some nightmares, friends, that leave us marked, scarred."

The ghost story took on a new dimension when something rose up behind the little man. The rubes didn't see it at first, but Jack did.

It was a shape darker than the shadow it occupied. Humanoid. Tall as Jack and painfully thin but somehow powerful. Its eyes gleamed red. Its nose was wide, chin exaggerated, ears awkwardly large flaps. A pair of two-inch horns jutted from its forehead. Its arms folded across its chest terminated in terrible, three-digit claws. Its lips drew wide in a soundless snarl, baring needle-sharp fangs.

Jack scrambled back. The rubes glanced his way, one giggling and the other gaping. The shape behind Mooney leaned in, stretching its arms out toward them. Its claws flicked their ears and cheeks, opening angry nicks in the Okies' faces with ease. They did not notice they were bleeding, but the creature's touches were enough to draw their attention. The two beheld the shape leaning over the storyteller, and the strength left them. They pitched to the floor, collapsing as one.

Mooney grinned. The shape behind him did not.

Jack pushed words out, as though they might shield him from similar treatment. "You killed them?"

"We gave them a little present to remember their experience by. Nothing too traumatic."

A costume. It *had* to be a costume.

Jack said, "That's Chauncy?"

The man had had plenty of time to change from his checked coat and striped pants. He had plenty of time to don a monster suit and come back, waiting for the others to arrive.

Mooney shook his head. "You see the resemblance, though?" Mooney cocked a thumb over his shoulder. "Meet the third Gambini, me and Chauncy's brother. We're triplets, even though we don't look *too* much alike."

Jack saw something in the face. Something in the mouth, which opened to lick Okie blood from those terrible talons. Its eyes were truly horrifying, red and gleaming in the lamplight. Costumes did not usually have working talons or forked tongues.

"Would *you* care for a mark to remember your experience by?" Mooney asked. Behind him, the horrible shape did a trick with its fingers, striking talons together, spitting terrible sparks.

Cold reality set in: *This is no costume.*

Jack responded the one way he could think of. He threw the half-full bottle of rye. It smashed against the floor, bathing the terrible thing's feet and legs in sauce. As well, it splashed in an unintended path to the candles and ignited. Soon enough, the terrible, terrible shape caught fire, and it let loose an awful cry. Jack clapped his hands over his ears.

As Mooney wheeled around, the creature's flailing set him alight as well. The stink of burning gasoline Jack carried back from the battlefield was invigorated by the stench of burning flesh.

The fright was almost too much to bear. Pain flooded Jack's chest, his ticker threatening to stop altogether. From the corner of his eye, Jack saw the rubes roused from whatever charm they'd been under, crawling away into the dark. He longed to escape as well, and that desire stoked a heat strong enough to thaw the icy paralysis in his legs.

He ran. Ran like his life—his soul, they'd said the attraction would cost his immortal soul—depended on putting as much distance between himself and that…that terrible thing…that Secret Showing…as quickly as possible.

History repeated itself. He was outracing flames. The last time, he'd been successful, diving atop sandbags before the flames licked his boots. They passed him by then, the stench pushing into his nose and refusing to leave. He ran back into the mirror room, mirrors showing a frightened man doing his damnedest to outrun the devil. He ran back into the haunted ballroom, where a figure in a pale gray shroud may have watched him from the dance floor, eager for another rube's soul.

It was a blessing when he slammed open the twin doors to the outside and ran through. Chauncy seemed to come from nowhere, appearing in his way. Jack rebounded off the man's big belly and broad chest. Chauncy grunted but did not stagger a single step. Jack, however, ended up on his keester.

"You see something that made an impression?" Chauncy asked. His yellow teeth and pale skin gleamed in the flickering lights, making him look like nothing less than a corpse.

Jack shook his head. Words failed him. Only dull terror flew from his yap—whistling screams and horrible moans.

"Can we still count on you coming back in the morning to help with rig-down?" Chauncy asked with a chummy laugh. Then, he sniffed the air, caught a whiff of the burning rye. His eyes bulged with terror. He ran into the Secret Showing, yowling, "Dante? Mooney?"

Then, the storm broke. Rain poured down upon the Midway like divine judgment or hellish reprieve.

Jack raced on. Rich spied him along the midway but did not try to stop him. Later, when Jack got enough sense to think about his flight, he recalled the cook shaking his head in a slow sad way. "I told you not to go, by gum. *I told you.*"

By then, he was racing up the road until the terror finally wore off. He waited out the storm in the bus stop, shivering each time thunder roared or lightning threatened to reveal a stalking, inhuman figure. Sleep came and, for the first time since returning from overseas, his dreams had nothing to do with trenches. Though they still stank of fire.

The next afternoon, Jack convinced himself the need for his belongings was great enough for him to return. He made his careful way back, to see if he might sneak onto the lot without attracting too much attention. The Gambini Brothers' Midway of Dreams was rigged down and gone. Moved on. In the field where it'd been, he found his ransacked valise. The clothes were still inside, both uniform and civilian duds. The medals were gone and the stash of cash, too. He had just the bucks in his pocket to live on and, as he fished them out to count out his life's savings, he discovered something else. That strange little poker chip with the Egyptian eye painted on it, a memento of the strange night and his terrible flight. He almost threw that poker chip into the grass and mud to rid himself of all reminders, but then he slipped it back into his pocket. His first brush with death left him no mementoes. This one, however, did. It seemed important to hang onto such a token for luck.

A few bucks ought to buy him a ticket away. Clutching his valise to his chest with both hands to stave off yearning for another bottle, he made his way back to the bus stop to see where he might go next. He hoped his trail would keep him as far from the Gambini Brothers, their Midway of Dreams, and their Secret Showing as possible.

CHAPTER NINE

SOBRIQUET

Sabrina Voerman

PART I
THE SHAME

S he was born with a caul.

When her mother, Vanessa, reached between her legs and picked up the baby she had birthed, she recoiled in horror. The blood and placenta that covered the thing she pushed out of her was much as she expected. Her sweat-slicked body crawled with the chill that slithered into the cabin. The bed linens were soiled—she couldn't afford new ones and would have to do her best washing them on the morrow.

Nessa picked up a blade on the oak table. When it clattered, the infant began to cry underneath the veil of flesh. Before she cut the cord that tied their lives together, Nessa placed her hand over the baby's head. The veil sloughed off with ease.

Underneath the caul was worse. Looking nothing like Nessa herself, the baby was a deformity. She hissed, leaning back as though the thing she created was a monster; killing it would be a mercy. Its eyes were closed, mouth agape, its wail filling the otherwise empty cabin. Even if the neighbors did hear, they would not come. They had not come as she shrieked when the labor pains had ripped through her, as though tearing her in half.

With the caul added to the bloodied linen, Nessa palmed the blade again. It was a simple kitchen knife—not very sharp, but sharp enough. The baby rested between Nessa's legs, still wailing, as she cut the cord that tethered them.

The moment the spongy bond was cut, the baby stopped crying. The child had black hair and matching eyes, so dark they appeared to have no irises. Not the cornflower blue of Nessa's, nor her soft brown locks. She blinked up at Nessa, searching for motherly affection.

"A girl," Nessa said. "What a pity."

The baby wriggled as if in response. Her mouth opened, but no cries came.

Nessa sighed and picked her daughter up, slipping her shift to offer the babe a breast. To Nessa's surprise, the infant latched immediately. The baby's deformed body was warm like a furnace against her. She leaned against the wall and shut her eyes for a moment to rest. They said the pain of childbirth disappeared the moment a mother held her child, but every ounce of Nessa ached, down to the marrow in her bones.

The night stretched on. Howls in the woods surrounding the village were a cacophony of prayer to the moon. Odd chitters of creatures unknown to Nessa came near the windows. Night sounds. They had terrified Nessa as a child, and she never outgrew those fears.

When the baby was asleep, Nessa studied her face. Bright red cheeks on warm skin, straight black hair that likely belonged to the child's father—not that Nessa knew which john that was. Her lip was malformed and her nose a squat, piggish thing. The baby was an unfortunate sight. In fact, it was quite ugly.

"An ugly girl will do naught but suffer," Nessa whispered. "Perhaps a pretty name will spare you shame."

She brushed the back of her fingers against the baby's crinkled cheek. "I shall name you—"

"—Briar!" Vanessa's voice carried through the small yard behind the cabin that pressed against the woods where wolves wandered. Briar looked up from the pile of leaves she was nested in, dress and hands filthy, a lock of hair in her grip. She'd cut Mina Masterson's hair in a fit of rage. Mina was the mayor's daughter, and she was so, so cruel. She had called Briar a freak day after day until she'd snapped. It wasn't Briar's fault her body was all wrong. Her hands were gnarled, her fingers crooked, and her back was hunched, but she was just a girl.

A snake slithered from the shelter of the decaying foliage, forked tongue tasting the air for threats. Briar thought for sure it would dart away when it sensed her, but it turned its s-shaped body and moved with unparalleled grace over her hand, unafraid.

"BRIAR!"

Only when the snake finished its course did Briar get to her feet, knobby knees she never outgrew knocking together as she turned towards Vanessa's home. "I am here, Mama," Briar called in a raspy voice. Briar felt half-feral as she limped between skinny sycamore trees, her upturned nose bleeding over her mangled lip. She wiped at it with the back of her dirt-stained hands, bits of broken leaves stuck to her flesh.

"How many times must I warn you not to enter the woods, child?" Vanessa snapped.

Briar's black eyes fell to the earth. Scattered dead leaves crunched under her footfalls, crackling like flame-eaten wood. When she was near enough, Vanessa beckoned her close, then grabbed at her apron to dab at the blood on Briar's face. She would never find someone to love her or a good family to take her and make her a good wife. An ugly child with a whore for a mother—she had no chance in this world. The malformed daughter of the village whore would never be permitted to live. She could survive, yes, but she could not live. Only the snakes tolerated her.

"The woods be the only place I feel safe, Mama."

"What of your home?"

Sneering, Briar managed to look even uglier. "Where I am scarcely tolerated?"

"What more would you ask of me? Do I not clothe and feed you?"

"Praying to God that I perish so you may return to a life without me?"

The sound of palm on cheek ripped through the air as Vanessa slapped Briar. Her head snapped to the side and she inhaled sharply through gritted teeth. Vanessa hissed, "You are an ungrateful thing."

Fight back.

Briar teetered between retaliation and breaking. She grasped for the comfort of a loving mother for the last time. "They tripped me in the schoolhouse, Mother. Spoke nasty things about…me being the daughter of the devil," Briar said. "They hate me so much."

Vanessa glowered at Briar. "You give them reason to! Every wicked thing you say and do shows on your skin—you're an ugly thing, Briar, inside and out."

Briar's tears were unleashed and, within a moment, she was a crumpled mess on the ground. Sobs shook her until her body hurt. "I-I was born this way. I was b-born with your sin on me, Mother!"

That only silenced Vanessa momentarily. "And I have repented."

The tears dried up and the space they left was filled with spite—seventeen years of it. She got to her feet, staring at her mother. "Every seventh day, with the bruises of the men on your flesh, with their seed in your rotten womb."

Vanessa smacked Briar's cheek again. Blood filled her mouth, velvet and sour. She spat at her mother, blood and saliva blended to make an ugly orange. It landed on Vanessa's shoulder, and she recoiled from her child, as though she might catch her ugliness. There was nothing left to say, for they both knew Briar was right; she bore the sins of her mother.

It was time she bore her own.

"You disgust me, daughter."

Kill her.

She asked not God to give her strength, but the devil himself. A spark in her belly nudged her, a little bit of hellfire. Briar raised her twisted lip and pushed her mother—hard. It was the first time she'd retaliated. Vanessa fell to the ground, brown leaves breaking into pieces below her fisted hands.

"Right where you belong," Briar said. "On your back. Just like the night you made me."

Vanessa's expectant gaze told Briar she'd known this day would come. "Get out, you beast, and never return. Run to your kind—be the wild thing that lives in the woods. You're a snake in the grass. I never want to see your hideous face again."

Briar bent at the hip and looked her mother dead in the eye. "I was born this way because you do not know how to love."

Vanessa let out a sharp laugh. "And you do, daughter?"

"No," Briar said, straightening as best her deformed body would allow. "But I understand how to hate."

She stepped around her mother and hurried into the house. Though she possessed little, she would take what she could. She filled a trunk with a few small books, a trinket made of sticks and twine she made for herself, a cracked hand mirror she hated to look in, and a few articles of clothing. She donned her warmest cloak and went for the front door. Her mother was there, staring at her with narrowed eyes.

"If you leave now, do not ever return," Vanessa said.

"Pray tell, Vanessa, why did you not drown me when I was a babe?" She recoiled at the question. Briar waited.

"You were my penance."

Briar's lips pulled tight. Though her mother was malicious, at least she was honest. If Briar took anything of Vanessa with her, it would be her sin and her honesty.

Part II
The Deal

Briar left home that day, determined to face the world alone and survive whatever came her way. Only she was met with disgust, hatred, and fear. The small village she was raised in tolerated her existence for seventeen years—the world did not. People looked upon her with pity on a good day, disgust on all others. She found no work, she could not even sell her body, as no one wanted to look upon or touch it for fear that they might catch her ugliness.

She soured inside, like milk left in the sun.

A clatter of coin inside the tin cup, nearly molded to her crooked fingers in the cold, startled her. The late-autumn chill ran its fingers along her body, underneath the rags she wore. She had been on the streets for just shy of a year, learning what earned her coin. A veil covered her face— passersby were more likely to give if they could not see what a hideous beast she was.

"You look like a woman who has seen better days," a man said.

Briar looked up through the lace caul. Before her was a tall man, lean but clearly muscular. His attire was strange to her—bright and adorned with gold tassels and buttons. His blonde hair was a bit messy, as though he hadn't bothered to comb it when he woke that morning. His soft blue eyes made Briar feel an ache that would never be soothed.

"I've seen worse days, but no better ones," she said.

"Would you like to?" he asked.

"I have nothing to offer you."

"Oh, that is where you are wrong." He crouched before her but did not reach to remove her veil. "I believe we can offer one another so much."

"You're mistaken."

"My name is Jacques. Let me give you something to eat, ale to warm you," he said, "then allow me to offer you a proposition. This is all I ask and, after your belly is full, your hands have thawed, and you've listened to my offer, if you turn me down, I'll be out of your life."

The promise of food and the soft smile on this man's lips compelled her. Within a quarter of an hour, she was seated at a table inside a fire-warmed tavern. Before her was a plate of meat, potatoes, and roasted vegetables covered in spices that she had never tasted before. Briar ate with the veil still covering her face, while Jacques sat across from her with a curious look in his eyes.

"Are you satisfied?" he asked. She nodded once. "May I lay my offer on the table?"

"You may."

"I am the ringleader of *Jacques's Requiem*, a traveling show catering to all sorts of desires. We have no animals, save for the snake that Madame Eve tells folks is the devil himself." Jacques laughed as though he knew something Briar did not. "I deal in people; a seer who tells people their future, a sword-swallower, a woman who is the master of fire itself—"

"What need do you have of me?"

"I sense a hidden talent within you. I need someone who can concoct tonics and potions for all our patrons' needs. Whether it be to make them smell like their lover's favorite scent, to have better eyesight, to give their enemy warts—"

"You speak of magic I do not possess."

"You speak as though you have tried and failed."

She opened her mouth to reply but could not. Jacques was right; she hadn't ever tried. Magic was something she had heard of but never seen.

"I ask you for one night, a trial of sorts. If you find any such reward, you can stay with my show. Should you reap no reward, I will give you enough coin for board for a month and food for two."

"What benefit will you reap?"

"A new attraction."

"And if I leave?"

Jacques smiled. "I suspect that a warm bed, the comfort of found family, and warm meals three times a day will be enough to keep you around. However, if you do not stay, then I will be out what I promised you. This is not trickery—I need performers for my show, and sometimes I must take risks to find rewards."

"Very well."

"You will need a sobriquet."

"A what?"

"A performing name. Something to draw in the crowd."

"My name is Briar."

He smiled wryly. "A beautiful name, certainly, but you will need something...catchy. I am Jacques the Diabolical."

"You think most highly of yourself, then."

"As should you," he said. His tone had shifted into a seriousness. "Your name will come to you in time."

Jacques rose from his seat and extended a hand to Briar. Hers were gloved, hiding how grotesque they were, but not how misshapen. She hesitated, not because she did not want to go with him and see what he had to offer, but because she did not want him to feel her hands. The veil protected her from the worst of it but, sooner or later, he would find out that she was a monster beneath the lace.

Accept.

She hesitated.

"Do me the honor of attending the show for tonight," Jacques said. "When you see what we do there, you can come to understand your role. And Briar, my dear, you have a role in this world."

Briar wanted a place in the world only so that she could burn it down—to unleash hellfire on those who treated her like she wasn't worthy of the air she breathed. There was a spark in Jacques's soft eyes that told her taking his hand was how she could achieve that. And so, Briar took it.

Music stretched her wondrous soliloquy through the air. Before Briar and Jacques set foot on the carnival grounds, she could hear it calling to her.

It was unlike anything she had ever heard. The music in the schoolhouse and church had been so monotonous, so saddened—as if pulling the joy from Briar's twisted bones and stealing what little she had. The realization that it had been suffocating her hit as this new music, bendy and fluid and playful, caressed her.

They stepped through the large sign that read *Jacques's Requiem.* The air seemed to change despite no real barrier separating the carnival and the rest of the world. It tasted like syrup on Briar's tongue, as though a cloud of sweetness had replaced the air.

"How long do you stay in one spot?" Briar asked over the cheerful din. The sun was still up, though slowly falling. Children ran all around with their buckled boots sinking into the trodden-on earth. Their shrieks of delight sliced through the cacophony of melody.

"A week at most," Jacques said. They walked alongside great tents with black and white stripes. The contrast from the green forest backdrop was startling—it would be impossible to miss if it rolled into town. There was a train in the distance, resting and waiting for the show to pack up and head for the next town. "We run two shows a day—though the grounds are open most of the day. We have two main events. One is family-friendly; trapeze acts and magic tricks. Occasionally, if the children are good, we add in a knife-throwing event."

A boy, about seven, stopped nearby, listening to the conversation with insatiable curiosity in his wide brown eyes.

"And if the children are naughty?" Briar asked loud enough that the boy would hear.

A laugh fell from Jacques, sweet like summer wine. "You don't want to find out." The boy scurried off, and Briar couldn't help but smile. "They're also permitted to see the tallest man and woman in the country, the hairiest, the fattest, strongest."

"What of the second show?"

"Ah, yes," Jacques said, guiding her to a handful of smaller tents clustered alongside the forest's fringe. "Somewhat more risqué, for adults only."

Briar felt her mother's hand wrap its claws around her heart, tightening. Everything she'd said of never finding love because of how horrible she appeared, inside and out, echoed in her head. That dull ache of knowing she would never have what others could—for why would anyone look past her physical state and see her as a human being aching for compassion?

Jacques, having never seen Briar beyond the veil, might come to care for her personality, but would certainly be scared away when he saw what she looked like. Briar bit her lip to hold back a sigh. She would stay a few nights and then leave, she decided. This was not the place for her. She would take what she could before she was caught in the act.

"Do go on," Briar said.

"You will have to see for yourself. I presume you are an adult?" Jacques asked, to which Briar nodded. People moved in and out of the tents—some in regular clothing, others in tight corsets that left little to the imagination. Jacques was detailing something about his seer, who told futures and fortunes—something about his name being Seven, for he had evaded death seven times so far. But Briar wasn't listening; she had caught sight of someone like her.

Her mother's words rippled through her thoughts. *Freak.* The nasty children at the schoolhouse taunted her. *Freak.* The whispers of neighbors in church. *Freak.*

"Oh, that's Eve, her sobriquet is Madame Eve. Isn't she a delight?" Jacques asked when he noticed Briar staring. "Born with most of her flesh marred and gnarled, hard and scaled like a snake's skin."

"She's…she's beautiful," Briar whispered. Eve had just emerged from her tent, wearing a snake-skin brassiere, shorts that went to her midriff, elbow-length satin gloves, and a real, live snake wrapped around her neck as though it were a scarf. Her thighs brushed together, her body shaped like a delicious pear, and her long black hair fell in lazy ringlets. Though she was shaped more like a woman than Briar, she bore her deformities with pride.

"A snake charmer—if you remain, expect to find snakes no matter where we go. They are drawn to her and seek warmth in our tents," Jacques warned. "But they will not harm you. You're not afraid of snakes, are you?"

You're a snake in the grass.

"No," Briar said, finding her voice again, despite how raspy it sounded.

"Excellent." Jacques clapped his hands and gestured to a tent. "This is yours. I've put provisions within. Clothing, jewelry, makeup, everything a young lady needs."

"I need none of those things," Briar snapped, then softened. "Pardon my outburst. I am not…"

"Used to charity?"

"I thank you for the gesture. I thank you for all the gestures."

"Wander tonight—get to know the grounds, meet the people. You won't find a better family; I can guarantee that. I'll put on a show I think you might find exhilarating," he said, stroking the whip that was attached to his hip.

Even though Jacques couldn't see it, Briar smiled as she slipped into her tent, one small lantern lit within. She studied the space; a cot with a few scratchy blankets folded at the end of it, a trunk tucked underneath. That was all she had, yet it was more than she had ever owned. She lifted the trunk onto the cot and opened it. Within was all-black clothing, similar to the rags she was wearing, but elegant—lace lining silk, elaborate embroidery along hems and collars. The jewelry would do her no good; the rings wouldn't fit upon her gnarled fingers, and the necklaces would only draw more attention to her hunched shoulders. Though, if she left, she could sell them.

At the bottom of the trunk, she spotted a handheld mirror. The handle was a carving of a woman, her arms holding the reflective glass surrounded by black filigree. Briar was stunned by its beauty. The irony of the mirror being far more beautiful than her wasn't lost on her. She sighed, putting the mirror back into the trunk and shutting it.

Heading back out into the night, she watched the cotton candy sky fade to blue. The stars came out to play, winking down at the carnival, and she followed the trodden path along to the main events. A carousel sat idle, and a giant man stood guard outside a tent labeled *Peep Show* while eager men queued. Purple smoke billowed from underneath a tent that promised futures and fortunes would be told. As Briar reached the big black- and white-striped tent, she heard Jacques's voice calling to the crowd and the crowd's thunderous applause and cheering. It was followed by the quick cracking of a whip, or maybe even two.

As she went to the entrance, another tent caught her eye. A soft sound of air being released from slightly parted lips, as though someone was blowing on her neck, lulled her. Her heels turned in the mud, and she cocked her head to the side. Following the impulse, she walked to the beige tent that had two torches on either side of the entrance, illuminating the snake embroidered on its front.

Briar looked around. There was no one lined up for this tent. *Curious.* Maybe Madame Eve had yet to start for the night. Parting the canvas, she peered in. Even with two torches right next to the entrance, inside was too dark for her to see anything. Despite the lack of any movement, something still beckoned her. She entered, letting the flap shut. Submerged in total darkness, Briar held her breath. All she could hear were the muffled cheers from the big top and the faintest movement all around the inside perimeter of the tent.

"Are you afraid?" The voice was husky, neither feminine nor masculine.

"Should I be?" Briar asked. She wasn't.

A gust of air filled the small space, like the entire tent was inhaling and then releasing one long sigh. "Do you fear nothing?"

"All my life, I feared," Briar admitted. "I've run dry."

The voice moved all around, as though it circled. "What do you feel now?"

"Hope, though I do pray I am not misguided."

"Pray? To whom do you pray?"

Briar felt a lump form in her throat. She thought back to when she prayed to the devil himself to give her the ability to fight back against her mother. "Whoever delivers," Briar said.

A faint glow appeared as though a candle held in a cupped palm was at the other end of the field, but the tent was not large enough for anyone to be standing so far away. As it grew larger or closer—Briar wasn't certain which—her surroundings took shape. The beige canvas walls showed themselves. Coiled around the surprisingly small space was a large python.

In the center of the room, Eve was lying upon a crimson chaise. She was nude in every sense, scaly flesh on full display. Her body boasted a perfection that Briar would never obtain—thick curves, rich black hair cascading in luscious waves down her body. One breast was covered by her hair, while the other was exposed. The only other imperfection was her hand, which was blackened as though burned.

It was in that hand that she held a bright red apple. Madame Eve brought it to her mouth and bit into the fruit. The crunch filled the small space. "I can taste your sin, Briar Black," Madame Eve said, "you taste of sweet nectar hiding a poison."

"An apple too ripe," Briar replied.

"No," Madame Eve said. She rose from her chaise, hair falling to her hips. Her blackened hand still held the apple and, with the other, she plucked a single seed. "Did you know apple seeds are poisonous?"

"I did not," Briar admitted.

"Sweet on the outside, poison on the inside." Eve smiled. "Tell me, Briar Black, do you ever hear the void?"

She shook her head. The sickly-sweet smell of a nearly rotten apple filled the air. Briar's head spun.

"Do you ever feel compelled to do something wicked? Something… evil?"

Briar swallowed. How many times had she wanted to hurt the people who hurt her? How many times had she stayed her hand to prevent herself from doing something she would regret? "Yes."

"Next time you hear the voice—listen."

Briar's first night as part of the Requiem filled her belly with fluttering moths. She had no knowledge of magic and potions, but Jacques promised her it would come naturally. Only time would tell whether he was fooling her for some malicious intent or telling the truth. But her belly was full, her clothes were new, and she had a roof over her head. A canvas roof, but shelter nonetheless.

Briar ran the comb through her sleek black hair over and over again. No matter how often she did it, the patches where it refused to grow showed. She was a child of autumn, a season so rich with color and beauty, but also the season of death's beginning. Her thin frame that refused to be perfectly upright, her hollow cheeks, her blackened eyes, her twisted lips—they were all proof she should not have been brought into this world.

She looked away from her hideous appearance and rose to stand in her living space—a tent so small that she could stretch her arms out and touch all the walls. A tiny cot with a trunk of clothing underneath was all she could call her own.

Half an hour later, she was seated on a myriad of pillows, rich reds and purples filling her performance tent. Jacques stood across from her.

"I simply request you give the people what they ask for. Whatever fleeting thought compels you to craft a potion, grind a pestle, whisper incantations…follow this intuition. You were born with a power you do not yet understand, but I promise you that, after tonight, you will have a richer understanding of yourself and your unparalleled abilities."

"We shall see."

"Oh, I love how you challenge me," Jacques said. He clapped his hands together and smiled. "I shall see you when the night has fled in fear of the sun." Briar rolled her eyes at his theatrics.

When Jacques left, her first patron ever entered. A young man her age sat down and wrung his hat in nervous hands.

"What is it you need?" she asked, uncertain.

"I, uh…" he stammered. "Tomorrow, I face a duel I am certain I will not survive. I need a potion that will make my adversary too ill to outdraw me."

Unsure how to concoct such a thing, Briar made a few hums and haws simply to give the impression she was thinking it over. Then a soft whisper filled her head, telling her to grind gypsophila. She pulled from the stores of dried herbs and flowers behind her, courtesy of Jacques. As she put the mortar and pestle before her to work, more whispers came. She added cinnamon, and the tent filled with its sweet smell. After she poured the contents into a small satchel, she handed it to the man. "Mix this with cream and ensure your adversary drinks his tea with it."

"Thank you," he said. As he reached for the satchel, Briar grabbed hold of his wrist.

"Coin is not the only cost," she said, uncertain where the command came from or what compelled her to say it. "I require a drop of blood."

"B-Blood?"

Briar grabbed a small blade from the array of items she had within reach. It glinted in the lantern. "One drop is all I ask."

The young man cleared his throat, then nodded. Briar flipped his hand so his palm faced her, then pricked the end of his fourth finger. The blood beaded like a snake emerging from hibernation. Briar slipped his hand underneath her veil and ran her tongue over the drop. He yanked his hand away in disgust, something Briar was at least used to, and fled the tent.

A shuddering gust of air escaped her lips, now painted with a drop of crimson.

The night continued this way. Patrons made strange requests, and Briar was somehow able to fulfill them. At the very least, she was giving them something they believed would work; she might never know how the potions and poisons turned out. Something told her that the whispers in her ear, however, were not leading her astray. With each patron, she took one drop of their blood.

Each one tasted sweeter than the last.

In her own tent, once the patrons had ceased visiting and the sky turned a soft blue, Briar pulled the veil back to wipe tears of exhaustion from her eyes. Her thumb trailed over her upturned nose and found it… smaller.

Her heart thundered in her chest as if it were trying to escape. She tore through the trunk of items Jacques purchased for her, digging out the handheld mirror she'd never intended to look into. Facing a dim reflection of herself, she wondered if perhaps her eyes were failing her.

Her nose had always been piglike. Until now.

Over and over, she ran her finger along the bridge, feeling no bumps or twists. Instead, she felt a nose that was perfectly straight, rounded at the end like a button. Her breath came in shudders, terror blended with fascination.

A movement of the canvas startled her. She pulled the veil back over her still-hideous face right as Jacques entered.

"What is this place?" Briar asked, her voice sharp as talons.

"A place where dreams come true. A requiem." He laced his fingers together. "Will you do me the honor of staying, Briar?"

How could she possibly say no?

Part III
The Cost

She cloaked herself in a black dress that hid her frame, her bulky shoulders. A veil that covered her face, like the caul she'd been born with, protected her from cruelty. Leaving her tent, she looked up at the stars smiling down from a sea of black. They mirrored the torches that lined the field where *Jacques's Requiem* was set up that week. It was her sixth week with the Requiem and the changes to her body were already noticeable. She stood straighter, her hair no longer had missing patches, her lips were perfect bows. She was not beautiful, but she was passable.

"Ah!" Jacques's voice rang through the air. "There is my eloquent dream queen."

Briar rolled her eyes, thankful for the veil. Jacques was in full dress—high black trousers lined with gold buttons. His tailed jacket was the brightest red, with gilded lapels and tassels, and black and white cuffs with golden trim. Attached to either hip were his whips.

"The crowd has lined up for you, my mysterious goddess," he said, slipping an arm around hers and guiding her to her small tent. As they neared, she could taste the sickening scent of the candles and incense. "Now, Briar, my bountiful beauty, will you be good tonight?" he asked, a pout on his lips.

"Good? Jacques, they do not come in droves for me to be good," Briar said. "They come and beg me for potions that will give their enemies warts, or spells to make the woman their spouses covet reek of sulfur. My sweet Jacques, how can I be *good* when all they ask of me is *evil*?"

"You exhaust me," he said. "But alas, your work proves to bring in coin and, for that, I accept your strangeness. Your refusal to let me gaze upon your face, your incessant need to wear this hideous *bag* of a dress, even your lack of a sobriquet perturbs me!"

"I exhaust you, but you respect me."

He smiled. "All my performers and showstoppers exhaust me, but only you interest me enough to frequent my dreams."

"Then let the thought of me continue to be a dream, lest the reveal of me haunt your nightmares."

"I suspect you are a beauty unparalleled underneath your veil." Briar shook her head in dismay. If only he knew. "Have you thought more about a stage name?" He broke apart from her and studied her frame for a moment. "You dress like a mistress of death…how about…the Mistress of Mystery?"

"Jacques…"

"The common people *love* alliterative names."

"My name is Briar."

"Yes, the thorn in my side."

"Do you not have a show to run?"

After Jacques had left and Briar had settled into her tent, people were let in one by one. They asked her for tonics, potions, spells, and all sorts of trickery to get their way. Her thirteenth patron of the evening, a pretty, young woman, sat across from her.

"What troubles you?" Briar asked.

The woman looked at her gloved hands, her round cheeks plump and full of life. Briar could see the divots where, should the woman smile, dimples would be prominent.

"My husband, he warms the bed of another woman, I'm certain of it."

"What is your name, child?" Briar often pretended she was an old crone. It made people believe she was more well-equipped for what they asked of her.

"Ana," she said.

"And what do you wish for me to do for you, Ana?"

"I want her…I want her dead."

Yes.

No one had requested such a thing before.

"Will you excuse me for a moment?" Briar asked, rising from the table and stumbling from the tent. She emerged into the crisp night air, free of incense and women asking for her aid in murder. Briar breathed deep, then hurried to Jacques's tent. She could hear the crowd cheering as he introduced the sword-swallowing act. Thunderous applause filled the air, and moments later, Jacques emerged. He ran his fingers through his slicked-back hair, then spotted Briar.

"Are you not occupied, Briar?" he asked.

"I am—I have encountered a strange situation I'm afraid I cannot face."

"Ah, ah, ah. You must give them all they ask for."

"She is asking me to murder someone."

"Tell me, Briar, what is it you wish for?"

She narrowed her eyes at him. "I do not know."

"To acquire what your heart desires, you must do all they ask."

"Even murder?"

"Is it your hand driving the knife? Is it your hand that pours the poison into their throats? Is it your intention to harm?"

"No."

"Then it is not your sin to carry but theirs."

"How can you approve of this?"

Jacques placed his hand on Briar's shoulder, no longer lower than the other, but even and sturdy. "My intent is not to serve the people, but to grant you everything your heart desires."

She tried to swallow but found only a lump in her throat, so large it felt as though an apple had been placed there. "You know, don't you?"

A charming, delicious smile crossed his lips. "I know the desires of all," he whispered in her ear.

Jacques strode off, beckoned by the applause from inside his tent. The sword-swallowing show was complete, and he had to announce the next performance. Briar turned and looked at her small tent. Over the past few weeks, she had changed, both in body and soul. With each cruelty she allowed, part of her changed into something beautiful. She wondered, as she walked back to the waiting Ana, what her insides must look like. Blackened and charred, damned to hellfire?

The wafting smell of lavender assaulted her senses as the dim candle-lit tent with the pretty blonde woman shrouded her. Without a word to Ana, Briar pulled herbs and liquids from the chest. The rank scent of carrion flowers overtook the lavender. The whispers told her to add a drop of her blood, so she grabbed a blade and pierced the tip of her smallest finger, letting a single red bead fall into the concoction. A cloud of smoke billowed, the poison bubbling violently, and then settled into a murky black death.

Briar's hand shook. She forced herself to steady it before handing the phial to Ana. "What is the woman's name?" she asked.

"Vanessa."

Briar's blood turned to ice in her veins.

Let your sin wash away the sins of the mother.

"Give me your hand," Briar said. Ana obeyed, and Briar went through the process of pricking her finger, then tasting the blood. Ana gasped not when the blade pierced her, but when Briar's tongue lapped up the sacrifice. "Do it tonight, before the sun rises," Briar told her through gritted teeth.

Ana nodded, slid a large satchel of coins across the table, and hurried out of the tent.

Briar closed for the night, exhausted by the weight of what she had done. The pit of her stomach was an empty void—a bundle of nerves that could not be soothed by drink. The show went on without her. Jacques's whips could be heard even in Briar's personal tent, where she sat on her cot and gripped the handheld mirror. Its ornate filigree was black like Briar's eyes. Though much of her body had smoothed out, she was merely passable. What she wanted was unparalleled beauty.

She waited until the night was kissed by dawn. As the sun began to rise, Briar watched the last of her ugliness slip off like the caul she was born with. It sloughed from her flesh—features changing right before her eyes until she was the epitome of what she considered beauty. High cheekbones, perfectly sculpted skull, proportioned nose and lips. Only her eyes did not change. Still black as tar.

Briar removed the veil from her lush black hair, rising from her cot. Leaving the mirror behind, she emerged from her tent, peeling away the layers hiding her beauty from the world. With each article of clothing, she found a plethora of confidence that radiated from her. She felt as though each footfall could singe the earth below her. Clad merely in a shift, she approached Jacques's tent. He was lying on his cot, tossing a bright red apple into the air and snatching it with quick reflexes. The veins in his forearms and slender hands protruded.

Beside him was Madame Eve, seated on a round stool low to the ground. She combed her fingers through her hair, snakes surrounding her feet.

"Must I become a mistress of death? Is this the cost of beauty?" she asked them, understanding now who they really were. The stories told in church were wrong—Eve was never tricked into eating the apple, into gaining the knowledge.

It was her choice.

Jacques sat up, apple in hand, and inhaled sharply when he laid his eyes on her for the first time. For a moment, he was speechless. When words finally came to him, they were breathy. "Beauty is pain."

"Not my pain, though, is it?"

"No," he said. "Theirs."

"Am I damned for eternity?"

"An eternity with me, should you have me," Jacques said. He stepped towards her and placed his hand on her smooth cheek, thumb caressing her bottom lip. Briar quivered. "You can still leave. Your soul is not yet tethered to mine unless you accept this gift."

"If I leave today, I lose everything I have gained here?"

"I'm afraid so." He held out the apple.

"Is it worth it?" Briar asked Madame Eve.

Yes.

"You know the cost. Do you accept, Mistress of Death?"

She slid her hands along his forearms, then grabbed the apple in his palm. He released it, watching her with the utmost respect as she brought it to her pink lips.

Briar bit into the apple, sacrament slipping down her chin.

CHAPTER TEN

THE UNVEILING

Erica Schaef

Miss Amelia Weatherford looked out the window of her private carriage. The sky was a deep, cloudless blue over the red-brick chimneys and slate rooftops. Brightly colored silk ribbons adorned the gas lamps lining the cobblestone street, catching the light of the early afternoon sun. The ribbons, she knew, marked the way to the carnival grounds, where a troupe of traveling performers had arrived nearly a full week earlier, causing a stir among the people of London.

At first, Miss Weatherford's mother, Lady Daniella Weatherford, had not wanted her to visit the midsummer amusement, deeming it a vulgar, low-class sort of entertainment. Eventually, Amelia's persistence, along with a promise to allow her strict and proper aunt, Lady Sarah Randolph, to be her chaperone, had been enough for her mother to permit one brief, afternoon excursion to the carnival.

Amelia found it hard to contain her excitement as the carriage continued. She was only able to do so by imagining her aunt's stern disapproval at any unladylike show of anticipation.

Lady Randolph sat across from Amelia, her face pinched in distaste as she watched the mass of pedestrians flowing toward the carnival grounds on either side of the carriage. "I did not expect such a crowd. And in this heat," she said, clicking her tongue, "it's absolutely stifling."

Amelia did not let her aunt's displeasure dampen her spirits. She only gave a polite nod and offered her fan to Lady Randolph, who declined it. When Amelia was finally helped down onto the stone street in front of the festival, she could not help the broad smile that spread across her face.

The air was alive with the smell of food and wood smoke. All around her, people were laughing and music was being played in loud, merry tones. She could practically feel Lady Randolph cringing beside her, but she paid it no mind. Today belonged to her, Amelia, and she was not going to waste one moment of her rare freedom. A thrill went through her as she allowed her senses to be beckoned by the sights and sounds of the carnival, and she wondered what adventures could be had.

Nicholas Gentry watched the tightrope walker's performance with waning interest. He had seen the routine dozens of times since the beginning of the season. Around him, the crowd let out a collective gasp as the performer feigned a loss of balance, only to right himself after a series of dramatic sways. Nicholas's eyes scanned the faces of the enraptured audience, stopping when they reached the beautiful countenance of a young woman in the front row.

Her wide, jade green eyes were intently focused on the performer, and her full, cupid's bow lips formed into a small 'o.' Nicholas sat up a little straighter, taking in the pale blonde hair neatly arranged beneath a pink sun bonnet and the slender, delicate neck exposed above a lace-embroidered collar. She had the youthful glow of innocence about her angelic, almost cherubic facial structure. The proportions of her upper body, from what he could make out, were *ideal*—her shoulders were slight above a tapering torso, which had been generously endowed with feminine curves. Though he could not see her hips, as she was seated, that was of the utmost importance.

Nicholas's gaze flicked to the older woman seated beside her. She wore a perpetual scowl in stark contrast to her companion's enthralled delight. Her beady, bear-like eyes looked out suspiciously from beneath the brim of her hat. She reminded Nicholas of a watchful scavenger bird, staring impatiently around her. He whispered something to the man seated to his right and then, for the first time in months, Nicholas smiled.

Amelia watched the equestrian performers with rapt attention. The way they balanced upon their mounts with nimble grace, leaping and spinning as though they stood on solid ground, made her heart race. It was like nothing she had ever experienced—a lively celebration brimming with music and color.

The end of the performance brought on a bitter edge of disappointment. As she stood, giving her enthusiastic applause along with the rest of the audience, she knew that her fun was over—that she would be returning to the constrictive, almost claustrophobic tedium of her everyday life. As she left the shelter of the tent, she saw that the early evening hour had brought with it a thin, low fog. It blanketed the ground, providing a mysterious, whimsical feel to the gathering twilight. Amelia slowed her steps, inhaling deeply as she savored the last moments of her reprieve.

Lady Randolph walked beside her niece, a delicate handkerchief held over her nose and mouth. "There is an awful stench out here. Make haste, Amelia, we are to have you home before nightfall."

"Yes, Aunt." Amelia stifled a sigh and quickened her pace with much reluctance.

She looked at the people around her as she moved through them. She noticed that they were of every class and social standing—something her mother most certainly would not approve of. Amelia, however, found the variety refreshing. She had grown tired of the same expressionless faces and indistinguishable drawing rooms in her mother's social circle. One face in particular caught her attention.

A tall, handsome man with dark hair was smiling at her from the periphery of the crowd. His eyes, so blue they were almost violet, caused her heart to skip and her breath to catch. Amelia felt herself blush and immediately averted her eyes, stifling a budding smile with the back of a lace-gloved hand. She gave her aunt a sidelong look, to see if her chaperone had noticed the wordless exchange between her and the handsome stranger. Fortunately, Lady Randolph's eyes were directed ahead of her, not at anyone in the crowd.

As they neared the front of the grounds, where their carriage would be waiting for them, Amelia and her aunt passed a group of workmen carrying brushes and containers of paint. One of the men, who happened to be looking back over his shoulder when they passed him, walked straight into Lady Randolph, spilling a large amount of red paint over the front of her muslin dress. She let out an indignant shriek and raised her hand as though to strike the man.

"Oh, my lady, so sorry," he mumbled. "That was right clumsy of me."

"Indeed," Lady Randolph hissed between clenched teeth. "The sheer carelessness," she breathed.

"My lady, please, there is a washbasin in the tent just there. I will retrieve a costume seamstress from the performer's area to see to your dress, I'm sure she can prevent it staining."

Amelia watched in astonishment as the man ushered a sputtering Lady Randolph toward one of the tents near the front of the grounds. She knew she would have to follow her chaperone but, for the moment, Amelia only stood, breathing in the balmy evening air.

"Do you like magic?" The voice was just behind her ear, making her start.

Amelia turned to see the handsome man she had noticed only moments before. "I'm sorry?" she asked, taking a step back.

"Magic," he repeated.

Before she had a chance to respond, he held his hand up to her, showing first the front, then the back of it. He reached toward her, brushing her cheek very gently with the side of his thumb as his fingers bent against the hair at the back of her ear.

She gasped at the contact and began to pull away from him. He retreated though, holding a large silver coin between his thumb and forefinger. Instinctively, Amelia reached back to feel behind her ear, but nothing was out of place. "How did you do that?" she asked, not bothering to stifle the grin that accompanied the words.

He looked down at her with those striking eyes and winked. Amelia's stomach fluttered in an unfamiliar, anticipatory sort of way. The sun was setting behind the stranger, streaking the sky with hues of pink and purple, their tones obscured by the rising fog. Crickets were beginning their nightly song in the park by the grounds, adding a melodic chorus to the approaching night. Amelia felt restless, eager for more of the excitement she was just beginning to taste.

"Are you intrigued?" the man asked, leaning back to study her face.

"Perhaps," she said, looking back over her shoulder to hide her blush. "I ought to see to my aunt. A man spilled paint on her dress, and she's been taken to—"

"What's your name?"

When she looked back at him, Amelia knew that the last thing she wanted to do was excuse herself from his presence. "Amelia," she said, biting her bottom lip as she considered the impropriety of their interaction. Her mother would be downright horrified if she could see her now. The thought amused Amelia and she gave a little laugh.

"What is it, Amelia?" the stranger asked, a smile forming on his own face.

"Nothing." She enjoyed the way he said her name. "It's just been quite an afternoon. And what should I call you?"

He studied her for another moment. "Come with me," he said, holding his hand out to her. "I want to show you something."

"Don't be ridiculous," she snapped, though her heart gave an elated little skip. "I asked what I should call you. What is your name?"

"Come on," he said, his deep blue eyes looking directly into hers, making her feel weak in the knees, "and I'll tell you."

Without pausing to consider the action, Amelia placed her gloved hand in his, looking back to make sure there was no sign of the imposing Lady Randolph behind her. "Only for a moment," she whispered in a breathless voice, "then I really must see how my aunt is faring."

She thrilled at the way his hand felt as it closed over hers; warm and strong, though he was being gentle. He led her back toward the center of the carnival grounds, to the entrance of a tent she had not had time to explore. Outside, there were painted signs reading *Magic, Oddities,* and, finally, *Witness the Astonishing.*

"What is this?" she asked, when the man stopped to hold open the flap of the tent for her.

"Something I think you'll enjoy, Amelia."

"But, sir, you are being really most absurd. You do not even know me," she argued, though she did not pull her hand from his. She knew what she was doing was not wise, but there were still quite a few people moving about at the carnival, and she did not see the harm in viewing just one more attraction before departing. Still, she felt like she ought to protest his brazen behavior.

"It's Nicholas," he said, looking into her eyes as his thumb exerted the slightest pressure on hers. "Come."

It felt like a dream—the fog, the man, the almost magical air the evening seemed charged with. Amelia bit her bottom lip again, telling herself that she would stay only a moment.

Inside, the tent was cramped with display cases and various pieces of furniture. Lit by candlelight, much of the space was cast into shadow, so that Amelia could not yet make out what was in the display cases. Nicholas released her hand to pull the flap of the tent shut behind him. "This is my collection," he said as he walked to stand in front of a glass display case.

"Your collection?" Amelia asked, taking a step forward. "Do you mean that you travel with the carnival?"

Nicholas turned to face her. "Does that surprise you?"

Amelia hesitated for a moment, allowing her eyes to adapt to the dimly lit space. "Yes," she said finally. He smiled, and Amelia felt the strange fluttering in her stomach again.

"I used to study medicine," he told her, crossing his arms. "In America. I was particularly fascinated by the anatomy of the human body and was immensely interested in coming to understand how it functioned. My studies were where I thrived, where I was the most…myself. In many areas of my life though, I was feeling restricted, weighed down by the expectations of others. A sentiment I think you may be able to sympathize with, Amelia."

She nodded. "I understand exactly. So, you gave up the study of medicine?"

"In a way, yes. Though, I am still able to pursue my interests through a more independent study. In any case, it was the freedom the carnival offered which really drew me to it. It came through the city I was living in a few summers ago, and something about the lifestyle, and the feeling of escape it provided…I never wanted to leave, so I didn't."

Amelia's heart beat wildly. The thought that a person could simply abandon everything that was stifling them and escape to this life of freedom and travel excited her greatly. Thoughts she knew she ought not be having sparked to life within her imagination—thoughts of herself as part of this mesmerizing, vibrant festival. She could so easily go with the carnival when it left the next day…

The thought was an absurd one, she knew, but she did not doubt that she would see this place again, over and over, in her dreams.

"Anyway," Nicholas was saying, "I did not bring you here to talk about myself. I wanted to show you my collection. I think you'll appreciate it. Here," he said, moving aside and gesturing to the display case he had been blocking, "have a look."

Amelia obeyed and approached, seeing that the case held the skeleton of some small animal. She bent to examine it. It was a very formidable-looking fish, with teeth like nothing she had ever seen. They were thin and sharply pointed at the ends, like exaggerated sewing needles. "What is it?" she asked, peering at the fish's unusual vertebrae.

"It's called a piranha. They are a carnivorous, freshwater species native to South America."

"Incredible." Amelia straightened, then moved to the next display case. The skeleton inside looked as though it consisted of one long, thin spine with dozens of symmetrical ribs running down its entire, winding length.

"A boa constrictor," came the response to her unspoken question.

"How did you get these?" Amelia asked, moving to the next display case, which held the skeleton of a small primate.

"Some were inherited from the man who ran this exhibit before I joined the carnival. Others I happened across in my own travels."

"How wonderfully exciting it all must be," Amelia sighed.

"It's getting dark," Nicholas said, cutting through her happiness like a blade. "But there's one more thing I would like to show you, if you are agreeable?"

"Yes." She nodded, attempting to keep the bitter disappointment from her voice. "Please do."

He held her hand again and led her to a large wooden cabinet at one end of the room. Excitement built with every step Amelia took. When he opened the door, she was surprised to see that the inside of the cabinet was empty. "I don't understand," she said, frowning.

"You want to stay here, don't you, Amelia?" Nicholas's breath on the back of her neck caused her skin to erupt in goose pimples.

She had not realized that he was standing so close behind her. He moved forward, so that she could just feel the gentle touch of his body against her back. Her breath caught. "Wh-what?" she stammered. Her mouth had gone dry.

"You want to stay. With me." The last two words were a whisper.

"Yes," she answered, surprised by the sound of her own voice uttering the word. "But—"

A hand clamped down painfully over her nose and mouth, pressing a damp cloth against her face. She struggled to turn her head, gagging on the sickly-sweet taste of whatever the cloth had been soaked in. Her arms were roughly pinned to her sides by one strong arm. She could not understand what was happening; it felt like she was drowning. She had one last glimpse of the empty cabinet in front of her before her world went black.

Nicholas worked quickly to bind the arms and legs of the unconscious woman. He even gagged her with a length of cloth, not that he thought the action especially necessary. She was unlikely to wake anytime soon.

He opened the false back of the magician's cabinet, then placed her limp body in the small space between that and the actual back. He watched her slow, shallow breathing for a moment to be sure she would not suffocate in her cramped position, then closed the false back.

He looked around at the tent. There was no sign, other than the pink sun bonnet at his feet, that Amelia had ever been inside. He picked up the hat and took it to a large trunk in one corner of the tent. Opening the case, he pulled out a new, more expensive suit, as well as a pair of round-rimmed spectacles, a briefcase, and a false, ginger-colored mustache. He applied the faux facial hair and removed the black wig he had been wearing to reveal cropped, ginger hair that matched the mustache. He changed into the suit, put on a bowler hat, and retrieved a cane. He placed the sun bonnet, as well as his original suit jacket, in the briefcase. Adopting a markedly stooped posture as he leaned on the cane carrying the briefcase, Nicholas exited from the back of the tent.

Night was falling. The fog threw everything into a strange, bluish haze. He walked toward the park at one edge of the carnival grounds, keeping to the shadows as much as he could, though there were not many people left strolling between the tents. When he reached the pine forest at the far end of the park, he hung the bonnet and the cheap suit jacket on a branch of one of the trees, so that they would be easily visible in the daylight. Inevitably, the young woman's disappearance would be investigated, the grounds would probably be crawling with policemen before midnight, and he wanted to leave this red herring to draw attention away from the carnival itself.

Perhaps they would conclude that Amelia had decided to run away with the handsome stranger she had doubtlessly been seen walking hand-in-hand with. Those sorts of scandalous things did happen in London—couples of different classes would occasionally elope, very unexpectedly, to Gretna Green. He really did not care what conclusion the investigators came to, so long as he was kept from suspicion. With any luck, the carnival would be allowed to depart from its current site in the morning, as was planned—taking him, along with his collection of oddities, and his slightly heavier magician's cabinet far away from here.

The first thing Amelia became aware of was the strange sensation of being rocked—a swift, unrelenting motion that made her feel sick to her stomach. She tried to let out a groan, but she couldn't. Her throat was incredibly sore and strangely…empty. Alarm brought her to full consciousness. Her eyes opened, only to be assaulted by a bright, blinding light. She tried to scream, but she had no voice—tried to open her mouth, but the muscles would not function. She could move her eyes and flare her nostrils, but the rest of her face had gone strangely numb and rigid. She tried to sit up but found that her body had been bound to whatever hard surface she lay on. Terror gripped her like an unyielding vice, and she struggled uselessly against her bindings. Everything hurt. She could smell blood; its harsh, coppery scent rising above others she didn't recognize.

"I think she's awake," a voice said from somewhere to the right.

"Good, she's come through the first portion of the operation surprisingly well." The second voice, Amelia knew, though her brain was too muddled by shock to place it. "Give her the chloroform."

A rag was held over Amelia's nose, and she remembered everything that had happened at the carnival quite clearly. The flash of memory lasted for only a moment before darkness overcame her once again.

Nicholas made careful incisions on both sides of the young woman's neck. He needed to be precise, but he also needed to move quickly. The swaying of the ship added another layer of complexity to the delicate operation.

Once the incisions had been made—two slanted, crimson lines—Nicholas used blunt vascular clamps to spread the subcutaneous tissue, creating pouches. With a fresh scalpel, he extended the pouches through thin layers of muscle, until he reached the spinal column.

"I need the gill arch implants," he told his friend and long-time assistant, George Wheeler.

"Here," said George, opening the box containing the implants, as well as a preservative liquid.

Nicholas washed the gill arches in a saline mixture before placing them in the pouches he had created. They had to be meticulously affixed to the spine by use of metal clamps. Nicholas was sweating profusely by the time he finished.

His next step was to add a row of gill filaments, which he had extracted from the same shark as the arches, and cut the gill slits in—five on each side. Then, finally, came the most dangerous part of the procedure. He was going to have to sever the young woman's trachea and attach it to the brachial system of the gills, then immerse the entire neck in salt water—all before she became hypoxic to the point of permanent brain injury or death.

He took a breath and looked down at the body on the table. The snake skin grafts, which covered her entire body and fused her from the thighs and downward, oozed bright red blood. That was a good thing; they were being oxygenated. Her lips he had excised, then sutured the muscles and subcutaneous tissue of her mouth together and covered the injury with snakeskin. He had amputated both of her feet at the ankles and attached the shark's tail fin there, the attachment points also covered in snakeskin. She looked so *believable*—this blood-soaked mermaid—that he could not abide the possibility of failing in this last portion of the operation. Once his new attraction was unveiled, he was going to be world-famous.

In the brief moment when her wide green eyes fluttered open, he knew he had made an admirable selection. The eyes looked nearly as amphibious as the rest of her, especially with the fish lenses he had painstakingly covered them with. His little mermaid was going to be the star of the show.

The pain was excruciating. It radiated over every part of Amelia, inside and out. It blocked out almost all conscious thought, though she was fighting to remember what had happened to her.

She had been badly injured somehow—perhaps on fire. That was what it felt like. Yes, that must have been it, because she was now immersed in water. Someone must have rescued her from a fire and submerged her in water. She did not remember it, but she did remember feeling panicked. Amelia wondered how long she had been in the water. It was all around her, even above her head. Her heart raced; in too much pain to even attempt to swim, she would drown if no one came to her rescue.

No one came. Still, she did not drown. She was completely underwater, but she was *breathing*. There was no act of inhaling through mouth or nose, yet she was not suffocating. Her throat and chest burned and ached, as though they had been scorched. She opened her eyes, her vision obscured by some kind of film, and reached up toward her face, but her arm felt strange and light.

As it entered her peripheral vision, Amelia was horrified; a wide, greenish fin moved up as she was trying to move her arm in the same direction. No…it could not be happening—this awful, hellish nightmare. She tried to open her mouth, but there was no mouth. There was nothing but fused muscle. She tried to move her head, but the action was exceedingly uncomfortable. Her neck held some strange weight, like a pressure that pressed directly on her spine. What had happened to her body, her face? Then, she remembered…

She remembered the hand clamping down on her mouth and nose in the carnival tent and waking up to the scent of blood as she lay upon a cold, hard table. She remembered the confusion, the pain, the pure helplessness of her situation. She remembered the man, Nicholas, and his striking blue eyes. His had been the voice she'd recognized when she had briefly woken, the one who'd ordered that chloroform be used on her. A surge of pain splintered through her body, shattering her thoughts into a thousand tiny fragments.

She peered through murky water. Was it truly murky, or was her vision strangely blurred? Her body was still rigid with pain. Chunks of algae floated nearby, drifting close to her face. There was glass a few feet in front of her. Beyond it, she could just make out the blurred image of a face staring back at her in astonishment. It moved away after a moment, only to be replaced almost instantly by another awestruck countenance. Amelia moved her legs—they were like one inflexible limb now. Nothing about her was familiar. Even her skin felt foreign and unnatural.

She cried with no voice, her tears welling up only to disappear into the cloudy water.

Nicholas beamed at the crowd surrounding his new attraction. They had come by the dozens—filing into the tent, money-in-hand, to see a real, live mermaid. Most of them, he could tell, had been expecting some simple hoax and were absolutely stunned to see the creature in the water tank.

She was beautiful—her torso, neck, and head having retained their shape, despite the snakeskin. Her gills and fins were seamless additions, and even Nicholas himself was impressed by the overall effect of his modifications. She was looking back at the crowd now, much to their astonishment.

"Can she talk?" one little boy near the front of the tank asked.

Nicholas shook his head. "She is more animal than human on the inside. As you see, she is perfectly content to be kept in captivity, quite like a goldfish in its bowl. Though, she does *look* rather more human than a goldfish, doesn't she?"

The little boy nodded, wide-eyed. "She sure does."

"Where did you find her?" a man near the back of the tent called out, craning his neck to get a better view of the mermaid.

"She was found in the Indian Ocean, near a small, previously uncharted island," Nicholas recited automatically. He had planned for such questions and had already fabricated a tale to account for the mysterious creature.

"Are there…more of them?" a young woman near the middle of the crowd asked.

"I believe that must be the case. Trust me when I tell you that we are working diligently to learn as much as we can about this phenomenal species. I am the first person in the world to have successfully discovered a mermaid and coaxed her into captivity. I intend to build my collection as I build my knowledge and understanding of her."

"Fascinating," the woman said, turning her gaze back to the tank.

Amelia was moving, bringing her tail up and down in a swift, jerking motion. People gasped and applauded, some even looking at Nicholas with undiluted admiration. His chest swelled at it. Finally, he was receiving recognition. Soon, he knew that he would have it on a global scale, with hundreds and then thousands of people pouring into the carnival to see the new attraction. Eventually, he would be able to give up traveling altogether—once word got around that the mermaid was a genuine specimen, the people, he did not doubt, would come to him.

He moved to the front of the tank, turning to see the display that would make him famous. Amelia's green eyes flashed to his, surprisingly vibrant and clear beyond the veil of salt water. His eyes fell to the blank stretch of snakeskin where her mouth had been. Yes, he truly was an amazing surgeon.

Then, he turned back to face the enamored crowd and smiled. They respected him, and he...he deserved this.

CHAPTER ELEVEN

ONE LAST CHANCE

Alexander Pearce

The remnants of Joe's final meal are stacked on the bare concrete floor, cold, congealed. He sits on his bunk, staring at the clock.

His execution is scheduled for ten P.M., but the clock in the hallway stopped long ago. For Joe, it's impossible to know if the clock's demise is a cruel, final torment or a blessing in disguise. He has spent two years in bare and familiar cells like this, during the many trials and retrials, until he was finally convicted. In those lonely hours, his mind always turns to Eliza.

He can conjure her azure eyes and blood-red lips with ease. He will never forget the way her red hair fell across her face when she laughed, or how she brushed it behind her ear, like it was such an inconvenience but would never wear it in any other style. The thought makes his stomach flutter in a way he doesn't deserve.

The Carnival Killer, the press had dubbed him.

Joe had been found guilty of killing four people, yet the papers hadn't focused on the carnies who died. Instead, every word they printed was about Eliza. They printed stories of Joe and Eliza growing up together, going to school together, and falling in love. They had photos of them from their yearbook, and long-winded accounts of their relationship from people who had no right to give them. But no one felt the pain of her loss like Joe. Since her death, he had wanted nothing more than to join her on the other side.

Now, he sits and waits for his wish to be granted.

The familiar sounds of the guard's boots on the concrete floor, accompanied by the tapping of more expensive shoes, disturb his macabre thoughts.

Out of view, two voices speak.

"He's in the next cell, Mayor Anderson."

"Thank you, son. I can take it from here." The mayor's unmistakable voice reverberates down the corridor.

"Are you sure, sir? This whole block is empty, seeing as no one's been executed in Massachusetts since '47. It might be dangerous."

"I assure you; I'll be fine. Joe and I go way back." Venom laces Mayor Anderson's every word.

When he comes into view, his expensive black suit is creased, and his eyes are puffy and red. Even from the other side of the cell, Joe can smell old booze. Before the mayor speaks, he pulls a small pistol from his jacket and rests it on the bars.

"What's that for, Mayor Anderson?" Joe asks, with little defense against the gun.

Mayor Anderson looks ready to shoot him, but takes a breath before speaking. "It's a way out, Joe. I've heard the electric chair is one hell of a bad way to go."

Joe shrugs, not risking a smile. "There are worse ways to go, I reckon."

"You sure? Because if they get the current wrong, it might take three or four goes to fry you. By then, your head will be nothing but molten flesh and bone. Your eyes will feel like lava in your skull, and every organ in your chest will burn as you've never felt before. How does that sound to you, Joe?" The sick pleasure on Mayor Anderson's face is palpable.

"Not good, I guess."

"No, not good. But this here, this is a way out." He taps the gun on the bars.

The hollow clang echoes in Joe's chest. "How so?"

"I ain't gonna spring you if that's what you're asking. But I know the warden here. He's a good friend of mine. He said that if you ended up with a bullet in your head, the report will say some overzealous guard thought you were trying to escape. For you, that means no long walk to the chair, no rubber diaper, and no pain. Just a blink and goodnight. Which, for the record, is more than I think you deserve."

"Is that why you're here? To save me from a bad death?"

"Not at all, Joe. I'm here because I want to know what happened to my baby girl the night you lost it. I want to know why you killed my Eliza."

Joe shakes his head. "I didn't kill her."

"I don't believe that, no one does. So, here it is. One last chance. Tell me everything. If you can persuade me that you didn't kill my daughter, then maybe I can get the governor to stay your execution while we look into it."

"I already spoke to the cops and the judge. My story hasn't changed."

"Oh, I know your story well. I had to listen to it in the courts for days at a time. It was an angel, right? A fucking angel killed her. Even though you were the only one alive at the scene, your arms wrapped around my Eliza." He chokes back a sob, wiping his nose with his sleeve.

The barrel of the gun never leaves Joe. "Mayor Anderson, I'm sorry that Eliza was there. I'm sorry for everything I've put you and your family through. But you must know I loved her more than anything. I didn't mean for this to happen."

"Don't you dare. Don't you dare even say her name. You got one chance, Joe. Tell me what happened at that carnival. Persuade me you're not the monster the world thinks you are."

"You sure you want to try again?" Eliza smirks as Joe rummages in his pocket for another dime.

The pyramid of cans at the back of the technicolored stall still stands even after four attempts to knock them down with a baseball.

"Of course, I do. You want a teddy bear; you're getting a teddy bear." He winks at her, and she rolls her eyes, trying to suppress her smile. Joe hands the money over to the carnie.

"Maybe you should listen to your girl, pal. I ain't seen anyone throw this bad since Texas."

"Hand over the ball, old-timer. I got this."

The carnie hands over three baseballs, shrugging his hunched shoulders.

"Kiss it for good luck?" Joe asks Eliza, and her face finally cracks into that perfect smile of hers.

"Just throw it!"

He throws the ball hard and straight, scattering the cans across the floor. Eliza jumps for joy, her Lemondrop-yellow summer dress rippling in the breeze. She throws herself into his arms and kisses him deeply.

The carnie throws Joe a bear, who gives it to Eliza. With dusk behind her and the orange sun falling beneath the horizon, she is more beautiful than he could ever imagine.

"Alright, alright, kids. Break it up. Take the prize and go get an ice cream to cool down after all that hard work."

Eliza laughs, letting Joe wrap an arm around her waist. Her hair brushes his face and smells of strawberries. The skin on the back of his neck prickles with delight. "Thank you, Joe."

"You're welcome."

They find a quiet part of the carnival and watch life pass by, enjoying some ice cream.

The carnival had arrived in Littlewhisper, Massachusetts, to great fanfare a few days ago. With the Cape Cod summer already in full swing, the place had been packed every night since they opened.

There are still plenty of people walking around, even as the cool sea breeze blows through the stalls and the sun settles over the horizon. Some pull on their jackets, others shove their hands in their pockets to fight off the chill.

"What do you want to do next?" Eliza asks as they watch a woman wrangle all five of her kids toward the exit with incredible efficiency.

Joe checks his watch and pulls a face. "We should probably go soon. Your dad said to be home by nine."

"I'm eighteen years old, Joe. My dad can wait."

"You know how your dad gets when his princess is late."

She knocks her hip into him, and he nearly drops his ice cream. "We can't go yet. We haven't even seen the freakshow."

"What freakshow? I didn't see a freakshow?"

"It's away from the rest of the carnival. I guess the owners didn't want to scare the kids."

"I'm not sure if—"

Before he can stop her, Eliza is already walking away. "C'mon, follow me."

Cursing how much trouble she always gets him into, Joe dutifully follows her into the darkness.

They buy their tickets to the freakshow from a small, well-lit booth and join the waiting crowd.

The eclectic group includes a pack of teenagers in leather jackets, huddled together, laughing amongst themselves. Other couples nod their hellos to Joe and Eliza. Most wait patiently, but a few tap their feet or check their watches like they have someplace else to be.

The show is held within a few tents connected by tunnels, all looking like they've seen better days. Seeing how only muck and grime hold the tents together, Joe starts to think that he's just been conned out of fifty cents. "Last chance to pull out if you're a chicken," Joe whispers in Eliza's ear.

She elbows him in the ribs. "Oh, hush now. This'll only take ten minutes. We'll be back in time."

Before Joe can respond, the lights are cut and a disembodied voice rings out. "Ladies and gentlemen, I commend you on your bravery."

One of the teenagers shrieks in mock fear. The sharp noise sets Joe's teeth on edge.

"You are about to enter a world from which there is no escape. Where nothing is what it seems. Please, come this way."

They soon find themselves in a tent with an uncomfortably low ceiling. The sickening smell of tobacco infects the air, threatening to make Joe's head spin. A single spot lamp illuminates a man on a small stage. He's much shorter than Joe, but his faded red velvet jacket and white shirt and braces strain against the muscle on his shoulders.

"My name is Chester Junior, and I am your guide for tonight's journey through the strange and macabre." He has a Midwest accent not often heard in Cape Cod. When he speaks, everyone listens. "I must warn you, those foolish enough to enter our freakshow only have themselves to blame for any repercussions. As I guide you through our terror tunnels,

189

I ask you to stay close to me and not touch any of our freaks. They don't like to be disturbed."

Eliza laughs as Joe raises one eyebrow at her.

"Come, now. Our story begins in an ancient and foreboding forest."

The crowd moves to the next tent, where Chester Junior climbs onto another stage that lights slowly. The backdrop is a painted mural of a full moon hanging over a forest of black trees. In the distance is a castle, its turrets piercing the night sky.

"Come closer, ladies and gentlemen, and allow me to regale you with our first tale." An expectant hush falls over the crowd. "The ancient forests of Germany are no place to be alone at night. They are full of the unknown and unseen, and the trees lean in, listening to your every word. The stars move while your back is turned, ensuring you never find your way home. And when the full moon rises in the east and casts an unholy light, it reveals other forest dwellers that should be avoided at all costs." Chester Junior cups his ear theatrically, listening to the silence. "Do you hear that?" His voice is quiet but clear. "I think something is coming."

A piercing howl shatters the silence.

Some people cover their ears. Others search wildly for the source.

A deep and throaty growl follows the howl. Even the teenagers stop their snickering.

"It's here! Stay back!" Chester Junior moves quickly as a wolfman tears onto the stage.

He is covered head-to-toe in coarse brown and black hair that pokes through tears in his clothes. Blue eyes stand out in ridiculous contrast to the black fur covering his face. The wolfman bounds from one side of the stage to the other, forcing the crowd to back away. He throws back his head and howls again, louder than before.

"Fear not, ladies and gentlemen, for this creature is chained and secure. You are all safe." True to his word, a chain is clasped around the wolfman's ankle.

"Have you ever seen anything like that before?" Eliza asks.

Joe shakes his head.

The wolfman throws his head back to howl at the moon. Only, this time, the wolfman chokes on the howl and starts a long and wet coughing fit.

"Must be a furball," someone shouts from the back.

The whole tent shakes with laughter, and Joe watches Eliza double over with it, her hands on her knees to catch a breath.

The wolfman pats his chest, still coughing, while Chester Junior starts to move them to the next tent. "I guess even the wolfman can get sick sometimes, folks. Let's move on."

As they leave, Joe hears the wolfman whisper to their guide, "Sorry, Junior, I've been howling all day. My throat's killing me."

Chester Junior gives him a withering stare before effortlessly switching back into character.

The next tent is smaller than the last, and the crowd stands uncomfortably close to fit inside. To Joe, the room smells of sticky and sweet cotton candy. An even more nauseous odor than the last tent, if there ever was one.

The backdrop is not as elaborate as the last. Instead of a forest, it is painted like a gray stone wall, with dripping green slime. Three skeletons are chained to it with their hands above their heads, bones stained yellow with age.

"Well, ladies and gentlemen, we're in trouble. Did you notice a castle back there with the wolfman? Way off in the distance? We're now entombed in its dungeon. Here, prisoners are chained and left until their skin and flesh all but rot away. But wait, is there still life in these ancient bones?"

A rattle of chains causes Eliza to start, her hand squeezing Joe's hard.

Bone clicks against iron with each slow and jerky movement as one of the skeletons begins to climb to its feet. The chain drags along the ground, keeping it in place.

A woman screams, hugging her boyfriend, who laughs with the rest of the group.

"I have to admit; it looks pretty real," Joe says to Eliza, who is standing slightly behind him.

"I-I'm not sure I like this." Her voice is quiet, the words meant only for him.

"We assure you that you are all safe," Chester Junior shouts as the skeleton gets close to the end of the stage. "This pathetic creature can no longer harm any of us. It can only watch as the world goes on around it. Maybe one day, it will find peace. Until then, it is time for us to move on."

But Joe can't leave, not until he figures out the illusion. He approaches the stage for a closer look.

To his dismay, the living skeleton is nothing more than a man so skinny that he has taken on the shape of a skeleton. His body is painted in an ancient yellow, with black used to hide his skin.

One of the teenagers throws a handful of popcorn on the stage, breaking the illusion for everyone else. "You look hungry, pal. Maybe you need to get yourself a burger."

The teenager throws more, and the skeleton stops his jerky and erratic movements, speaking to Chester Junior in what Joe assumes is German.

Chester Junior raises a hand to silence him. "Alright, kids. No more of your horseplay. Let's go to the final room so we can all call it a night."

They are led out of the room, and Joe can't help but mouth an apology to the skeleton man on stage.

He shakes his head in response. "*Kein problem, mein freund.*"

A closed curtain stops the group before they can enter the final tent. Eliza stifles a yawn, her hand falling back into Joe's.

"What's the holdup?" someone shouts, but Chester Junior shushes them.

His face is flushed with anger, and it's clear he wants to get the tour over with. "Please, ladies and gentlemen. We have visited the dark forests of Germany and the dungeons beneath an ancient castle. But the living skeleton is not the only creature to reside within its stone walls. In that very castle, fallen to earth a thousand years ago and confined forever by man, is a real-life angel." Chester Junior pauses with the nerve of a well-practiced orator. "I warn you; this is not like any creature you have seen before. It is dangerous, it is frightening. You may want to throw yourself on your knees and pray. I assure you, all these feelings are normal. We only ask that you do not approach the angel under any circumstances."

The curtain parts and they are walked into the biggest tent yet. It is divided in two, separated by a small fence. The other side of the fence is in total darkness. Their side is set up like a faux church, with pews and dog-eared bibles strewn about. Shafts of colored light pour in through fake stained-glass windows, and the smell of incense is thick.

Joe expects disappointment again, but Chester Junior has a wicked smile on his face. "No more stories, folks. Keep your voices low; we don't want to anger the angel. Now, let us pray."

The lights of the house of false worship slowly grow. Joe can see a shadow moving in the darkness, but little else.

As the lights rise, the angel takes form.

"Oh, my god." The words fall from Eliza's mouth.

In an ancient-looking cage is the creature called an angel.

But Joe fails to see any resemblance to the blonde, robed figures that adorn the frescoes of the Vatican.

This creature is nearly fifteen feet tall, its skin unnatural porcelain white. Black eyes take up much of the featureless face, and it is entirely hairless.

It raises a taloned hand to stop the glare from the harsh lights, letting out a soft groan. Joe feels a streak of pity for the creature, locked in a cell barely big enough for it to stand.

A bucket of popcorn flies over their heads and the group of teenagers pushes to the front. "That's not an angel; it's just a big, ugly guy."

The creature tries to spread its enormous, curved wings, but the cage is much too small, and the wings hang limply by its sides. They are not birds' wings as depicted on so many paintings throughout history; they are wings of impossibly-white skin stretched over sharp bones.

The terrifying sight rattles the crowd. Some look uneasily for the exit, crossing themselves. Others mutter quiet prayers under their breaths.

The creature snarls a guttural sound like nothing Joe has ever heard. It vibrates in the pit of his stomach, and he realizes the beast is speaking an ancient and unknown language.

Then the creature takes a step forward, leering down at the teenagers, who go quiet.

As it speaks, the mouth that stretches from ear to ear is teeming with teeth that are for nothing more than tearing flesh from bone.

Chester Junior drops his act as he starts pushing people towards the exit, harder than many of them expect. "Okay, show's over, folks. Come on, time to leave." Some linger, waiting to see what will happen. They crane their necks or push to the front, but Chester Junior pushes back. "I said it's time to go!"

One of the teenagers, quick to recover from the primal fear the creature instilled, jumps the barrier between them to get a better look. He knocks on the cage's bars, then howls with laughter. "Look, it's all phony!

The cage is made from wood!" He grabs the cage, pulling the wooden bar from its fitting. It comes off easily in his hands.

That's the only opening the creature needs.

It dives at the gap, throwing its arm through the cage and gripping the boy's head in one colossal hand.

The boy's squeal is cut into a choke as he is lifted off the ground.

Without thinking, Joe rushes to help. He clears the small fence in a leap and feels Chester Junior close beside him. Eliza shouts but he can't hear her words.

Joe grabs the boy. Chester Junior pulls a nasty-looking blade from his jacket and slashes at the creature's arm. A spray of something warm and black hits Joe.

The creature lets go of the boy, who lands half on his feet and half against Joe. Joe's only thought is to drag him back to the fence, but he can't turn fast enough.

The creature takes a final swing, catching Joe's shoulder with its razor-like talons.

A searing pulse of pain scorches through his entire nervous system, taking the wind from him and dropping him to one knee. He has just enough time to see Chester Junior shove the bar back in place on the cage before Eliza drags him over the fence and out into the cooling night air.

Joe wipes the creature's blood off his face with his sleeve and checks Eliza over. The boy he helped runs off into the night with his friends, keen to be anywhere but the carnival.

"Are you okay?" Joe asks Eliza, seeing that she is a sickly shade of green.

"Me? I'm fine! You're the one who's bleeding!" Eliza turns him around to look at his shoulder.

He winces as she touches the tender flesh near the wound. "It got me pretty good." The searing sensation that had racked his body leaves lingering needles of pain in his joints, but the worst has passed.

Chester Junior appears from the tent, his face is red with effort. From inside, they hear men shouting and the angel screeching.

Eliza rushes at him, jabbing her finger in his face. "What the hell happened in there? Why did that thing attack us?"

"We'll give you a full refund, miss. Now lower your voice, alright?"

"'Lower my voice? Why? Don't you want people to hear how dangerous this place is?"

Chester Junior squares up to her. His calm words don't match the rage on his face. "I said to stay behind the fence. Your boyfriend here ignored me. He's lucky I don't press charges."

Joe steps between them, placing a hand on Chester Junior's shoulder. "Take it easy, pal. That kid was about to get really hurt."

The other man shoves him away, causing another burst of pain in his shoulder. "No one was going to get hurt, stop making a scene about it, alright? All that happened here was our actor got a little too carried away, and those fake claws of his are pretty sharp. That's all. Just go sleep it off, kid, you'll be fine."

Chester Junior smooths his hair down as Joe holds Eliza back. When he spots the wound on Joe's shoulder, a flash of fear passes his face but disappears as quickly as it appeared. He steps close to Joe and whispers so only he can hear, "I don't want to make a problem for you or your girl, alright? So beat it, or the pair of you will be limping home."

Joe pulls his fist, ready to deck the nasty little man, but Eliza grabs his hand. "Don't Joe." Her wide eyes stare up at him, and the anger melts away.

It might make him feel better to break the guy's jaw, but he can't put Eliza in danger. If she got hurt, he could never forgive himself. "C'mon, let's get out of here," he mutters.

She nods and they make the slow walk back to Eliza's home, where Joe hopes Mrs. Anderson can stitch up both his jacket and his shoulder.

Their walk home had been slow, following the roads instead of cutting through the forest.

With the wound cleaned and dressed, Joe quickly falls asleep in the Andersons' spare room. Never in Eliza's, that's Mayor Anderson's golden rule.

But Joe's sleep is not restful; he is assaulted relentlessly by wicked dreams.

He watches as the angel falls to Earth from a crack in the sky, cast out from somewhere else. It's so real, Joe can smell the burnt foliage and feel the heat pumping from its porcelain skin. Lying there on the forest floor, the crack in the sky closing rapidly, it feels pain for the first time in its existence.

As it tries to fathom all the information in this new plane of existence, a group of hunters comes upon it. The angel can smell the fear encoded in their every cell.

They attack in panic, and it tries to fight them off. Some men die, but the angel is still getting used to pain. They eventually subdue it, locking it away, ensuring daylight will never again touch its skin.

The entire thousand years of bondage are shown to Joe in the blink of an eye, and he hears the angel calling out to him in its unknowable language. It calls across space and time to be freed of its damnation.

When Joe wakes, slick with sweat and his shoulder burning like hellfire, he feels a thousand years older. But the angel's voice is still in his head, calling for him to save it from its torment.

Listening only to the angel, he pulls on his torn and bloody clothes, and sneaks down the stairs of the Anderson mansion.

The clock in the kitchen says it's two in the morning.

Before he reaches the back door, a voice from behind makes him jump.

"What the hell are you doing?"

Eliza stands in the kitchen doorway wearing a nightdress that ends just above her knees. In the dim light, worry is etched on her face.

"Go back to bed, Eliza."

She covers the kitchen in five nimble steps, grabbing Joe's arm. He nearly lets out a scream as she twists it just enough for the scabs on his wound to break. "You can't go anywhere like this. And it's two in the morning, for Christ's sake."

"But I have to; it's calling to me." To Joe, it sounds like someone else is borrowing his throat, so alien are his words. "We need to set it free."

"Set what free? Joe, you're not making any sense."

"The angel, from the carnival! I can hear it calling out to me."

She steps back, crossing her arms. "Do you have a fever? Maybe I should call—"

Joe puts his hand over her mouth. The usual smell of strawberries clings sickeningly to the back of his throat. "No, call no one. I need to do this."

She shoves him off. "The hell you do. The angel wasn't even real. As Chester—or whatever his name was—said, it was just a guy in a costume who got over-excited."

Joe shakes his head, smirking. "No, you're wrong. I saw it up close; it touched me. I know it's real. You don't have to believe me. But you will when you see the angel flying over Littlewhisper. You will."

Eliza knows him well enough to know he won't change his mind. "Well, I won't let you go alone. Not the state you're in. Give me one minute. I'll be back, I promise."

She doesn't wait for a response, leaving him alone with the constant calling in his mind. The angel can feel him not moving, and it sends a surge of nervous energy through his body, demanding he leave her.

But he holds off, fidgeting on the spot as the seconds tick by.

True to her word, Eliza is back and dressed within a minute. She opens the back door soundlessly. They don't speak until they are at the top of their long driveway and well away from anyone's earshot.

The night air is cool and damp on Joe's skin, helping with the fever that has crept up on him.

"Are you sure we can't wait until the morning?" she asks.

"No, we have to do this now."

"Okay then, well, I brought this just in case." She pulls her dad's old army service M1911 pistol from her waistband. The silver gun, glistening in the moonlight, looks so big, too big.

"Holy shit, what are you going to do with that?"

"That thing—whatever it is—nearly took your arm off today. We need protection."

With no time to argue, Joe follows Eliza into the night.

It takes nearly an hour to get back to the carnival. Each step towards the angel is uncomfortable as the fever spreads through Joe's body. With it comes a dull ache in his bones that he can't shift. Every time Eliza tries to support him, he brushes her off with a grunt. All the while, the angel calls to him, each call more desperate than the last.

Standing in the shadows of gnarled pine trees, they survey the carnival. Most tents and trailers are cloaked in darkness, but some still have oil lamps dripping light into the night.

"Do you know where we're going?"

The sky is moonless, and the stars seem dull, but Joe will find the angel blindfolded if he has to. All he must do is follow the agonizing calls of despair he hears in his mind. "This way." Joe's words are a whisper, masked by the rustle of an ancient pine tree.

Eliza follows close, her short breaths sounding impossibly loud to Joe.

When they reach the sealed exit in the tent, another voice begins to whisper to Joe. It's the same voice that told him to ask Eliza to kiss the baseball for good luck. Somehow it makes itself heard over the angel's constant wails of torment. The voice tells him he's sick, and the wound on his shoulder is infected. He needs a hospital, not to be sneaking around in a tent.

The voice is his own.

But the angels sobbing drowns it out swiftly, bringing tears to Joe's eyes. He wipes them away subtly.

"What's the plan?" Eliza asks, taking the pistol from her waistband.

It makes Joe uncomfortable. "It's simple. Get in there, break the bars to set the angel free, then run like the devil is chasing us."

And to Joe, it does sound simple, and Eliza nods.

When they cross the tent threshold, only one oil lamp burns next to the cage. To both Joe's dismay and joy, the creature is precisely where they left it.

The angel is lying in its cage, knees tucked up to its chin and wings folded around itself for warmth.

An excruciating rage ignites in Joe. He wants to smash the wooden bars to pieces and end the millennia of torment the angel has suffered.

Eliza grips his shirt before he can charge in.

He winces at the sharp pain in his shoulder. "What?" he demands through clenched teeth.

"Look, that's the guy from before."

Chester Junior is sitting near the cage, his cap pulled down over his face. He snores quietly.

"Why would they guard it if it's just a man?" Joe asks, smugly.

"I-I don't know."

"You know why, Eliza. C'mon, let's do this."

"But we don't know what it really is. Please, Joe. Let's go back and speak to my parents. This is too much for us. My dad can get Littlewhisper police in here to—"

But no such thought can enter Joe's mind. He is focused on his mission now, nothing else matters. "You've got the gun, so keep it pointed at him in case he wakes up." Joe starts down the offensive faux church, ignoring her hissed pleas for him to stop.

The angel stirs in its cage, standing noiselessly. It looks different now, different from the creature he saw in his dreams. The angel's black eyes stare down at him, and Joe sees no fear or emotion. Just a dark void.

In the flickering shadows of the oil lamp, the angel looks like a creature that should be locked away from humanity. But it knows Joe is here to help; Joe hears its voice again and the anesthetic calm of its words washes over him. He reaches for the wooden bars, only halted by the sound of a bottle skittering across the floor.

"Shit, sorry," Eliza whispers, but Chester Junior is already leaping to his feet, kicking his chair away in the process.

"What the fuck?"

Eliza fumbles with the pistol, pointing it at his chest, and Joe's stomach drops. "Don't move, please." Her voice is barely a whisper, quivering like tears are close.

"What's going on here?" Chester Junior asks, his eyes flickering between the two of them.

"We're setting the angel free, as you should have long ago." Joe's voice sounds more assertive than the queasy feeling in his stomach should allow.

Chester Junior raises his hands. "You don't want to do that, kid. Seriously, step away from the cage."

"Look at it. It can't even open its wings." Joe watches the angel bare its teeth. There are no tears on the outside, no calling for help. But inside, the angel is in such insufferable torment, he's sure of it.

While Joe is distracted, Chester Junior shouts, "Hey, Pop! You might want to come in here."

Two men enter the tent and Eliza steps closer to Joe.

The first is unmistakably the skeleton from the freakshow. He looks more like a scarecrow without the greasepaint. The other man looks about sixty, with thin, gray hair and a slight beer gut that comes to most men at that age. But his arms are still broad, bulging under his shirt. The tattoos that cover them have turned blue with age.

"Would you care to tell me why you're pointing a gun at my son there, miss?" The older man's gray eyes flicker between Joe and Eliza.

Eliza stammers, "I-I'm sorry. We didn't want it to be like this—"

Joe cuts her off. "We're here to set the angel free. You've imprisoned something ancient and beautiful for so long, against the will of God."

The angel towers over them all, its wings twitching noiselessly.

The old man runs a hand over his stubble. "Boy, let me tell you now, God has nothing to do with this creature."

"He's the one who got scratched today, Dad." Chester Junior's eyes, gray like his father's, are fixed on the angel. It licks its lips, and Joe thinks he spots a forked tongue like a lizard.

"Christ, not another one. Let me guess, kid. You went home, had nightmares that this thing needs rescuing? Now it's speaking to you and telling you to rescue it? Got a fever as well, by the looks of it."

"H-how did you know?"

The old man shrugs. "It's what it does. It's what it always does when someone gets too close to the bars. Some type of infection is my theory, but I ain't a doctor."

"Then it is real? It's a real angel?" Eliza asks uncertainly.

The old man looks thoughtfully at her before nodding. "I think so, or at least it was an angel. So does my friend Oskar here. He and his whole Order did."

The skeleton man nods, his eyes not moving from Joe's hands on the bars.

"Then how did you find it?" Joe asks, wanting to catch them in their lies.

"You already know the story." The old man points behind them.

"What? That shit about the castle?"

"It's not shit, kid."

"I don't understand." Eliza starts to lower the gun, but one look from Joe steadies her hand.

"That forest my son told you about? That was the forest surrounding Buchenwald. I was there in 1945."

"Buchenwald. I know that name." Eliza looks to Joe, unable to hide her fear any longer.

"I was with the 6th Armored when we liberated the concentration camp there. People think the fighting stopped when the war ended in September 1945. But it didn't, not really. We had to comb every scrap of the woods for the SS bastards that tried to escape. I got separated one evening after a heavy firefight. There was this castle, the turrets just about visible over the trees. We held most of the castles in the region, so I thought, so I made my way there. On the way through that cursed forest, I was attacked by a pack of wolves like nothing I'd ever seen. Those things were as big as horses, and bullets all but bounced off them.

"I managed to take one of them out, but they chased me to the castle portcullis then stopped dead, slinking off into the night. Because it wasn't no castle, you see. It was a monastery. And an old one, at that. The door was open, but the place was empty. Plenty of army stuff, though. Guns, radios, and flags. The usual. I looked for survivors. There had to be someone left, I figured. So, I followed the wiring and the electrics down into the dungeon. That's where I found Oskar here chained to a wall. He was close to death, left for days with nothing but a trickle of rainwater coming through the bricks."

Joe looks to Oskar, who stares unflinchingly back.

"He was part of an order of monks who had been guarding this beast here for centuries. Then the Nazis came and tried to weaponize it, but it never worked. When the Nazis got wind of Buchenwald falling, they scattered like rats from a sinking ship."

Joe's head thuds heavily with the old man's words. But the angel's voice comes back almost immediately, soothing the sickness in him.

"Of course, I didn't believe him when he told me about the angel. I had to see it for myself. I carried Oskar further down into the tunnels until I found our angel in a wooden cage. The same one it's in now."

Joe's rational mind tries to push through the fog obscuring it. A million questions come through but are blocked in his throat.

Eliza isn't having the same issue, though. "But why did the monks lock it up in the first place? Shouldn't an angel be, I don't know, revered? Instead, they locked it up with wooden bars?"

Oskar speaks, his accent heavy, but his pronunciation is perfect. "The Order imprisoned the angel because we knew it to be an unholy abomination. We spent centuries trying to kill it, using all methods of death developed by scientific advancement, but it always survived. As for the wood, I must be honest. I am not sure why the angel will not break those bars. They are inscribed with a language lost long ago, which repels the creature by burning it at the slightest touch."

Oskar's words are a garbled mess in Joe's ears, yet he is certain every one of them is a lie.

Eliza turns to him, lowering the gun slightly. Her eyes question everything he knows to be true about the angel.

"Don't believe them, Eliza. They're monsters! They're the ones who should be in a cage!"

"You don't believe me?" Oskar shakes his head slowly. "I watched my entire order get fed to this creature. I watched the Nazis try their best to control it but fail on every attempt. I assure you, the story is true."

"Joe, this sounds wrong. Monks kept this thing locked up. Even the Nazis were scared of it. That's not an angel. That's something else."

The old man speaks again, his arms crossed tightly. "There you have it, kid. We know that you won't believe us no matter what we say. You got scratched, and that means you're sick. You need to go home, rest and, in a few days, you'll be fine. I promise."

Chester Junior takes a step closer to Joe, who grips the bars harder. "Fuck you! Stay back!" he shouts.

"Joe, I think he's right. You need a doctor. That wound looks bad."

"He's lying to us, Eliza! Don't you see?"

"No, it's you who can't see Joe. Whatever that creature is, it's not an angel. It's something dark. Step back from the cage. Let's get you to a hospital."

But Joe can't—won't—abandon the angel.

"Is it still calling out to you?" Chester Junior asks. "Is its voice full of human emotion? Look at that thing and tell me you see anything close to human emotion."

"All lies, Eliza. Just shoot him and shut him up."

"What? It's not even loaded."

The carnies exchange a look and Joe feels his window of opportunity closing.

"Yours might not be loaded," Chester Junior says, reaching into his jacket, "but mine is." His hands dwarf his stubby revolver. It looks old and worn.

Or well-used.

He thumbs back the hammer with a mechanical click. "This can go one of two ways, kid. Either you take your hands off that cage and we get you to the hospital. Hell, I'm sure your girl's daddy will want to know where his pistol got to."

Eliza flashes him a nervous look.

"Or I shoot you and your dead hands fall off the cage. Either way, the results are the same."

Joe knows he's lost Eliza as she lowers the useless pistol. Her eyes, usually so vivid, are clouded with fear.

But the angel grips him once more, infecting his mind.

He gives in.

"It's too late. The angel must be free."

Joe yanks two of the bars hard. They snap like twigs, falling away in his hands. He quickly pulls the third and fourth away.

The angel dives for the gap, hitting Joe like a bull and throwing him ten feet backwards. He lands with bone-crunching force on the fake wooden pews. The world around him swirls in a vortex as blood trickles from a wound on his head. Through blurry eyes, he watches the angel stretch to its full height.

Chester Senior fires the pistol twice before his body is torn to pieces in a dense cloud of crimson. The other men do their best to attack it but are dispatched with nothing more than a swipe of its claws and a bite through Oskar's neck.

Their screams are replaced with wet, sickening ripping noises. As unconsciousness beckons, he feels Eliza's hand slip into his, slick with the blood of those who had tried to warn him. The warmth brings Joe's sight back for a final moment.

"Joe, please help me."

Then she is gone, wrenched away by the angel.

The world fades to black for Joe, but Eliza's screams accompany him into an unconsciousness that he hopes he never wakes from.

Mayor Anderson is quiet when Joe finishes speaking. Tears pour down his face, but his fists are clenched so tightly, his knuckles turn white on the pistol. "So that's what you're sticking to?"

"It's the truth." Joe stands, leaning against the cold concrete wall.

"Bullshit. Do you know what I think? I think you killed them all. I think you killed them and chopped them up into little pieces. I think you killed my Eliza."

The last sentence hurts Joe as much as it always has. Shame burns his face, but he doesn't break eye contact. "No, sir. I would never hurt her."

"Oh, but you did, Joe Ludlow. You hurt her in so many ways." Mayor Anderson looks up and down the corridor before aiming the pistol barrel on Joe again.

Joe doesn't move; he has nowhere to go. "Even after all this time, you don't believe me?"

"Of course not. It was all some pantomime to save your sorry ass from the chair."

Joe smiles with only his mouth. "And look how that turned out." Joe laughs humorlessly, then turns to rummage under his pillow. "Have you read much of the news recently?" Joe asks, approaching the bars with a copy of the Littlewhisper Herald newspaper.

The mayor doesn't take it from him. "Where did you get that?"

Joe pushes the paper through the bars. "Fifth page, bottom left corner."

Mayor Anderson relents, accepting it. It's dated only a few days ago. He flips to page five, to a small article hidden beneath a vacuum cleaner advertisement.

It's about the bird of prey attacking livestock on the east coast. In an unrelated occurrence, the number of missing people cases in rural Massachusetts has increased by twenty percent in the last twelve months, with no bodies found.

"It's still out there. That thing that killed Eliza. The carnies were right. It may once have been an angel, but it's not anymore. The whole world is in danger with it on the loose."

Mayor Anderson screws up the newspaper, throwing it back at Joe. "You sick son of a bitch. After everything you've done to me and my family, now you try to pull this shit? My daughter died because of you, at least have the decency to do the same."

Mayor Anderson pulls the trigger.

The bullet hits Joe's stomach like a truck. He feels muscles split and bones shatter. The noise seems to echo forever in his ears. Doubled over with pain, he drops to his knees. Hands tacky with blood, he reaches for the discarded newspaper.

As Mayor Anderson lines up a second shot, he spots a picture of Eliza that he had given the Littlewhisper Herald long ago. It's small, but it's certainly her.

Joe holds it tight to his chest and whispers her name. "I'm sorry. I'll see you soon."

Then he's gone, his eyes glazed over, his legs twitching uselessly.

The racket of the guards charging towards him, demanding he drop his weapon, sounds dull to Mayor Anderson.

As rough hands shove him to the ground, he does not feel satisfaction, as he had expected. Instead, there is only a gnawing sensation, like rats in his stomach, that Joe Ludlow may have been telling the truth.

ACKNOWLEDGMENTS

As with all our publications, Carnival Macabre would not be possible without the help of some dedicated Crows. I would first like to thank our Assistant Editor, Damon Barret Roe. This anthology would not have been possible without her. Assisted by our Acquisitions Editor, Stephen Black, we were able to sort through the mass quantity of submissions to pick out these amazing stories. I am grateful for them both. Damon also tirelessly led the Editing Team through this process, and I would like to extend my gratitude to the members of this team, including K.R. Wieland, JayLynn Watkins, and our newest Novel Editor, Eli Hayden Loft. I am always so honored to work alongside the Quill & Crow Editing Team, and this project was no exception.

Back for her fourth and final anthology, Marie Casey led the creative design efforts, from the perfect antique cover to the beautiful eBook. As with all our anthologies, this one would not be possible without her, and I hope you appreciate the unique artistic touch she brings to Quill & Crow projects.

Lastly, I'd like to thank all the authors who contributed their stories. After a few strictly Gothic collections, I was looking forward to getting back to our horror roots. I thoroughly enjoyed every one of these tales. I love when writers are able to capture the vibe I'm looking for in an anthology, and each one delivered. Working on this anthology has been an enjoyable experience through and through, and I hope you've enjoyed reading it as well. I appreciate everyone's efforts and look forward to seeing what more we can come up with as a publishing house.

Dreadfully Yours,
Cassandra L. Thompson

AUTHOR BIOGRAPHIES

BRAD ACEVEDO is a self-published horror writer, also featured in publications by Jazz House and Quill & Crow Publishing House. Geocacher, purveyor of the odd & quirky, may or may not be a Wendigo.

VALERIE ALEXANDER has been published in a number of anthologies, as well as outlets like LampLight, Dark Moon Digest, and others.

FOX CLARET HILL is a transgender horror fiction writer who aims to aid the representation of the LGBTQ community in his favorite genre via his work. Born in America and raised in England, Fox currently resides by the beach in Australia with his husband and their two dogs, Herbie and Gizmo. He also hosts two podcasts, Goreporium & The Web Surfers, with his younger sister. Despite writing fiction secretly for years, Fox primarily worked with non-fiction as a proofreader and honed his typing skills as a transcriptionist and captioner. Only in 2021 did he push himself towards the goal of being a published horror author and was first published in February 2022.

KATERINI KORAKI is a speculative fiction writer based in New York. You can find her work published in Luna Station Quarterly and Alternating Current, among other places. When she's not writing, you can find her drinking iced lattes, rearranging her bookshelves, and crocheting up a storm. Say hello to her online at katerinikoraki.com

ALEXANDER PEARCE was born in 1990 near Liverpool in the UK. He lives in a small industrial town in the northwest of England where he has been a fan of Gothic and the macabre for as long as he can remember. When he's not editing his debut novel about a beautiful Cape Cod town that has enough skeletons in its closet to fill a graveyard, he is gaming or working through his backlog of unread books.

DANIEL R. ROBICHAUD lives and writes in Humble, Texas. His fiction has been collected in Hauntings & Happenstances: Autumn Stories as well as Gathered Flowers, Stones, and Bones: Fabulist Tales, both from Twice Told Tales Press. He writes weekly reviews of film and fiction at the Considering Stories website.

CRAIG E. SAWYER is an American writer known for horror, crime, western, and sci-fi. He is a direct descendant of the McCoy family that famously feuded against the Hatfields over a stolen pig, and has been published by Shotgun Honey, Weirdbook, Schlock Publications, Crystal Lake Press, Nightmare Press, Monkeys Fighting Robots, Levy-Gardner-Laven Productions, and Skull Dust Press. He is the creator of the horror/adventure comic "The Forbidden Museum," and the RPG sci-fi board game Escape from Dulce. Craig traveled much of the United States, eventually settling on the West Coast, where he slept on rooftops in Venice. Before becoming a writer, he worked as a bartender, carpet weaver, roofer, bouncer, Shakespearean actor, and stagehand.

ERICA SCHAEF is an author of dark fiction and Affiliate Writer member of the Horror Writers Association. Her novella, "This Cold Night," will be released from Brigids Gate Press in December of 2022. She lives in rural Tennessee with her husband and two wild children.

EDDINS SINCLAIR is the pen name for Russell Brickey, a poet currently living in the Rust Belt with his wife and two little dogs. Eddins Sinclair's two novels about the war between the Vampire and Zombie nations, *Z vs. V: The War of the Undead* and *Z vs. V: At the Forest Edge*, can be found on Amazon. Russell Brickey has poetry collections out from

Spuyten Duyvil Press, Wild Leaf Press, and Kelsay Books. Both authors grew up in Oregon where their stories take place.

SABRINA VOERMAN is a pantser in life and in her writing. While she loves almost every genre under the sun, she often gravitates towards the dark, macabre, and morally gray. She is currently publishing her *Blood Bound Series*, which are dark fairy tale retellings for adults. When she isn't writing, reading, or studying, she is exploring the expanse of nature on Vancouver Island.

AMY WESTPHAL is an artist of canvas, cake, and words. As a former gallery artist turned cake designer, now author—this Mrs., Mama, and sometimes dragon, lives for creativity and excessive em—dashes.

TRIGGER INDEX

- Addiction & alcoholism
  Goblin Market
  The Secret Showing on the Midway of Dreams

- Alcohol/drug use
  Goblin Market
  The Secret Showing on the Midway of Dreams

- Animal cruelty
  Taman Shud

- Blood-letting
  Humbug

- Burning
  The Bone King
  Humbug
  The Secret Showing on the Midway of Dreams
  Taman Shud

- Cannibalism
  Sorry

- Coulrophobia (clowns)
  Sorry

- Curing of disability
  Sobriquet

- Death
  The Bone King
  Goblin Market
  Humbug
  One Last Chance
  Raclure's Curiosity
  Sorry
  Taman Shud

- Electrocution
  Raclure's Curiosity

- Gore & Mutilation
  Goblin Market
  Sorry
  The Unveiling

- Physical abuse
  Raclure's Curiosity
  Sobriquet
  Sorry

- Prejudice
  The Bone King

- PTSD
  The Secret Showing on the Midway of Dreams

- Self-mutilation
  Humbug

- Slurs
  The Bone King
  The Secret Showing on the Midway of Dreams

- Suicide
  Sorry

- Torture
  The Bone King
  Goblin Market

- Vampirism (Children/Adults)
  Taman Shud

DISCOVER MORE GOTHIC HORROR TITLES AT
WWW.QUILLANDCROWPUBLISHINGHOUSE.COM

Printed in Great Britain
by Amazon